Ox Bells
and
Fireflies

Ox Bells
and
Fireflies

A Memoir by Ernest Buckler

Drawings by Walter Richards

Introduction by Alan R. Young
General Editor: Malcolm Ross

New Canadian Library No. 99

McClelland and Stewart Limited

Copyright © 1968, 1974 Ernest Buckler
Introduction © 1974, McClelland and Stewart Limited

All rights reserved
0-7710-9199-0

The Canadian Publishers
McClelland and Stewart Limited
25 Hollinger Road, Toronto

Printed in Canada by Webcom Limited

Contents

Introduction   xi

1   Seven Crows a Secret   3

2   Memory   19

3   Wildcats, Tetrazzini, and Bee Beer   42

4   Slate Rags, Tudors, and Popocatepetl   60

5   Chords and Acres   79

6   Plow, Scythe, and Peavey   89

7   Seed, Forges, and Rising Bread   104

8   Wicks and Cups   118

9   Goose Grease, Death, and Parables   126

10   Soft Soap and Drawknives   137

11   Drop Mail and Diplomats   151

12   As the Saying Went, or Slugs and Gluts   160

13   Antics and After   169

14   Houses   185

5   More Memory, or The's and And's   196

16   A Man   234

17   A Woman   243

18   Another Man   251

19   Like Spaces, Other Cases   264

20   A to Z   276

21   Fireflies and Freedom   293

*The author wishes to thank
the Canada Council for assistance
while this book was in progress.*

FOR *Claude Bissell*

Introduction

Ernest Buckler's *Ox Bells and Fireflies: A Memoir* (1968), his third full-length prose work, marks a significant departure from the direction in which his two novels, *The Mountain and the Valley* (1952) and *The Cruelest Month* (1963), seemed to be leading. As one turns from the first to the second of these earlier works, one discerns an increasing concern on Buckler's part with problems of plot and structure and more especially with the portrayal of the inner psychology of his characters and the complexities of their interrelationships. However, in *Ox Bells and Fireflies*, a portrayal of the author's childhood experience in rural Nova Scotia, Buckler not only veers away from such preoccupations, but virtually abandons conventional novel-writing in favour of a special kind of prose memoir that by his own admission deliberately fuses fiction and non-fiction, an experimental process since developed further in his *Window on the Sea* (1973).

As a work of art, *Ox Bells and Fireflies* may be categorized as a Regional Idyll, which, according to Desmond Pacey, was "the chief of our prose forms" in Canada during the first and second decades of the twentieth century. Buckler's *The Mountain and the Valley* and to a lesser extent *The Cruelest Month*, along with such works as W.O. Mitchell's *Who Has Seen the Wind* (1947) and Wallace Stegner's *Wolf Willow* (1955), attempt to revive in various ways this idyllic strain, familiar from such earlier works as Stephen Leacock's *Sunshine Sketches of a Little Town*, Lucy M. Montgomery's *Anne of Green Gables* and Mazo de la Roche's *Jalna* novels. However, though *The Mountain and the Valley*, *The Cruelest Month* and *Ox Bells and Fireflies* are indeed "regional" in their conscious attempt to portray the life and character of a recognizable locale within a specific historical and social framework, at the same time all three belong to the much wider literary context known as "pastoral" and partake of a mythology that transcends the bounds of what is merely national or regional. Consequently it is as pastoral that I here wish to discuss *Ox Bells and Fireflies* in the belief that, though part of the book's appeal derives from its "regionalism," its primary appeal derives from something much greater.

What chiefly matters, I feel, is the way Buckler manages to evoke that universal human desire to return to some lost paradise world, the memory of which appears to lie within our collective subconscious, providing a model against which the spiritual poverty of our present existence may be evaluated. Such a desire is basic to the inspiration of what is known as pastoral, which, at its most recognizable, will tend to evoke visions of the Golden Age, Arcadia or the Garden of Eden, those three forms of earthly paradise associated in Classical and Judeo-Christian mythology with a now lost state of human happiness and innocence. In a more general sense, however, a similar inspiration is recognizable in literature wherever one perceives the longing for any kind of lost innocence and happiness that can only be recovered by retreat into memory, or by a shift into a different environment or social setting. Such longing, by its very nature, affects those outside the temporal, geographic or social boundaries of the imagined pastoral world. Consequently most pastoral literature tends to be built around dramatic juxtapositions and comparisons. Commonly, for example, a writer will set the simplicity and innocence of childhood or of a primitive people against the consciousness of the complexities of adult experience or of so-called civilized society. Or he will contrast a rural setting with an urban and more technologically advanced one, or the juxtaposition may be sociological as William Empson so tellingly revealed in *Some Versions of Pastoral* (1935). Invariably too the values of naturalness, communal fellowship, non-competitiveness and contentment will be set against those of sophistication, individualism and capitalistic enterprise.

In *The Mountain and the Valley* Buckler exploited such tensions to the full by depicting his semi-autobiographical hero, David Canaan, as torn between the conflicting values of life in the rural confines of the Annapolis Valley and life in the larger world beyond. In *The Cruelest Month* he mixed his native Nova Scotians with sophisticated urban outsiders in a similar local environment by bringing them all to a guest home called Endlaw (an ironic anagram for Thoreau's Walden), a place "exempt from the arithmetic of time," a kind of asylum-paradise where the characters are "continuously free to fit together the pure, unalloyed fabrics of Time, Place, and Sentience, as never before." Though the characters of *The Cruelest Month* may be "free" in Endlaw as never before, they nevertheless learn that self-discovery is painful and frightening, and none leave their rural retreat unscarred. *Ox Bells and Fireflies* does not explore the psychological conflicts of a David Canaan, nor does it involve itself in the complex unravellings of personality that occur in *The Cruelest Month*. Its drama derives instead from the juxtaposition of an unacceptable present against the remembered pleasures of a past that is now lost. On one level, loss of past is merely the product of the author's having grown up and having left behind the innocence of childhood. On another level, so Buckler would have us believe, the world he once knew has since been destroyed by the forces of urbanization, crass materialism and the general depersonalization of all facets of human intercourse.

As Buckler describes it the present is epitomized by "the cluttered roadside lunchroom on the day when 'with' has become 'without' forever" and by the counter inside with "the artificial flowers beside the yellowed cactus plant beside the bowl of stagnant water where the feet of two small turtles clutch stuporously for footholds on each other, not knowing each other from rocks…" Throughout *Ox Bells and Fireflies* there is a steady flow of such images of sterility, spiritual blindness and isolation, often reminiscent of T. S. Eliot's *The Waste Land* and culminating in Buckler's final vision of the present as a world in which all men are sleepwalkers "among the things that now are all alike, shorn to their one feature of going from one moment of sameness to the next…" But such indictments of the present also serve to emphasize through contrast the splendours of the past to which the author returns through his memories. The qualities of the world that memory reveals are very much those of pastoral. It is a world that is timeless, one in which "everything was always and forever Now," and in which "the day itself has all day long to model its dayness under the eave of Time." It is a world of carefree happiness, non-competitiveness, uninhibited wonder, human fellowship ("neighbours were that much like brothers then"), harmony between man and nature, peace and inner contentment, a world in which a sense of family and community provides the guiding moral principles and in which people and objects are characterized by an honesty and inherent integrity that is incorruptible. Though death is present on almost every page, "its great sabled presence" coming "over the rim of Never" and taking back "in its closed hand the breath of someone its hand would never open on again," the quality of life in Buckler's rural world is only the more vital as a consequence: a far cry from the city-world of present time in which men are, in the narrator's view, no more than living corpses occupying a brutalized and spiritually arid urban landscape.

The presence of death in Buckler's pastoral world, something the child soon learns to acknowledge ("the black horses drew the black-tasseled hearse so slowly through the August afternoon and suddenly you knew what doomsday was"), is of great functional importance for it largely prevents the black-white contrasts between present and past from being sentimental. However timeless the experience of Norstead (Buckler's "no more place") may seem, death remains its most constant inhabitant. Indeed one of the central tensions which holds *Ox Bells and Fireflies* together as a work of art is the author's counterpointing of a sense of timelessness against the paradoxical flow of the irresistible forces of time which transform "then" into "now," youth into age, and the living into the dead. Though the passing of time (whether in the form of the changing seasons or human mortality) is on the one hand acceptable as part of the natural rhythm of the pastoral world, and as such bears no real threat, on the other hand Buckler never quite lets us forget that it is this same force that has ultimately destroyed his rural Eden and brought about the waste land he so painfully evokes in his closing pages:

> We no longer see the things we used to see: our own pulse in the lapping of the lake, our own snugness in the kitchen fire, our own eyes in the window pane. We see things we never used to see: the iron in the band of winter-cloud behind the factory chimney, the prison eyes in the dry blade of weaving sidewalk grass, the death mask of time in the rag of newspaper blowing down the gutter.

Yet, as already implied, though *Ox Bells and Fireflies* is often elegiac in that it mourns the loss of a way of life and mode of experience that Buckler associates with the rural Nova Scotia of his childhood, its dominant tone is joyful and the book actually ends with a coda that returns to the prevailing idyllic strain, the final chord being an allusion to "Fireflies," the joint symbol along with "Ox Bells" of the peace, freedom and joy that lie at the heart of Buckler's pastoral world. Such a paradise, though not available directly, is approachable through memory, which ultimately, as the book seems intended to show, is capable of transcending the forces of time and of making Norstead live once again. Appropriately Buckler several times discusses the processes of memory and even includes a whole chapter on the subject, recognizing at the same time its hidden trap of sentimentality and the fact that "the act of memory has a mesh all its own" which of necessity can only select "a medley of fragments" while letting "events the size of lives slip through." What *Ox Bells and Fireflies* does is to collect this "medley of fragments" and arrange them into a composite portrait, which, as I suggested earlier, is particular in its depiction of a specific locale at a specific time in history while at the same time it attempts to be universally representative ("I'll call the village 'Norstead,' the boy 'I.' They stand for many. The time is youth, when Time is young"). The pastoral world of *Ox Bells and Fireflies* is indeed everyone's dream of childhood, of the past, of the country and of an ideal existence.

The form that Buckler imposes upon this visionary world is at one level an obvious one. Through twenty-one short chapters he touches in turn on such topics as school, games, religion, politics, sex, language, buildings and people, allowing his collection of vignettes and portraits to suggest by their very heterogeneousness the rich variety of the way of life he is evoking. At another level, however, the form of the work is shaped by its inherent pattern of cyclical time. It begins with the innocence of childhood ("I was ten and I had never seen a dead person") and progresses through the stages of puberty, marriage and parenthood, ending, however, with a return to childhood ("My father walks over the golden oat stubble...He is young and strong"). Such a cycle seems intended to demonstrate the power of memory to fuse different moments in time as it moves backwards and forwards within the human time-scale. At the same time, since the "I" of the book is representative only, the movement from childhood to adulthood and back to childhood is an expression of the recurring rhythm of human life, that endlessly repeating progress from birth to death that subsumes the individual life-span within a far larger pattern. The recognition that there is such a pattern then provides consolation for a human time-scale that to the individual commonly appears threateningly linear, one-directional and limited in duration.

To assist him in his handling of time, Buckler deliberately employs a multiple point of view. He begins with the first person "I" of his child narrator and ends with both the child's voice and the first person "we" of the elderly survivors who can look back collectively at the past and mourn for what is lost. Elsewhere, however, he uses the third person "he" and "she" in more distanced analytical passages in which he exposes the minds and characters of the different men and women who make up the population of Norstead. Occasionally he also uses the colloquial second person "you," a device which tends by contrast to draw the reader into a more intimate relationship with the narrator and the objects of his description. We thus see the world of Norstead from different angles, distances and perspectives corresponding to the different points of view. This multiplicity in turn corresponds to Buckler's flexible time-scale, which itself is the product of his understanding of the way in which memory functions within the human psyche.

My final comment concerns Buckler's style, the chief characteristic of which is its daring and innovative search for metaphors and verbal effects that will express precisely the complexity of ideas and feelings that he wishes to communicate:

> In the dream it is afternoon and the snow, thick as eyelashes, begins to fall so silently the trees are mesmerized. The sky is the great dome of a paperweight and the snow is the snowstorm inside it. I hold my head back, staring into its swarming fleece as if to penetrate the secret of "up," where all the mysteries are. I feel sudden worlds in my blood, both hushed and glossy.

Ox Bells and Fireflies is full of such passages and they tend to be uncompromising in the demands they make of a reader, for it must be said that the richness of metaphor and description in Buckler does not make for so-called "easy" reading. However, allied to Buckler's love of slow-moving and densely textured poetic description is his gift for capturing the rhythm and idiom of his characters' speech which frequently reveals to us in its primitive economy as much about the quality of the life he wishes to evoke as any of his finer descriptive passages:

> "Hadn't I better hitch up the team and snig her closer the foundation there?" he says. "I don't want you fullas to come over here and lift yer guts out."

> "Hell, no. There's six of us here. If we can't raft a sill that size into place, we ain't fit to pick shit with the hens. Come on, boys. Come *on* there, Willis. You only bin married two days, yer back can't be *that* weak!"

Admittedly there are times when Buckler fails to breathe the necessary life into a word or phrase, but this is perhaps the price to be paid in reading an author who has been willing to take risks. To my mind it is a price worth paying.

Alan R. Young
Acadia University

Ox Bells and Fireflies

1 / Seven Crows a Secret

I'LL CALL THE VILLAGE "Norstead," the boy "I."
They stand for many. The time is youth, when Time
is young.

I was ten and I had never seen a dead person. I
did not think about any of it with these words, but
this is the way I remember it.

It is the night before the death. I am dreaming that it is winter, and snowing.

In the dream it is afternoon and the snow, thick as eyelashes, begins to fall so silently the trees are mesmerized. The sky is the great dome of a paperweight and the snow is the snowstorm inside it. I hold my head back, staring into its swarming fleece as if to penetrate the secret of "up," where all the mysteries are. I feel sudden worlds in my blood, both hushed and glossy.

The snow eyelashes the tufts of brown grass lingering friendless in the fields and comforts them like a blanket. The plowed land is smoothed white, and each twig on every bush is a white pipe cleaner. There is not a breath of wind. The snow shawls the spruces and ridges the bare branches of the chestnut trees with a white piping.

And now the only markings on the sheeted day are the sudden blackness of the barn gables, the bundled blackness of a figure walking out of earshot (and as if out of earshot of himself) on the road, the immaculate ink scrawl of the leafless apple trees in the orchard. When the lamps are lit the eddied snowflakes blur the light they cast outside the window into short-stemmed yellow flowers.

The dream changes.

Now the fields and the houses are stunned with midnight and the wind comes snarling and scowling across the fields. Knived with cold and rolling its savage breath about in its bodiless throat. It wakens the snow from its dream of itself and enslaves it. The snow, swept helpless before its bitter broom, is at first bewildered, then joins the wind's vicious rage.

The wind blows all night, drawing back the armies of its breath almost to the core of silence, then sends them plunging across the fields in a keening and sepulchral thunder. It lashes the snow and spins it in dervish rags of bluster higher and higher into the air. The cold hardens to brutality.

The bed shudders a little. I stir, cat-cozy, then burrow deeper into my dream . . .

The dream shifts and it is morning.

The morning dawns morningless as falling night. Outside the frosted and besieged windows the air is a white, tossing sea. Fury battles itself in all directions at once, and when two breakers of snow clash against each other the explosion blots out everything in sight.

I go out to the shop for wood. The shop door lashes at me, and the air inside is driven solid with nails of cold.

There is no stroke of noon in the day, not a second's pause for it. Gibraltar-shaped drifts are packed hard as rock against the barn. In spots the crust is shelved like lava, tongued with white welts. Across the plowed land there are sculpted waves of drift large enough to swamp a whale, and off their overhanging edges, sharp and precisely curved as scimitars, the spindrift sifts continuously like some infernal steam. Next to them are the jagged Everests, with the snow that climbers perish in swirling about their cliffs and craters. Tips of the far-off mountain trees that edge the sky are frozen blue.

In the afternoon, a Bible sun blazes once through lemon clouds. And later, blood-red Old Testament towers and firmaments burn colder than ice along the horizon.

It blows and blows. And then it stops.

I go out with glee to test the altered landscape. Still blue shadows line the undersides of the drifts. Only the cold remains to keep a stony order . . .

And then it is morning again.

I run to the window and look out at the scattered farmhouses riding the trackless drifts. There is nothing moving anywhere except the smoke curling upward from their chimneys as if each family had just elected a new Pope.

The Pope of this day is Light. The sun strikes prisms of light from the igloo caps on well curb and fence post (to be knocked off with the jubilant swipe of a mitten). From the side of the canister in the pantry with the picture of the King and Queen on it. From the one piece of gold in the house, my mother's wedding ring, as her hand dips into the canister for the drawing of breakfast tea. From the weather vane on the peak of the barn . . .

I follow my father to the barn. I stretch my legs to the utmost to fit my feet into the giant holes his feet make in the snow that is white as weasels.

We open the barn door. Two shafts of light from

the opposite peak windows intersect like bands of light on a Sunday School card. They nest themselves in the English hay on the scaffold and the meadow hay in the bay. I touch the beam of light from the dung-window where it falls on the yellow oat-straw bedding in an unused manger.

The oxen rise like prophecies and stretch hugely, hollowing their backs downward and curling their rigid tails straight upward, like the tails of lions.

The horse glistens with energy. My father says he will hitch him up in the sleigh, for exercise. We'll drive down to Gus Jordan's to pick up the ox shoes Gus has been corking for him in his hand forge. My heart leaps.

I hook the tugs onto the shafts as my father lifts the horse's mane free of the martingale and flips his tail out over the crupper. The horse vibrates his whole body once as if he had trodden on lightning. The sleigh bells shiver like spoons in a tumbler.

And then we are on the seat, taken out and warmed beforehand beside the kitchen stove. We tuck the warm "buffalo" around our knees and head for the gate. The horse plunges through the drifts in rabbit jumps that rock the sleigh like a cockleshell. I hang on for dear life, manufacturing danger to delight me further.

And then we are on the smooth road. The runner tracks glisten in the sun between great walls of snow cubed out of the drifts by the road-breakers' shovels. Father just touches the horse's flank with the tip of the whip, and with a spring of his haunches and one brilliant fart the horse is off.

Father takes a twist of rein around each wrist to hold him steady, but our speed surprises a breeze from the air. It sings past my stocking cap. If I close my eyes for a moment we are really flying. The balls of snow from the horse's hooves spanging against the lip of the sleigh are like a delicious bombardment by the morning's very light and splendor.

Crowned with the royalty of speed, I wave exultantly to everyone we pass. Jim Stedman breaking the ice in his well. Rachel Anson taking a pan of oats to the hen pen, her crimson scarf a stab of color. Ben, the Portuguese storekeeper, whose back-door drifts will soon be spoked with yellow holes the shape of broom handles because he never goes farther than the sill to "water his donkey" . . . All of them patriots with me in this morning just by breathing it.

I don't feel the cold. I look at my father's solid face as the horse slows down to a walk, and there is no shadow then on anyone or anything of their not lasting forever . . .

I AWAKEN. Actually awaken this time. It is not winter, as in the dream. It is the first of May.

The sun is just coming up. It tints the air and the white birches the color of young flesh.

Light, finding things, draws their shadows from them slantwise on the ground, then gives them light.

The tin pails shine. Diamonds are discovered in the pebbles of the road, emeralds in the branch tips of the firs, rubies in the idol eyes of roosters, ebony in the black horse's glistening flank. Dandelions dazzle themselves with yellow. Shingles glow gray, with fatherly knowledge. Thistles sparkle with a family wit. Spider bridges, cantilevered as light as glances, twinkle between the plum tree twigs. Auntly hens shine brown on the glinting straw. Swallows shimmer, hills kindle, and the fields sheen themselves with resurrection and internal rhyme.

Of wind, the day's worry, there is none. Of cloud, its uncertainty, not a trace. Of rain, its brooding, not even a memory.

Windowpanes, disinherited by the winter, are given back their kingdoms of contentment. Meadows, disavowed, are recognized again. Bushes, banished to only initials of themselves, are given back their total beings. Kingfishers bright as rings draw perfect parabolas on the air and sing of them. Clocks brighten at the thought of company, the bread knife awakens, and plates become transitive. A hush of freshness walks on the air like Christ.

My blood springs with the hallelujah of downstairs and outdoors. I race downstairs.

My mother is scalding the wooden churn. The steam from it glistens in the sunlight from the open door. She cools the scalded butter tray with water pumped from the deep well in the cellar. As I eat, I watch the mesmeric motion of the dash in her hands and listen for the "breaking" sound that means the kernels of butter have begun to separate.

Lit velvetly with food, I don't know whether to stay with her or go out with Father. It is a morning for being with everybody.

I go out where Father is taking away the sawdust banking. I pick up handfuls of the tiny yellow cubes and let them sift through my fingers. I feel the sun sifting through my hair.

I go back into the kitchen. I watch Mother press the shining butter into the mould that has the pattern of acorns carved on it by my father.

Father comes into the kitchen and pumps himself a drink. "Aaaaaah!" he says, as he pushes his cap back and takes the dipper from his lips, so sweet and cool is the well water after all Mother's pumping.

I go out again with him. I take the brush off the long flower beds that run from the house to the road.

In a little while Mother comes out with us. I can see that this is a day when Father and Mother too like to keep the perimeter of their presences touching.

Mother picks up a head of poppy seed from the ground, missed when she gathered them last fall. She breaks open the outside sphere to see if the tiny round seeds inside, each in its small compartment, are still good. (I've heard of opium dreams. I think: How are they contained in these tiny globes? Where in the dappled foxglove is the power to soothe heart trouble?)

I pick up a marigold head. Its seeds are like little commas (as its blossoms are like commas in the solid prose of a summer afternoon). They radiate from the center to form a perfect circle.

"Do you want to save this?" I ask Mother.

"No," she says. "I never have to worry about planting marigolds. They seed themselves."

"I'm glad," Father says. "I like yellow flowers."

It is not like Father to say anything like that. He never says anything like that. I am standing beside him. He puts his hand on my shoulder for a moment and draws me against his leg. He never does that. I am almost trembling with self-consciousness, but I've never felt so alive and happy in all my life.

And then, suddenly, I have to see the brook. As if to stamp its voice, the voice of the very morning, on me, like the acorn on the butter.

I walk down the road, past the brother-faced houses, down the long hill, to the bridge across the brook where it runs through the meadow. I sit on the bridge and watch the brook.

Wine-light is solid from the white stones on the bed of the brook to the surface where the twinkling leaves of silver flash. The brook is never for an instant the same, yet more than anything it stays itself, close and chatting. I shred pieces of bark off the bridge rail and drop them into the chuckling current. I drop pebbles, one by one, into the water. This is the kind of day when it is wonderfully pleasant to do meaningless things like that.

Warmth, warmed by its own welcome, spreads everywhere.

I see a small trout suspended between the surface of the water and its shadow on the pebbled bottom beneath, more electric with motion than if it were moving. Once or twice it flicks itself an inch ahead, like an impulse to certainty that sees itself as soon mistaken. And then, hitting the answer fair, it flashes straight into a dark cavern beneath the bank.

I open my shirt and let the sun touch my chest. I listen to the brook and there is not a cavity of any kind within me. I fit into myself like the brook to the bank.

I listen to the brook, and my own flesh and I are such snug and laughing brothers that I know we are forever mingled with the sun's pulse (or the wind's or the rain's) and forever unconquerable . . .

I WALK BACK up the hill. I hear a strange voice in the kitchen. The way Father and Mother are talking sounds strange too. I have a funny, still feeling, as when you hear a clock stop. I go in.

A neighbor is there. All three are standing, or moving purposelessly about. The neighbor's eyes are out of breath. His face looks as if he were carrying it rather than wearing it, like a garment snatched up. He is still white with the news he's brought: Jim Stedman just fell off the staging on his barn roof and broke his neck on the rocks beneath.

I look at Father. He looks as if his breath had toppled. And then he looks at Mother as if otherwise his look would have no place to go. Her look locks hands with his in the same way.

There seems to be some sudden terrible question in the air. In this great stroke of silence from the dead that even the leaves hear, it shrieks to be answered.

I am stunned. I go outside.

I look at things. And look at them. But they don't tell me anything. This is nothing like the snow in the dream or the sun in the dream. They've retreated inside themselves, inside that ring of deafness, where they only talk to each other. In silences. The wild roses seem bowed with their own helpless color. I pick up a stone. I stare at it. It doesn't tell me anything. I drop it. I see Jim breaking the well ice in my dream. It doesn't tell me anything.

That night, we go to the dead man's house. Its windows do not speak.

Mother has cautioned herself not to "break down." Father opens the kitchen door as Mother slips her rubbers off, to leave them on the porch. Jim's wife Annie is sitting by the stove, pleating her handkerchief, her stricken face almost a childlike pink from tears parched dry.

"No, Mary," she says to Mother, with a faint smile of greeting even now, "don't leave your rubbers out there."

There's something about this being so much their ordinary exchange that Mother breaks down. She controls herself, but later when she says to Annie, "If you want that black hat of mine . . . ," she breaks down again.

The men sit in the kitchen, cumbersome with solemnity, looking like children who don't know their lessons. They spring up too quickly to offer their seats to a newcomer, themselves perching on the woodbox or standing, in a pose that tries to look at ease but instantly becomes awkward. They do not look at their wives in a way that is suddenly like the way they hadn't looked at them in a crowded room when they were first courting. The family of the dead are awesome to me in their grief, almost regal with it.

Visitors are shown into the parlor, where the coffin is. They move as if walking is a precarious thing they've just learned. Their eyes are kept in sober check, as if to take notice of anything in the room but the dead man would be shameful.

I stare at the dead man. His face is whiter than water could ever wash it. The lamp is turned down to the color of his fingernails. I stare at his hands. They don't tell me anything.

THE AFTERNOON of the funeral, I sit on our verandah steps. I hear Mother and Father talking inside the house. My father is to be one of the carriers.

"Mary," he calls to her from the bedroom. "Where's my fine shirt?"

"It's in the second drawer there," she calls from the kitchen, "under the . . . Just wait a minute. I'm coming up to change now, myself."

"Is these the right studs?" he says to her in the bedroom.

"Yes. Here, I'll put them in for you." It is strange, this feeling they seem to have today for each other's clothing. They never help each other dress. "Have you got a clean handkerchief?"

"Yes."

"No, that's the one I got the iron rust on. Better take this new one."

"Which dress are you wearin?" my father says. He never says anything like that. "The blue one or the brown one?"

"I think the blue one'd look better today. It's old, but . . ."

"I always liked that dress on you."

"Did you like that old dress? You never said."

"Yes. It always looked good on you. What's my boots look like? Are they shined all right?"

"Yes. They look like new. That sock don't hurt where I darned it on the heel, does it?"

"No. Not a bit."

"Poor Annie!" Mother says. "She's takin it so hard. I don't know, some said she drove her pigs to a poor market when she first married Jim, but . . ."

"I never saw nothin wrong with Jim," Father says. "Do you mind that morning it darkened up so when I had all the clover down and Jim never said a word, he just come over and started rakin with his own horse?"

"Yes, I remember. Does my skirt hang even in the back there?"

"Turn around. A little more. Yes, it looks straight to me." They never do this.

"And those children certainly thought there was no one like him," Mother says. "You never looked out and saw Jim in the dooryard or anywheres without you saw young Jim at his heels."

"I know. Do you want your beads?"

"Yes, I think so. They don't look gaudy at a time like this, do they?"

"No, they look nice. Here, I'll fasten that ketch for you." Father *never* does anything like this. "Does us carriers set all the time, like the mourners," he says, "or do we stand up for the singin?"

"No," Mother says, "the carriers sets all the time. Oh, Joe . . . when I think . . . if it was you . . ."

Father doesn't say anything for a minute or so— and when he does speak his voice sounds different. "Well," he says, "I guess I better get my coat on and walk along. The people'll be getherin soon and the carriers is supposed to be there a little early. Maybe if you and Mark go out bime'by and stand by the gate you'll get a ride with someone."

"No," Mother says. "I want to go with you. We'll walk along with you. And wait."

"Maybe you'll get a chance back."

"No. We'll walk back with you. Unless *you* could get a chance. You've been workin up there in the graveyard ever since daylight. You must be tired."

"No," Father says. "I'll walk along back with you."

THE FIELDS are still. Even the nostrils of the coal-black hearse horses are still. The mourners, in the front pew, are still.

And then when the first notes of the organ sound the mourners themselves seem to break a little at the neck. It seems as if the clouds I can see through the church window are black-capitaled with the word NEVER.

The singing begins. "Shall we gather at the river/ The beautiful, the beautiful, the river . . ."

I close my eyes and try to see, really see, the river that "flows by the throne of God." They sing "In the sweet ('In the sweet,' the two splendid basses echo) bye and bye ('bye and bye')/We shall meet at that beautiful shore . . ."

I cry.

At the grave, a leaf from the poplar grove blows onto the coffin and dances the length of it. The carriers pay out the first slack to the straps that let the coffin sink. I see my father's hands tremble. I notice a wrinkle in my mother's face that the sunshine seems to engrave there. I feel like running.

WE WALK home together. Father's face looks like I've seen it when the plow would turn up some object of long ago. The shard of an adze or a musket ball that the French or the English had used when they were fighting for Port Royal. He'd hold the object in his hand a moment and look far off, as I have since seen men look when they heard a bell toll, the breath of his face suspended. I would want to grasp his hand as if to rescue him from something. But then he would look toward the house, where my mother might be gathering up an apronful of splints from the chipyard to kindle the supper fire, and I would know that we were all safe.

He looks at Mother now. For a moment they look the way they do when they are working in the fields together, sowing seeds. When something comes out of them that is neither one of them but more than both. I take both their hands. I have never done this before.

"I remember when Jim and I was kids," Father says. "We used to put green apples on the end of a withe and flick em at a bottle we'd set up on the stone wall. And every time there was a fresh snow we'd go back and try to track a fox to its den . . . And hot afternoons I remember we'd strip our clothes off and wade into the lake for the white water lilies."

"I remember those lilies," Mother says. "You used to bring em to us girls. They always closed up at night, didn't they."

I look back at the churchyard. A flock of crows is circling overhead. I count them. One crow sorrow, two crows joy; three crows a wedding, four crows a boy; five crows silver, six crows gold; seven crows a secret never to be told.

2 / Memory

I'LL CALL THE PEOPLE of Norstead family and neighbors. They stand for many too.

No single description can contain them. They could be harsh as the gravel under the sled runners in patches where the snow had turned to slush, and gentle as moonlight on the wild cherry blossoms. They could seem as cheaply comic as "stage Irishmen" and as finely strung as pain of death. Their faces could be as scraggy as turnip knurls or as handsome as apples. Their talk could be a dull rosary of empty shells they ticked off like parrotry or like a flash of eyelight that showed the whole blood-mesh of feeling behind it. They might be a thing and its contrary at the same time.

But not in the unicorn sense: it was just these opposites that made them real. Sometimes rough as oaths, they yet had a kind of poetry—if poetry can be taken as the bottom skin of whatever in all its differences is all itself. One mood could turn them frivolous as wrens; another could hold them speechless in its galling fist. But they were always intensely alive.

As, it seemed, were all the things around them. Surely the trees exulted and sorrowed. Surely the rocks often longed to be rhododendrons. And each storm, each fine day, each sundog of event was different from every other—and as different to each watcher as the watchers' inner weather differed among themselves. Plow, cow, crow . . . rock, cock, clock . . . everything, animate or inanimate, cast a different shadow of itself as its context varied.

These people were miles and guiles away from the wide world, but each and every form of existence was there in its own translation. The feather and stone of hope and foil are the same everywhere. The rooster's comb is the same color as the Cardinal's biretta.

This is memory then. And though memory may be a miracle—that you can sit where you are and send the mind skimming back over the rails of time and space, at will—there's no denying that it can be harping, misleading, and treacherously sentimental. That it often conjures all sorts of things into a vanished way of life that were never there to begin with. (Especially when a writer's mind dives back into his country childhood is he most apt to come up with a jam jar of candied guff about Crokinole sprees and taffy pulls that were, in fact, mild horrors.) The heart, far less misty-eyed than the mind, despite its sentimental name, is a far sounder witness. Once in a while it leaps of its own accord—through the skin, through the flesh, through the bone—straight back to the pulse of another time, and takes all of you with it. You are not seeing this place again through the blurred telescope of the mind: you are standing right there. Not long enough to take it all down, but long enough to give memory a second chance.

What triggers these leaps? You never know beforehand. No pressure of will can force them—but a slat of light surprising the dust on an empty chair can do it. The sudden glimpsing in the look of an age-changed face of the one familiar look that has never outgrown itself. The moment when the mind is crouched and sodden, like a cat in the rain, before the stare of the cold lettering of where you've irrevocably come to, in the silence of it that no one else can hear. A day in the crowded street when all things, even the scales of curling paint or the cracks between the bricks, are heavy with bearing no self-explanation. The coming dusk of a winter Sunday when the sun on the snow-patched roofs looks almost like Spring sun but the sky has that red, cold-burning archipelago in the west where the dead are . . .

And however they come, it is only this sleight of heart that can unlock "ago" like the master key of dream.

One way or another, I remember Norstead.

It was a sixteen-mile hush of forest away from Champlain's first landfall at Port Royal. Port Royal itself was hushed with history, solemn as a mountain with it. A joke goes around that one of the new crop of villagers was lately heard to remark: "Last night I had my first drink of Champlain." I had my first drink of Champlain from my grandmother. She was one of those tiny women distilled by age and bright with the gist of things, who could dance a jig at ninety, and with her gift of story write picture books in a child's mind clearer than ink.

I listened to her, and I could feel the earth give a sort of tremor when Champlain, bringing Time with him, set the first discoverer's foot on this whole time-less land. I could see the map-red Micmac blood Rorschached on a folded leaf. (And I could hear the laughter of the English dukes who later danced in the long, low mansion next to the garrison, where the

Negro slaves were taught submissiveness by having their fingers thrust into the jamb of an open door whose sharp edge was then squeezed tight on them.)

I listened—and I heard the stroke of the first settler's ax on the first astonished trees, which would give him both his home and his heat. I could see the lynx eyes smoldering at night at the edge of the tiny clearing he had made in this midnight of strangeness. I could taste the faint trace of smoke in the burntland potatoes that gave him his strength. I touched the first blade of grass that brought the first living smell where there had only been the closed forest breath of endlessness and secrecy . . .

But the past was only reading then. Whenever I closed its book, everything was always and forever Now.

Sometimes when I walked ahead of the oxen as they planted their great slow feet like sorrows on the land and my father guided the plow, I would pretend that there were still Indians in the thickets; but my father was too real for this fancy to last.

Sometimes I would pass the church at night when all the lights were out in all the houses. The dark trees would be whispering together their primeval messages that were not for man's knowledge. And I would feel at my heels the chill of lateness that haunts every hour—something I'd never noticed before. But the moment I ran in past the big hackmatack at our gate and saw the lamp turned down for me on the kitchen table I instantly forgot my fear.

Something stilling came out of the ancient graves in the cemetery too. Their borders traced as if with some invisible brush of chapel light and chapel deafness, they were like tablets of inscrutability written on the ground. But who would linger to decipher them, when the inscription the sun made on all the daisies and in all the green meadows of the blood was freshness everlasting?

And if Port Royal had besides its open and living eye another one, lidded but with the gaze of centuries behind it, the winding road that led there was as warm and present as the morning kitchen.

The road was not like the trees. The trees slept somewhere deep inside themselves and awoke before anything else; the road slept beside us and awoke when we did. Men looked at it as at their own hands; women as at their own thoughts; children as at their play. It was a family road and we gave our names to it.

Just beyond the knot of houses were the cool Lattimore Hills, named for Steve Lattimore. He made all the child coffins and carved the lambs on the sides of them with the same knife he used when he came to cut the calves. His talk was peppered with two odd oaths: "By the King Judas!" and "By the Good Thunder!"

And then you came to the bridge over Little Tim's Brook. *Big* Tim Carter was so short the other men used to tease him when he mowed naked in the coarse meadow heat, warning him not to hang his scythe in too far or he'd behead the thing he'd miss most; but his son Little Tim was six foot seven, with arms like flails and fingers like backbolts—who could yet sew a larrigan together with the waxed end neater than a woman could hemstitch.

And then you came to Grandmother's Hollow. Grandmother Wentworth was a matriarch who put every penny the family could save into more and more acres of Crown Land. No one was quite sure why this stretch of road was named for her and not for her husband, but Grandfather Wentworth had a recognition of his own. People from miles around came to see the huge boulder that with the bare grip of his arms he had heaved on top the stone wall at the edge of the barley field. If you work your way through the thicket of second-growth hemlock the field has now become you can still see it there—but where is the strength in the muscles that once overcame it?

Yes, the slat of sunshine surprises the dust on the chair—and I am suddenly back in the slant-roofed bedroom, to which the wind and the rain gave an added snugness.

I run to the window and look out. It is a shadowless day in June. Wide awake, but as lazily self-contained as the tiger cat that walks the top pole of the zigzag pasture fence. The cows, great bulks of contentment, are grazing near the bars. Their sides are covered with outlines of Tasmania and Zanzibar where the patches of white hair alternate with the brown.

This fascinates me. What mapmaker beneath the skin can cause the hair to grow white and then, once across the irregular but precise edge of the patches, to grow brown?

As if at a signal the scattered cows stop their grazing. They wind in single file back the cowpath between the alders, to sprawl motionless in the shade of the two giant maples that stand at the crest of the blueberry slope. (And why do the green blueberries have their roundness puckered into a little frill at the top?) The cows' huge liquid eyes squint tight, then open wide, with the rhythms and logarithms of satiety and peace.

Nearer the house, the wild crabapple tree foams with blossoms and bees intent as theologians. Its branches patiently scrawl the lesson of universal branching on the stainless air. The blue half-shell of a robin's egg lies on the ground beneath it, like a tiny fallen sky. Swallows, with a bit of glistening mud or a hyphen of straw in their beaks and a murmur in their throats as of deliciously soft-edged "x"s tumbling together, swoop toward their purse-mouthed houses building under every eave.

The day itself has all day long to model its dayness under the eave of Time.

(There is no shadow on it—no shadow at all of any day to come when there may be no one you love left to turn the corner of the house and break the envelope of loneliness that encases every object in the room. Like a bird's nest full of snow.)

Sounds do not disturb this day. The rushing of the brook, the cow bells, voices in another field—none of them roams out to claim the ear as on other days; they are content where they are. Each object and all its case inflexions—the slope of a hill, the curve of the road, the up-and-downness of trees, the back-and-forthness of clapboards on the house—bask in being exactly themselves. Even the lawless bushes that live for nothing but to trespass on the cleared land are forgivable in their froth of green.

A flock of crows, their wariness and their portent suspended, configure nothing but crow flight above the drowsing churchyard.

The air smells of sunlight and grass. Of cup towels on the line and the clean angles of gable roofs. Of warm-rock breath and the cloth over rising bread. Of tree sap and leaf spine. Of wild roses on the stone wall and creamers in the well. Of the imminence of apples and the hair of children . . .

We are planting.

The ground has been ribboned into dark brown furrows. They lie like brothers side by side, the earth's rich secrets exposed willingly to the sun.

The horse's fiery nerves are subdued to usefulness. He grazes in harness at the edge of the field while my father cuts the seed potatoes. My father studies each potato for a moment, then with a surgeon's skill slices it into sections that will each have two eyes.

My mother goes up and down the rows, drawing a light chain behind her to smooth the seed bed. A neighbor notices this. He is himself full of the strange amity of planting time.

"Joe," he calls across to my father, "did you know that Mary was loose?"

We all laugh.

I think: Isn't it wonderful that he'll be living right next to us all our lives! And I think: If we get our potatoes dropped first, why don't we go over and give him a hand with his?

I picture how it will go. When he sees us coming with our baskets he'll know we're coming to help, but he'll pretend we're just coming to talk.

"Does it matter which o' these bags we take the seed out of?" Father will say.

"No," he'll say then, "not a particle. But now you fullas don't have to . . ."

He knows we will, though. And when we do, won't there be a tingling fellowship among us!

I walk along the rows my mother has chained. I drop the seed almost sedately, to make sure the spacing never varies. It is as if with each seed I am marking off another interval of pure balm in this humming day. My body rejoices: its own total inspiration.

(Not yet a crevice in its blood for the bat wings of ache to penetrate and fasten themselves. No place for worry to encamp with all its belongings. No fang of doubt, bleeding the day itself the white of love forgotten. No thrombus of promise dead. No poisoned sting of rivalry. No knowledge of an elsewhere world where even the ticks of time are each a cold stranger to the other—with all the crying in it of the invisible tears that dissolve nothing and all the soundless screaming.)

My mother's face wears itself gently and becomingly and my father is stronger than anyone I know. She moves up close to him to ask about the "small seeds." She always sows the small seeds. They make no special sign of intimacy you can see, but all at once something about their nearness fills up that little hollow in the perfect day put there by the day's very perfection.

My last row is finished and I watch her sow the small seeds. The ground is warm enough for her to kneel.

I watch and I marvel. Potato seeds are no mystery: they just grow more potatoes like themselves. But how are the plumpness and the redness of the grown beet contained in that tiny brown burr? The greenness and the warts of the cucumber in that tiny white eye lens? The cone and the tartness of the parsnip in that little oatmeal wafer? The cheek-flesh of the turnip and the leaf-pack of the cabbage in those miniature purple spheres so alike that you couldn't tell which was turnip seed and which cabbage unless they were marked?

She covers the seeds with just a skivver of sifted earth and pats it down.

I look at her hands . . . and I look at my father's

hands as they guide the handles of the plow so skill-
fully that the wave of earth the plow tumbles onto the
potatoes covers each of them to exactly the same
depth . . . and from every detail of everything I look
at comes the sudden exclamation of its falling exultantly into place with me . . .

Another time, I glimpse the scaling paint and the
cracks between the bricks on the homeless street . . .
and it is April in Norstead.

The season has been late. This is the first morning of the year when the rooster's crow is liquid, not
piercing, in the air. The light on the woodpile has
turned from winter glass to a holograph of armistice
on the scrolled birch bark. Overnight the whole camp
of winter has been struck and everything has come
over to our side. The repentant sun touches everything as if with the hand of reconciliation. The doorstep. The sides of the milk pail frothing to the brim
with the milk of the cow just freshened. The rocks,
which this day are somehow delivered of their self-
stunning weight.

Things stretch deliciously in the warm-springing
air. There is a kind of sumptuous yawn of all things
recognizing each other and mingling closer and yet
closer until their breaths touch. They become as
partnered as mouth and eye. Even the breeze (sudden lamb of the winter winds that tried to shout
things down and bend them down, fighting against
their roots) listens and bears messages from one to
the other.

The cat boxes a ray of sunlight that dances off a ladder rung. Birds perch on the very tops of trees, their notes dazzling in the air like coins. For the first time, outside-the-kitchen and inside-the-kitchen meet, hands out, at the open door.

Wagon wheels smile inside themselves at their own roundness. Walls, gentled by the sun, preen themselves on their own uprightness. Waves of something benevolent and dissolving of all solemnity come out of everything, as if each thing was its own godparent.

(Not yet—not for a long time yet—the faintest premonition of that later gust which comes from other objects when the brand of parting or of buried chances smokes inside you. You stop at the cluttered roadside lunchroom on the day when "with" has become "without" forever and it comes at you from the missing letter in the swinging metal sign. You step inside and it comes at you from the slush stains tracked into the floor. You go to the counter and it .comes at you from the artificial flowers beside the yellowed cactus plant beside the bowl of stagnant water where the feet of two small turtles clutch stuporously for footholds on each other, not knowing each other from rocks . . .

No slightest inkling yet of the multitude of places where it can lurk. Loose tarpaper flapping. A leaning post. The rack of twigs and bottle caps and stones in a sidewalk gutter. The fixity of decorative pattern in a traveling garment the pattern cheapens.

The rusted iron bolts that hold the train rails down. Last fall's dead grass between the sleepers . . .

You step into the bus and it comes at you from all those faces. The instantaneity of youth painted off them by middle age. Their features crumpled in a patch of haggard sunlight. Bleak as asylum walls for your never having had the lifelong nearness to them that would make the mask of flesh invisible.

It comes at you from the meaningless mysteries of all those faces. The empty history of all that clothing. The bruising enigma of each particular of the day—an enigma which yet has at the core of it that everlasting nothing that stares out of the faces on playing cards . . .)

This morning, the windows of each house have their eyelids up. Each front door is held open to the air by a smooth round stone. (Every stone not the shape of shapelessness becomes ornament.) The hill beyond the houses talks softly to itself. Root sap, still obeying its call, glazes the stump tops where my father cut wood last winter. The hill talks to itself, and this one day in the year the morning talks *about* itself.

I think (exquisitely safe) of people I have seen in town looking as if their faces were dragging themselves behind themselves. As if their bodies had gone out. How could they ever let themselves fall into that dreadful numbness, as if they didn't see what they heard or hear what they saw? . . .

ANOTHER TIME, another street—and I leap back to that regal day in October when we gather the crops.

I see the hardwood hills blazing (though not yet haunted) with remembrance. Golden light plates the skin of everything.

(Not yet is the skin of things seen through to the naked viscera beneath; the light itself not yet a skin of burning sadness that casts those invisible bars of shadow on the heart.)

The air is as still as the Bible; pure and clear as the brook in a psalm. The velvet afternoon light sprawls in this once and total gift of itself, bemusing the senses. I glory in its dreamy ambience.

(Not yet the ravage of the perfect moment by the need to grasp it entire, knowing that all you ever find in grasp's palm when its fingers open up again is echo.)

My father is digging the last of the potatoes. I have gone ahead in the row, pulling the blackened stalks. He follows now, tumbling the potatoes back between his legs and spreading them to dry with a single expert motion of the hack sunk before each hill. My mother pulls the single-minded carrots and the good-natured turnips from their smooth sockets in the earth and tops them. She cuts off the tortuous clumps of root from the cabbages and lifts clear their solid hearts, where each leaf has so flawlessly sealed the other in a compact of certainty.

The digging done, Father piles the turnips into

cairns. They will be left outside until the first freezing nights, to sweeten their taste.

(Quickly I load my arms full of their lush tops and dart to the barn. I watch the cows lash up a greedy mouthful of them, their eyes as set with ecstasy as if they were feeling the bull.)

The heavy squash glisten like knobbly green bone. I break them off their labyrinth of vines and the stupored pumpkin moons off theirs, and make mounds of them. They too will be left outside a few days more to soak up the very last of the sun. I squint my eyes. They look like piles of emeralds and gold.

But it is the plain, clumsy-shaped, well-meaning potatoes that we love best. Of all growing things they seem the most kinlike. They lie there in the soft, bronze Indian light, patiently waiting to be picked up.

The three of us kneel together beside the rows. We assemble the scatterment of them into round heaping basketsful. The cleaned stretch behind us as we work our way along is like hours lived out to the full. The feeling of home is stronger in us than at any other moment of the year.

Father puts three basketsful into each meal bag. The bags are so full that he can just pleat together enough slackness at the top to hold the tie. I hold the pleating tight while he encircles it twice with the twine and turns the miraculously deft knot that holds so firm but can, with his equal knack, be so easily flipped free.

I have learned to count. I count the bags; there are twenty. All at once I know exactly what twenty means. Father carries each bag to the cellar window, one arm akimbo to support it on his powerful shoulder. I shiver with delight at the sweet thunder the potatoes make as he pours them down the sluice to the bins below.

The work is done. The first partridge drums on the fallen log. The afternoon light is drawn back inside the trees and the rocks. The rocks hold it the most secure because they are the same all the way through. Moisture, blood and brain of the ground, stiffens into clean bone. Stars glint in the sky like frost. I tingle all over, challenged, as the edges of things become hard and bright when twilight thickens.

The supper food this night is warm and supperly as never before. The teapot sits like a gentle sovereign at my mother's elbow. The dishes are like smiling accomplices in a pleasure about to be sprung on someone. Appetite shimmers. The meat and the bread and the tea are like the host of some affable religion whose only creed is the denial of sternness. The table is the altar of kinship between the stove warmth and the lamplight. The plainest of mysteries, facelight, knits its shield above the table and around us.

The moment the lamp is lit the room seems to be all gathered in from outside the window. Each object in it consents suddenly to its own shape and stands about like a messenger of faithfulness.

And somehow as I eat I still go through the motions of the afternoon—on that screen the body so deliciously sets up for a good day's work to mime itself on.

And now, supper is over and the table cleared away. A kind of muted resonance echoes in our bodies from the steady note of plenty that comes from the potato bins; from the carrots buried in sawdust to keep them firm; from the heads of cabbage laid out side by side along the big cellar beams. We own ourselves completely. Everthing around us seems to be the fruit of us.

My father draws his chair near the stove and rests. When he rests at night it is as if a great tree of ease spreads over the kitchen and shelters it.

My mother goes to the sideboard in the dining room. Inside it are the grace notes of our lives. The napkin rings. The small reading glass with the celluloid handle. The calendars that were too pretty to throw away when their year was over. The yellowed newspaper with the short paragraph about her wedding in it . . . She brings out the multicolored knitting basket she bought from an Indian at the door, with the multicolored balls of yarn in it, and puts it on the table. It is time to think of winter.

She sets up a mitten for my father. It is only a work mitten, but she interlaces the black yarn with the gray to form a fox-and-geese pattern and rings the wrist with two red bands. The soft rhythmic click of her needles takes any intentness out of the silences in the room, gives each of us that freedom for his own thoughts that knits us closer still. She ties off the thumb hole with a circle of string and continues along the palm.

In a little while she takes the mitten over to Father. She asks him to put his hand in it, so that she can gauge where the narrowing should begin. His bare thumb sticks out the hole and the needles quill about his knuckles. It looks comical, but somehow this is one of those moments when he and she seem so mingled together that even sight can scarcely separate them.

I sit at the table and lay out the alphabet blocks my father has made me from a length of two-by-two. I am learning to form words with them. Each cube has a different letter on each of its six faces, so that endless combinations are possible. I think, glancingly, how strange it is that everything in the world could be spelled out with these twenty-six little pine blocks. To chance on small wonders like that makes a fine sparkle in the blood.

(Not yet the compulsion to think hard. Not yet the discovery that too much thought about things stirs them up, until they dismay you with their infinite clamor.)

I make houses of the blocks. I put the letters of my father's name in the roof, and those of my mother around the door.

Then I make words. I make "thing." I change the *g* to a *k* and I have "think." I change the *i* to an *a* and

I have "thank." I see that vowels are the eyes of words. I see how they change the word's expression. I feel the first real excitement, to find that learning has a kind of daybreak behind each small door of it that opens to you.

I make "those." I change the *o* to *e*. I have "these."

I look about the kitchen and I think, surgingly: We are "these." We will always be "these." And I feel a pity so vast I almost cry with it for everyone and everything in the world that are "those."

And then right in the midst of forming the word "tomorrow" I feel the first flakes of drowsiness begin to sift through my blood. They thicken before the screen of daytime stir my muscles have been echoing; they caress each nerve as it lets go. I feel at once heavier and lighter. My whole body is slaked with luxurious yielding.

As I climb the stairs, I am half-tranced with visions of the blossoming, absorbing bed. I crawl under the blankets and lie there waiting for them to receive me wholly. I close my eyes. I will myself a few more waking moments to savor their welcome. I am rocking in the trough of a great woolen wave. And then the soundless breeze of satiety is behind us, the anchor is up in every limb, and the bed and I begin to drift toward some endless shore . . .

Yes, the winter sun burns cold behind that cloud island in the west where the dead are—and in one trans-

location after another, changing as swiftly as one sense
can grasp the lead from another, I am back where . . .

I see the unshed rain in the bundled clouds,
thinking its troubled thoughts when I have none.

For this is the day I have fished all afternoon in
the boat with my father on the sunstruck lake that
lulled the insistence out of everything. Now we are
snug inside the cabin. Now the rain, loosed of its
thoughts, dimples the lake with them like a million
fish jumping at once. It gently clouts the leaves of the
big maple that overhangs the cabin roof.

I stand quietly in the doorway, watching it. My
father fries the trout (he never peers at my quiet-
ness), and every crude utensil in the camp glows with
the comradeship of things that would be merely
dingy anywhere else. I feel splashes of pure happiness
as thick as the raindrops . . .

. . . and I see the swirling blizzard that caught
my father in the woods, hunting—with not five minutes now of daylight left outside the kitchen window
where we watch for him to find his way home in. My
mother has not lit the lamp. That would make it
really dark outside. And then I think I see a movement. And then I think I imagined it. And then I
know it is Father. I see him feeling his way along the
fence that leads up to the corner of the barn. And I
see my mother's face as she lights the lamp then . . .

. . . and I see that same fence in the spring after
all the sprawl has been so beautifully taken out of it
by the new posts, peeled and gleaming, which I hold
up straight for my father to drive with a titan swing

of the sledge, and the new wire stretched to such a singing alertness that the whole morning echoes with it . . .

. . . and the big buck vaulting the fence in the fall in a curve smooth beyond belief, its antlers like heraldry . . .

. . . and the criss-crossed tracks of the wagon wheels on the meadow moss, after the last strand of rakings has been tossed on top of the hay load and the binder tightened to the last possible notch as my father swings his whole weight downward from its projecting end while I knot the rope around the longwithe. He eases the wagon, inch by cautious inch, across the deep ditch to the main road, and then I ride the load. The soft supporting hay unlatches all my tired muscles and I am so high above the ground I feel like a king in a procession . . .

And I see the first purse I ever had, at the moment of miraculously finding it again after having lost it (I carried it everywhere) on my way to the old chopping where the wild raspberries always sprang up in the matted underbrush . . .

. . . and the kite, the day I made 100 in arithmetic, dipping and sailing in the sky so that it made flying of my running too . . .

. . . and the nakedness that glows from having shed all things but the living flesh as Stan and Howie and Dick and Jack and Lennie and I frolic together in the Baptizing Pool in the standstill August afternoon . . .

And I hear the ox bells cool as ax glint in the swamp.

. . . and the mesmeric tick of the stick I hold against the spokes of the turning wagon wheels the Sunday afternoon we drive four miles to the house of the man who has the tame crow that can talk . . .

And I smell the green smell of the white willows . . . and the yellow smell of yeast in the crock . . . and the pointed smell of spun fleece . . . and the round smell of purple plums . . . and the stately smell of birch bark . . . and the laughing smell of apples in a barrel . . .

And water tastes supremely like water. And nutmet like nutmeg. And bread like bread . . .

And my bare feet touch the dust in the road the first day the dust is warm all through and there is not a moth of disenchantment in any fold of the cloth of the day.

3 / *Wildcats, Tetrazzini, and Bee Beer*

I STARE AS THESE IMAGES VANISH. And then I laugh. I remember the fun there was in everything then. Just plain, thoughtless fun. And—what was a quite different thing—the funny *side* there was to everything. Later children seem to have been born bored. We never knew what a tiresome moment was.

Take the mornings again. They didn't *have* to be special. The most ordinary one we woke to seemed to be burnished with a sense of wonder.

If it was summer, there would be a flock of robins praising the air outside the bedroom window and the day seemed endlessly high and wide for things to happen in. If it was winter, the panes would be wall-papered from top to bottom with sprays and medallions of frost, but everything in the day would be near and touchable and guarding.

Downstairs, the kitchen would beckon with the smell of food and the pulse of living. Cereals had not yet been blown from a gun, refined to all but predigestion, and packaged about some object of miniature weaponry. We breakfasted on oatmeal bubbling like lava, and on bread browned in a wire toaster held over the fire itself. The boiled eggs would be peeled with great caution from their shells. Their glistening perfection of geometry would be admired for a moment before we plunged our spoons into the golden yolks. That children should have to be coaxed to eat, as if food were something as distasteful as fractions, we'd have found completely baffling.

As we ate, our thoughts sprang ahead to the fun awaiting us outside. That didn't have to be special either. It was enough just to open the henhouse door and watch the hens rustling their cuneiform feet in the straw, clucking like quilters over the scraps you threw them. Just to see the strands of sunlight strike gleams of iridescence from the tail feathers of the strutting rooster. (Once in a cold snap ours had his proud comb nipped by the frost. We had to install him in a box beside the kitchen stove, where, his pride of appearance laid low, he moped like Napoleon on Elba.) Then to stand on tiptoe to see how many eggs in all their porcelain splendor would be pocketed inside the straw-filled crate nailed to the wall. And then, as cautiously not to disturb her as if she were royalty, to ease down the boards that covered the mouth of the prostrate apple barrel the setting hen was enthroned in, replenish her food tin, and, this being the thirteenth day, crane to see if there were any small beaks poking out between her feathers.

(Should another hen at the same time show signs of brooding rather than laying, she was put into an open-meshed onion bag and hung on the clothesline until her passion cooled.)

Or, later, to knock out the wooden pin that held the cow's "stanchel" in position—so that in one deft movement she could now spread the posts apart and angle her trumpet-shaped horns back through them. And then to watch her race outside to the tub of water. Watch her gather such great quantities of it into her mouth before swallowing that you could see it tumbling down her throat like huge balls. Watch her turn away and rapturously sickle her tongue around the first tuft of sweet clover. Or, to stare into the horse's velvet eyes, as if into a bottomless pool of all that was quick and sleek and graceful, as his great lips delicately picked up every last oat held out to him in the palm of your hand.

In a pig's eye, it may be muttered. Yes, in a pig's eye too. To watch the pig's moneylender eyes above the flat button snout with the two thread-holes in it go nearly mellow as he scrabbled up the round, juicy apple you threw into his trough. Watch him maneuver it between his jaws for the first voluptuous, splitting crunch.

Yes, even in a hen's eye. We watched a hen's eye, occult as a fish's, to see if we could catch the lightning wink with the single lid that moved *up*ward instead of downward.

We stared, in fact, into the eye of everything. Flesh or plant or matter. And wondered.

Not that we floated about like damp little mooncalves. The clownishness of life was never lost on us either. Far more intriguing than watching the gluttony in the pig's eyes was the thought that maybe he'd get *out* again today.

I remember one morning our pig got out. When we first spotted him he was rooting seraphically in a row of stately zinnias that bordered Mother's flower garden.

Now you can no more steer a pig than a hurricane. The moment we surrounded him and tried to drive him back toward the pen he bolted straight between Father's legs and zigzagged through the clumps of bleeding heart.

"Oh, my bleeding heart!" Mother wailed.

"Oh, my bleeding ass!" Father roared, struck with more practical considerations. "Head him off before he gets into the cucumber patch!"

Father, who was never ruffled, who never came out with anything outrageous like that! We were knocked spinning by a sudden gust of laughter. Tottering with suppressed giggles, we couldn't have headed off a gnat. Even Mother shook only the harder when the pig bore down on the "embroid'ried" pillow slips Great Aunt Lena had sent her last Christmas. She'd spread them on the grass to bleach, and the pig's sharp toenails punctured one of them and it sailed off with him, flapping from a left hind hock. He landed smack in the middle of the cucumber patch, cleaving wide open each tender cucumber he trod on.

"Get the swill pail!" Father yelled at me.

I got the pail and sidled toward the pigpen door, tapping the pail and calling, "Here, pig, pig, pig . . ." The pig glanced at me briefly as if to say, "What foolish fellow is this?"—and then began to root among the vines.

"Get that rope hangin behind the shop door!" Father yelled again.

I got him the rope. He took it in one hand and grabbed up an apple under the Astrakan tree with the other.

"Stand back!" he called to the rest of us.

He advanced toward the pig in slow motion, holding out the apple in his hand and (though we knew he was seething inside) wheedling the pig in a kind of baby talk that sent us off into fresh spasms.

Now that we were apart we could give vent to our laughter.

My sister had a mild earache (that pipe smoke blown by Father into her ear had this time failed to cure). I remember her giggling and then moaning: "Oh dear, I wish I didn't have this cussed earache so I could *enjoy* laughing!"

Father got close enough to the pig that he could reach out and scratch behind its ears. The pig, as all pigs scratched there do, become almost jellied with delight. Father beckoned to me.

I took over the scratching, while he cautiously passed one end of the rope around the pig's body in a bowline knot behind its front legs. Then he paid out the rope as far ahead as it would reach and began to pull.

The pig immediately turned from jelly to steel. All fours braced like pillars, he couldn't be budged. Mother came up and, crouching over, began to push against its rump.

At last the two of them managed to snake him forward a little, step by jerky step. Until Mother, weakened by laughter, suddenly stumbled and sprawled headlong across his humped-up back. The pig shot from beneath her like a bullet and, with the tension on the rope so suddenly relaxed, Father tumbled backwards in a heap. The rope flipped out of his grasp. He sprang to his feet and scrabbled some tomatoes off the vines, hurling them at the pig without a second's aim.

None of them found its mark; but the pig, as if realizing he could never hope for a better send-off than that, simply headed for the pigpen door, rope, pillow case, and all, and disappeared inside.

"Well," Father said to Mother, himself suddenly grinning, "maybe you could ride him better if I got you a saddle!"

Yes, maybe the pig would get out again. Or maybe the same Aunt Lena would turn up for a visit and bring her violin.

Relatives were more engaging then than now. There was one who said "Good morning" to any cow he passed tethered alongside the road, nodding to her gravely. And another gentle soul who, in his cups, used to stepdance up and down the road proclaiming to one and all: "I'm your Uncle Billy Rippy-Tippy Ringle-Jingle Razzle-Dazzle Crip's Almighty God-dam!"

It was Aunt Lena's double distinction that she played the fiddle and was violently allergic to horse farts. She would arrive, wheezing like a bellows from her twenty-mile drive—but brave soul that she was, she never failed to oblige us with "Beautiful Isle of Somewhere" before getting her head down on the squawweed pillow that was the only real, or fancied, remedy for her condition. Each fall we youngsters scoured the pasture for a fresh supply of the knobby squawweed blossoms against just this emergency.

I remember one time she came to see us. There had been the usual preparations for her visit. Mother had made a blueberry fungy. The Almanac had been brought in from the outhouse and replaced with some old dress patterns cut into precise squares. The squawweed pillows were in readiness, and the tick she was to sleep on stuffed with fresh straw until it lay on the bed like a pregnant whale.

Her recital over, Aunt Lena retired early. In the middle of the night a mouse, which we'd unknowingly gathered up in the straw, popped through the slit on top of the tick, scampered over her belly, and sent her leaping from the bed like a trout. One foot (in a tasseled bed sock) landed square in the "chamber" and she rushed dripping and screaming into the hallway, the very "rags" she'd put up her hair with nearly alight with terror.

Whenever we had company we always left a lamp turned low in the hallway in case they might want to "go out" in the night. At the sound of these screams that seemed to argue murder at least, Father bounded out into the hallway in just the shirttail he slept in. Aunt Lena took one look at him in the spectral light—and fainted dead away.

Yes, maybe Aunt Lena would turn up again today. Or maybe you'd look out and see the boxlike "caravan" of the Levantine peddler topping the far hill. There'd be the prospect of all those bolts of yard goods, with their exciting store smell, spread out like a rainbow—and of his fascinating tales of life in the olive groves of Damascus.

Or maybe on your way to gather spruce gum

you'd glance up and there in the log road would incredibly stand a moose. A magical shiver would go through every one of your senses, for the great pan of its antlers and the primeval "bell" of gristle and coarse hair hanging at its throat were like relics of an animality untamed since the dawn of time.

Or maybe there'd be a woodsplitting frolic for the sick neighbor—and working alongside the men with the small ax your father had fitted up especially for you and the air constantly alive with the cloven sticks of rock maple hurtling toward the pile like gleaming Indian Clubs, you yourself would be a man with the others in all their gusty and ribald fellowship.

Or maybe down at Bill DeVarney's the professional barn mover would be setting up his medieval-looking winches and pulleys, and the three yokes of oxen would be waiting to pull the building down the treacherous slope that sober heads were sure could not be navigated without disaster.

Or maybe the wild geese would fly over and everyone would rush outside and watch them out of sight as if partaking in a mystery.

Or maybe someone would shoot a wildcat . . .

I remember one day in housecleaning time my cousin shot a wildcat six feet long. He carried it home, dumped it casually into the woodbox that had been lugged out into the dooryard for its yearly scrubbing with Gillett's Lye, and went off to water the horse. A few minutes later his sister came out and plunged her scrub cloth straight into the animal's jaws. She had just time to yell, "Help! A tiger!" before she, like Aunt Lena, keeled over in a dead faint.

But it didn't really matter whether anything *happened* or not. The days, just in themselves, seemed to glint with unexpected fireflies of what could only be called pure joy.

The morning you hurried over to inspect your small garden, and there were the first beans breaking through the earth like a row of tiny wickets. The exquisite lull in the back meadow, ringed and ribboned through by the brook, the moment you rested from turning the back swath of new-cut grass and saw that your father was breaking the dry twigs to boil the kettle . . . Dozens of things like these every day in the year; and as often in work as in play.

The moment after the last yellow birch in the last woodpile on the mountain slope had been piled on to the go-devil . . . and you had helped bind the load tight as a drum with the girdling chain, then sprung to your seat on the bag of straw at the load's pinnacle. Then to watch your father pilot the team with his matchless skill between the rocks and stumps along the edges of the narrow round-turn. And the moment after that, when you glided out on to the smooth snow of the main log road and your father passed *you* the reins . . . and as the brilliant muscles of the horses (a span this time) responded to the slightest gee or haw you tested your control with, an electric glee of power coursed from the tips of your fingers right down to the soles of your feet.

The moment after the peak thrust of your sled's

speed down the long hill bluing with dusk slowly exhaled, and looking up the hill again you saw the square of the kitchen window suddenly yellow with lamplight just as the pond ice began its chill night-booming, and the thought of the roasting spareribs glittered—yes, glittered—all through you.

And the moment in that same frozen night when, disembodied with weariness, your feet touched the hot flatiron wrapped in an old sweater under the blankets and you felt sleep stun you with its first delicious blow . . .

It was a kind of instant Zen, come by with no effort at all. Perhaps in the most humdrum hour it would strike you right out of the blue, and for the length of one dazzling pulsebeat lift you higher than a June of kites into that sky of skies where the glass between inside and outside melts completely away.

I mean, you'd be standing there on the bank of the brook and the current you couldn't see beneath the dark surface would be floating the water bubbles lazy as dreaming down the stream. The sun would be drowsing on your back. Sounds themselves would have a little pocket of stillness around them like rocks have. Your fishing line would be hanging slack from the alder pole into the pondlike stillwater. And then suddenly the surge of a trout would stretch your line taut and all at once your heart would seem to spread out like a fan and you would know exactly what trout-*ness* was. And *brook*ness. And *leaf*ness. And, yes, *world*ness and *life*ness itself. You would move right out—and gloriously—into everything around you.

The same thing might happen when, in October, with the crisp air stained with a painting's light, you crept so softly along the pine-needled path to the edge of the woods that now hemmed the old back orchard and there was the unsurprisable flock of partridges budding, this time unawares, in the very nearest apple tree . . .

Or when the January bluster moonscaped the frozen fields as eerily as the South Pole and you laced up the brand new larrigans to test their invincible snugness against the lashing snow . . .

Even when the black horses drew the black-tasseled hearse so slowly through the August afternoon and suddenly you knew what doomsday was—though not with any shrinking of the heart, because it would never be for you or for anyone you loved . . .

Or just to hear your father, who always "et whatever was set before him" without remark on it (or on anything else inside the house for that matter), say to your mother: "Someday, why don't you have a parsnip stew?"—and suddenly you'd see how one's light had become both the other's light and shade . . .

Not, again, that we were little puffballs of tender sensibility. We were not long innocent, either in knowledge or deed, of life's earthier side: and when we were by ourselves most of us used language that would have raised hair in a logging camp. Not to show off, but as part of the natural gusto (I remember one three-year-old who regularly bolted down not only his daily prunes, but the pits as well) that saved us from anything like wispiness.

[53

Of formal games there were few. Hopscotch courts checkered the dusty road in summertime and occasionally there'd be a fitful stab at blind man's buff among the cocks of hay put up against the dew in the shape of huge thimbles. There was a kind of baseball, played with a sphere of tightly wound sock ravelings (which sometimes broke apart in midair, trailing lengths of yarn behind it like a comet), and a kind of football played with a blown-up pig's bladder. But these didn't count for much. Who could be bothered with such nonsense as clouting a ball with a stick— when you could be walking the highest beam in the barn and tasting the spice of real danger while rain drummed its cozy tattoo on the roof? Or letting out the amazingly intricate beaver dam that was flooding the swale? Or building a lean-to, as exciting as Crusoe's, from the spruce boughs and maple saplings the choppers had left behind them in the mountain clearing?

(The girls' games seemed to us cold toast indeed. They played with dolls: small smooth-sided oblongs of rock which they dressed in petticoats carved out of discarded ironing-board covers. And when a new catalogue appeared, they would spend hours on end playing something called "Which Do You Like the Best?" That is, one after another would say which she liked the best among the items shown on each page, be they button boots or trusses.)

Books did not engage us. Perhaps because there were so few around. I can remember clearly only three. *She*, *Self-Raised* or *From the Depths*, and something called *Lady Scarsdale's Daughters*. But, strangely enough, we were utterly charmed by opera singers. Wherever it had its source I cannot even guess, but every so often would come our way a group picture of the divas then regnant. Alda, Galli-Curci, Melba, Tetrazzini . . . Each in the lush costumes of her most famous role. They held us like magnets.

Of spectator sports there were none. Unless you counted the friendly contest over whose ox team could haul the winter's "king" load to the stave mill, daily "scaling" figures going the rounds like news bulletins. Or the rivalry among young men away on the spring log drive to see who could grow the heaviest beard. The day they came home each beard was shaved off and weighed on the postmistress's letter scales. (The prize for the winner was a stickpin—and the worshipping glances of every girl in the place.)

But if there was nothing of the arena sort to amuse us, there was always some absorbing private operation to watch. Someone rocking up a new well. Or skinning a bear. Or hewing a ship spar. Or webbing a snowshoe. Or burning a chopping. You could watch the neighbor who was such a genius with animals pull a pig's "black teeth." Or, by his expert manipulation, save the cow with an apple in her windpipe. Or, with no curb but his gentling hands, shoe the plunging colt that no one else dared go near.

Strange children, with their flip questions, the men could not stand. ("That lookin snot, pimpin around, with his ears hangin out!") But with us, who had so often worked with them at the same tasks, it was quite different.

It was very nice, that special fellowship between adult and child then. You were never made to feel small and gawky. And watching a group of men working at their special crafts and ourselves being given some slight hand in them (how eagerly we fetched the chisel to pare the colt's frog or passed down the small chinking stones for the well!), with the yarns of moose hunt or log jam or sex capers threaded through it all, the whole thing was as hypnotic as a campfire.

Hero worship, the headiest of all childhood fevers, had its part in this. But our heroes were not of the usual kind. They were more apt to be the man whose woodsmanship was so perfect he could mark a tiny cross in the snow and fall a tree so that its tip struck that cross exactly, no matter which direction the wind was blowing. Or the brilliant (though never cruel or spiteful) "make-game" who could take off anything to a T. Our favorite was the time Curt and Sarah Lawson got into a tonguelash over the leach barrel. Familiar as it was, when he came to the part where she'd yanked out a loose corset steel and snapped it over Curt's head, and the part where Curt had yanked out the bung and then leg-bailed it toward the pasture, we could hardly keep from rolling on the ground. Or the fellow who could stepdance "Redwing" to a standstill and "tongue" the mouth organ into such throbbing tremolos that the girls almost burst their camisole straps in the polka quadrilles.

Not to mention the awesomely equipped gentleman who could bring off that staggering feat with not six, not eight, not ten, but thirteen pennies of the large size then in use.

More than any of this, though, it still remained the quite ordinary things that would for no plain reason stir us as if with the spark of marvels.

A calf's bangs. The Big Dipper. Huckleberry shine. A bluejay feather. The smell of oranges or pickling spice or britchen straps. An owl's eye. Looking down a deep hole. A snow crystal landing on the end of someone's nose. Seven 9's making 63. Everything being exactly what, where, and how it was at that very moment—stones being heavy, apples being round, water being cool. The touch of hand or sun or breeze. The taste of fern "meat." The sound of crickets winding their clocks. The fuzz on a bumblebee . . . Hundreds of things like these.

But the single thing, naturally, that best represented the blend of lark and wonder in our lives was Christmas.

I remember one in particular.

Waking while it was still dark, but feeling the special magic of the Christmas-morning darkness and smelling the intoxicating smell of fir and hemlock all through the house and the heat of the room stove that was never lit this early on any other day in the year. Eating breakfast by lamplight in a chatter of excitement. Then Mother taking the lamp and leading us all into the dining room, where, as if from a gesture of magic, the soft-shimmering tree sprang out of the darkness like a great warm emerald. And everyone's face somehow open to everyone else's.

All that long day I remember, each moment of it steeping with presents and the smell of oranges and roasting chicken and tenderloin, steeping with Christmas, until the Christmas daylight bowed out to the Christmas dusk gentler than light to dusk on any other day.

Just before dark (and before the Christmas concert, when King Herod's whiskers, spun from the tag locks of Uncle Billy Rippy-Tippy's sheep, would jiggle so comically as he talked that every parent in the audience, himself one muscle away from "snorting," would frown at every child not to giggle out loud) I went down the road, with Christmas everywhere in the yellow window light slanting out on to the snow and in the hushed, darkening trees, to see what Stan *Dexter's* sled was like.

It was plain that Stan's father, Jess, had got on to the bee beer.

You never hear of bee beer now, but it was a feature of nearly every household then. The "bees" were tiny cauliflowers of, I suppose, some yeastlike substance. You put a handful of them into a self-sealer of molasses and water and set the self-sealer on a sunny window sill. At once the bees began to course through the liquid. Up and down. Up and down. When, after a fortnight or so, they finally settled on the bottom the brew was ready to go.

Jess had also been raiding the apple cider and nipping at the beet wine. When I arrived, he was setting out to milk, with a pail of peelings for the cow.

A few moments later I happened to glance through the window at his progress and there he was: wearing the milk pail like a helmet now and tossing out the peelings from the other pail in great arcs to left and right as if he were sowing grain. It wasn't long before he came back.

"Jess!" his wife cried, as he opened the kitchen door. "For *praise's* sake, what . . . ?" For with him he had the cow.

Jess merely grinned and led the cow straight in through the door and across the floor to the dining room. "I thought she'd like to see the tree," he said.

Four happy hours later I took one long last lingering look at our own tree to provision me through the night and, drugged with the day as if with some charm in a fable, climbed the stairs and fell instantly into a school of dreams that carried me on their backs like golden fishes.

4 / *Slate Rags, Tudors, and Popocatepetl*

REAL SCHOOL WAS ALMOST ALL LARK. Honesty can only treat it as a joke. But a joke with a lining of solid values nevertheless.

The building was not a proverbial red, it was scribbler gray. It was not set in some quaint hollow; it sat on a solid ledge of bare granite that took a fearful toll of skin and breeches. We were not the poet's "little man," blessings on him, whistling all day as if he'd swallowed a bobolink. That we'd have considered mere empty-headedness.

And teachers were by no means all apple-cheeked and dove-brained innocents either: they were people. There was one who got so groggy from late courting hours every night that some days she scarcely knew cube root from board feet, and finally the trustees had to "speak to her." And another with a great sense of occasion. The afternoon Ruth Goldsmith's father "came to the door" and told Ruth her brother was home from France, she marked everyone's work 100 and we all knew quite well she set the clock ahead.

The teacher had a table desk with a dining-room chair; and our two rows of great-bellied double desks faced hers. There were also two blackboards, a globe, a clock with a pendulum like Poe's, a barrel stove with a game leg that was forever buckling at the knees and letting the whole works down on to the floor, a row of nails for the coats, and three maps—so chapped with age, and their backs so reinforced with gingham soaked in flour paste, that they made the world look like one huge delta.

No kindergarten tulips trimmed the window panes. We had no crayons, and for some reason all we ever drew was pears. Walls were decked with nothing but a picture of the reigning king and a feed calendar.

And yet we learned a great deal. Much of it by rote, maybe—but we did learn.

What did we learn?

Well, in grammar, we learn that "the subject is?" . . . "what we're talking about." (The teacher would start the question off, and everyone would chorus the ending.) "The predicate is?" . . . "what we say about the subject." "The object answers the question?" . . . "who or what." No matter that in the face of a concrete example anything but the simplest sentence could trip us up. In "O, when will the rain unleash the buds?," "O" was named as subject almost every time. Whereas "analyzing" a complete sentence or "parsing" its nouns was a problem that found the teacher herself on such shaky ground that she'd move on quickly to "figures of speech." "Synecdoche is?" . . . "using the part for the whole." "As in?" . . . "All hands to the pumps!" we would shout as one man.

Reading was our strength, and right from the start we hadn't the least trouble with it. Even Grade One (despite a drilling in their ABC's which would now be looked on with horror) picked it up as naturally as breathing. Probably because the stories in their Reader had such real interest that they couldn't wait to puzzle them out. No dreary Janes and Dicks with no more zest than skim milk.

Instead there was the perky Little Red Hen, with her wonderfully tart reply to those who would help not at all to grind her grain of wheat but were only too eager to help her eat the bread she finally baked of it. Or the crack-brained Chicken Little on whose head fell the acorn that she mistook for the sky—and on whose journey to tell the King about it was taught how the Foxy Loxys of this world can fatten on the Goosey Looseys. Or "Belling the Cat," a trim little parable that covered in three short paragraphs the whole matter of courage under fire.

Later we met the woman in the scarlet dustcap whom the beggar asked for one of the cakes she was baking. Each cake she took from the oven seemed to her too large to give away. So she'd bake him a smaller one. But when that was done it too seemed too large. So she'd bake him another that was smaller still. Until the beggar, who was of course a magician, eventually lost his patience and turned her, much to our delight, into the first scarlet-crested woodpecker. There was also the one about the old woman whose pig balked at the stile, with its truly witching prose. Suspense kept us on edge until "the ox began to drink the water, the water began to put out the fire, the fire began to burn the stick, the stick began to beat the dog, the dog began to bite the pig, the pig began to jump over the stile . . ." so that the old woman did after all "get home tonight."

And who could forget *The Wise Men of Gotham*? *The Prisoner and the Flower*? (The sting of that one was almost more than we could bear.) *Diamond Cut Diamond*? *The Brahmin, the Tiger, and the Jackal*? *Hans Brinker; or, the Silver Skates*? Just their titles were enough to fan our curiosity to white heat.

Poetry was turned as far as possible into prose. The thing was (heresy of heresies!) to get the gist of

it and let the moonbeams go. This was done by looking up certain random words of the poem in the dictionary and writing in their no-nonsense meanings
over the top. Carried too far, this could give some odd
results. "Like a feather is wafted downward by an
eagle in its flight" gains clarity maybe, but little else,
by becoming—as it did in an old Reader of mine—
"Like a feather is 'to convey effortlessly through air or
water' downward by an eagle in its 'act or manner of
hasty departure.' "

And yet poetry did get under our skins. When
the teacher read Gray's "Elegy" aloud, even the hel-
lions who'd just been "snapping" each other's ears sat
still as mice. We took the poet's pleasure in peculiar
sound effects too. "Pernambuko." ("A wind blew up
from the Pernambuko/Heave-ho, the Laughing Sally
. . ."). "Noch nicht" ("notch nitched," according to
the teacher) in the story about the Tyrol. Or, best of
all: "Popocatepetl." These became bywords in all our
conversation. "Hi, Stan, how's your Popocatepetl?"
Roars of laughter!

In geography we learned that the world is round,
because if you "sailed constantly in the same direction . . ." Or was it that if you "dropped an object
from a high tower . . ."? In any case, we weren't quite
convinced. But we could rattle off the capitals of
Europe without thinking. France? Paris. Spain? Ma-
drid. Montenegro (where is it now?)? Cetinje. Bul-
garia? Sofia. ("Sophia who?" More laughter.)

We learned that England had a temperate? . . .

climate . . . and exports? . . . "cuttelry"; that India lies
on the E? . . . quator . . . and exports? . . . precious
stones; that Baluchistan is inhabited by? . . . Mongols
. . . and uses the yak as a? . . . beast of burden. "Hi,
Stan, how's your yak?" Clowning a lesson stapled it to
our minds like nothing else.

English history was our favorite subject. We
were less than bloodthirsty but we did like action,
however grisly—and there was plenty of it there.
Waging war, smothering little boys, setting out on
expeditions, a Cranmer burning off his own hand because he'd "recanted" . . . ("Recanted," we'd ponder.
That must be one of those *secret* words, like "fornication" in the scripture readings. If we sneaked a look at
"fornication" in the dictionary while the teacher was
out sweeping the porch, we merely got another long
word we didn't know the meaning of. And if we
looked that one up, we simply got "fornication" again.
This was a topic of endless discussion on our way to
and from the spring under the clump of roots where
we got our daily pail of drinking water.)

History had its dull stretches up to Henry the
Eighth. But Henry, of course, had those six wives—
including Katharine-Parr-Who-Outlived-Him. (We always thought of that end clause as part of her actual name.) And the Tudors, one and all, held us in
that strange spell they've had for every imagination
before or since. The poor luckless Jane Seymour. The
blazing Elizabeth. And who could not be struck still
by Bloody Mary, with the "callous" on her heart?

(We knew it was "Calais," but somehow it was far more in keeping with our awe to picture it as a kind of regal stone bruise.)

It was these touches that made them all so real. As, later, Cromwell would stick with us because he had warts on his nose, and Queen Anne because she had twenty-children-all-of-which-died-in-infancy.

Stodgier matters got scant attention. The Rump Parliament was good for little more than a smirk when the teacher mentioned it. The Reformation couldn't hold a candle to the Gunpowder Plot. The Industrial Revolution was shrugged off except for the spinning jenny. ("Hi, Stan, how's your spinning jenny?") But the string of personalities of which history is the sediment lived in our minds like a glittering parade.

We also had good heads for arithmetic. As early as Grade Three we could say our thirteen times table backwards. Grade Four could reckon the cost of papering a room; Grade Five, the volume of a grindstone. We learned as well how to arrive at an H.C.F. or an L.C.M.; when to "set the decimal over"; how much change to bring back if eggs were selling @ 15 cents per doz.; how to "express £5 12s in terms of pence"; and that, if you wanted any painting done, A rather than B, and certainly rather than C, was the man to hire.

To say nothing of the extra lore gleaned from the back covers of our "Big Beaver" scribblers. That they weighed with grams in Troy (was that the same place they had the wooden horse?); that a stone was fourteen pounds, an ell forty-five inches; and that five and a half yards was, of all things, a perch.

We were equally captured by the fact that the conversion rate for the pound sterling should be such a strangely un-round figure as 4.86-2/3, and that anything as smooth as a circle should always be such an odd 3.1416 times the length of its diameter.

Basic tools for mathematics were a slate, a slate pencil, a slate rag, and a vanilla bottle to hold the water for washing the slate clean. Pieces of flannel shirt tail were favored as slate rags by the children themselves. They had he nice nap that best soaked up the drip. But for reasons of motherly pride we were usually given the showiest gingham "remnant" in the house. Slate rags, in fact, became almost a caste mark.

At the back of Grade Eight's arithmetic was a group of Miscellaneous Problems (numbered 1 to 100) of such fiendish difficulty that they sometimes daunted even the teacher. Daunted her, but never defeated her.

Asked for help with one of them, she would check first whether or not its number had been heavily ringed with black pencil by a previous teacher. If it had, this meant that the key to it could be found in a scribbler of solutions to "hard questions" that made its furtive rounds among the teaching sisterhood of all the nearby schools. She'd tell us to skip this one for the time being—and hope that we would not press the matter until the scribbler came her way again.

If it was not so marked, and if the answer she

worked out remained stubbornly different from the one the book gave, she'd simply write "Wrong Answer" above the one in the book and substitute her own. Leaving us overjoyed to have bared the flaw in a printed text.

Of course what the "D"s and "C"s—that is, Grades Nine and Ten—learned was purely occult. We touched the compasses and protractors they used for something called Mechanical Drawing with as gingerly a reverence as if they were the bones of saints. Anyone could see that the things we overheard them discussing were plain guff. How could x plus y, two letters, be the number of days it took to build a house? But they kept us wide-eyed nevertheless.

There was no chemistry equipment, but one teacher had somehow got hold of a small ball of sodium. She would put this into a muffin tin of water and tell the "C"s that "hydrogen was escaping"—although you couldn't spot a sign of it. It was sheer magic. (Until the trustees got wind of what was going on and put a firm stop to such dangerous cantrip, with all those young children there.)

Except in arithmetic, our examinations consisted of a line of questions written on the blackboard, each beginning: "Write a note on . . ." In arithmetic the teacher took them straight from the book.

One day she fumbled her copy and asked us to express two thirds (instead of the intended two fifths) as a decimal. This question looked like the easiest of the lot, so Howie tackled it first. He was still adding more naughts to the dividend and getting more sixes in the quotient when the bell rang an hour later.

No one worried about examinations, however. You knew you'd be sure to grade no matter what you put down, public feeling against the teacher's failing anyone being so strong. And if you had no grasp of the subject whatsoever, you could always have your mother write an "excuse" saying that you couldn't be there for the test that day because they needed you at home to help sweep down the flue, but she'd vouch that you knew your work. This would do.

Grading everyone was *one* earmark of the good teacher. The other two were: she was "strict"; and if the son of the household where she boarded tried to "go with her," he must be given first claim. Break any of these unwritten rules and she wouldn't be asked for a second term.

This matter of ask or be asked was a ticklish proposition. If a teacher was forced to "apply" for a second term it was a kind of disgrace. Sometimes as late as June neither she nor the school authorities had shown their hand.

"Maybe she don't *want* the school agin," people would sputter, "but I think they ought to *ask* her. They're makin a fool of the poor girl."

If the girl did swallow her pride and ask, a hard-and-fast verdict was still a long way off.

The Secretary was little help. He acted only five times a year. Quarterly, when he made a drive on sluggish taxpayers to meet her salary ("I just can't face the girl unless I have twenty dollars, anyway, to offer her—why, she's buyin her own chalk now!") . . . and on the night of the lantern-lit school meeting, when he pressed, always without luck, to have them vote five dollars for repairs to the outhouse.

If she asked him, he'd say, "It ain't up to me, it's all up to the trustees." If she asked Trustee Tom, he'd go right on paring his apple with a jackknife and say, "It's all right with me if it's all right with Bill." Bill would say, "It's all right with me if it's all right with Tom." This deadlock might go on for weeks before a firm "yes" could be pried out of anyone.

Naturally, a "home" girl must under no circumstances apply for the post—even for a first term. She could let it be known by word of mouth that she would "like the school," but to urge her suit more than that would have been a shameless "presumption" on the claims of acquaintance. She could only hope that the trustees would come to *her*. They almost always did, but here too they took their good-looking time about it.

Perhaps the most common criticism of a teacher was that she "put all her time on the higher grades." That is, the "D"s and "C"s, who had to write the Provincial Tests in town.

She didn't, actually. And yet there was a clannishness between her and the "C"s that didn't reach down to the rest of us. When she heard their lessons she sat on the top of an empty desk facing theirs, or squeezed in alongside them, three to a seat.

There was a keen air of conspiracy in their open plotting of every possible trick to outwit the Provincial markers. She told the "C"s to write *something* about everything, whether they knew what they were talking about or not. On the grounds that enough fire, however chance, would be sure to hit the target somewhere. (I, when I became a "C" myself, once described the Caxton press as "one of the greatest battles every fought, both sides advancing and retreating, and the ground covered with wounded and slain.") And "C"s had it constantly drummed into them that, no matter how early they finished their papers, they should cut off the final answer in mid-sentence and write "Not enough time to finish" at the bottom of the page.

The week the "C"s went off to "write" (in their brand-new corduroy reefers or clouds of organdie) they were the center of everyone's thoughts. And the week in August when they were due to "hear," the whole community quaked with each approach of the mailman. Hands trembled so they could scarcely open the envelope and draw out the sheet inside.

If in no case was the "top torn off" this sheet (the top scrolly part proclaiming it to be a PASS certificate), a jubilant shout went relaying from hayfield to hayfield and these "licenses," as they were called, were brandished aloft in the post office doorway until the aprons of congregating women filled the air like a swarming of butterflies.

If one *were* torn off, however, hearts sank like

stones. There was nothing quite like the sympathy for a failed "C," save that for the teacher whose "Returns" (after three days and nights of struggle and near-hysteria over the tricky Average Daily Attendance section) came back from the Inspector with all the percentages marked Incorrect.

Once a year the Inspector called—and that was another dread day.

No one had minded the old Inspector. He used to tether his horse to an iron ring in the clapboards, doze a few minutes by the stove, suck a lozenge for his asthma, "sign the Register," and then leave without asking anyone a single question. But this new man was as prying as a new broom, and notorious for the relish he took in heckling a fledgling teacher, especially, to the point of tears.

By keeping close tabs on his passage through neighboring sections the date of his visit could be pretty well forecast. And each day of the week in which it was likely to fall the schoolhouse floor was swept twice, the stove got a coat of "Rising Sun" stove polish, and we all wore clean starched blouses.

But we could never preguess his catechism. If Grade Five had been drilled in fractions as the likeliest bet, he'd come at them with the War of the Roses. If the teacher tried to steer him toward Grade Seven's knowledge of the Gulf Stream, which they'd rehearsed letter-perfect, he'd ignore her and spring "Abou Ben Adhem" at them.

It was a monstrous ordeal, but the glee when it was over made it almost worthwhile.

The moment he'd gone, discipline vanished. We all bounded from our seats and clustered about the teacher's desk; and she hashed the whole thing over with us like a general, all rank aside, with his victorious troops.

"Dick, what was it he said when you said . . . ?" it would go. Or, "I *knew* it, Miss Crockett, I just couldn't think." Or, "I saw him grin, *honest*. He grinned twice." Finally she'd say, "Oh, it's pretty near recess time anyway, I guess you can go out and play *now*."

These were the routine features of our education. But that's not to say no room was found for the more delicate arts.

We sang—with the teacher always taking what was known as "top line." And our songs were no limp confetti like "Lazy Willie, will *you* get up." They had meat and punch. "Jim Blake, your wife lays dying / Come over the wires tonight . . ." Or another splendid knell (our favorite) whose title I forget but whose most gripping lines, at the point where a jilted sweetheart hangs herself, still cling: "He took his knife and he cut her down / And in her bosom these words he found . . ."

Acting talent was given scope in the yearly concert, which was never without its rousing mixture of accident and glory. There was one flag drill in which the leader's crepe-paper leggings began to unwind, loop by trailing loop, until the whole battle formation turned into a tangled rout. But this calamity was more than redeemed by the number that came next.

In this the teacher recited verses about the Titanic while two girls sang "Nearer My God to Thee" outside on the porch, with their heads inside a pork barrel to give the impression of sounds over water.

One teacher thought it would whet our taste for literature in general if she read aloud to us from books that had nothing to do with school. But, again, no pap. No winsome rabbits in a cabbage patch, no flighty Alices. She simply read us whatever *she* was reading. Our favorite here was a story of love and horror called *Flames in the Wind*, with the startling first line, "My God! Oh, my God!"—although she did water this down to "Gracious Me!"

As a last mercy we were never asked to muddy our minds with indigestible scraps of information about Current Events in the world at large. The world outside, and its sour lessons, could wait.

WHAT KIND OF CHILDREN did all this make of us?

Well, for the most part we were strangely adult. No Tom Sawyers. (We'd have taken his bogus drolleries as the mark of a ninny.) No bullies. No vicious nicknames. We were always rassling; but if two of us ever came to real blows, it was as serious as if our fathers had clashed. More often than not because in some way they had. For this reason, the teacher never interfered. It would have meant getting herself mixed up in a far graver issue.

Nor did parents interfere much with the teacher.

The only time I can recall a parent's "coming to the road" was in the case of Lennie Whitman. And then in no bristling mood.

It seemed that Lennie's recitation for the day was "An Arab's Farewell to His Steed." Which began: "My Beautiful, my Beautiful, that standeth meekly by /With thy proud mane and arching neck and dark and glittering eye . . ." His mother merely asked if Lennie could be let off his assignment this once because their old driving mare had died last night in her sleep and he couldn't get past the first two words without choking.

Our noontime games were seldom games of fierce contention either.

Not even the kind of ball we played. There were no bases; only opposing fielders scattered about wherever they chose. You hit the ball and then made a dash to touch the outhouse. If these fielders couldn't scrabble up the ball, throw it at you and strike you with it (the yarn it was made of was soft enough that it didn't hurt) before you got back, you stayed at bat until they did. There were no ground rules other than that, and no score. It was a point of honor with the pitcher to throw balls the batter could get the best crack at. "No wonder you got us out," one side might scold the other, "you didn't give good balls!"

We much preferred Moose. The "moose" were given a five-minute start to take cover in the barrens and then the "hunters" came after them in full cry, with their alder-whittled muzzle loaders.

Or Oxen.

We made our own "oxen." The method was simple. Fill a liniment bottle halfway to the neck with water. Girdle the bottle, at the level of the water, with a piece of string soaked in kerosene. Set a match to the string, let it burn all the way around, then lift off the top of the bottle (which would separate in a perfect circle) and you had an ox. Strap his neck into the hollow of a miniature yoke, tie a string to the yoke, stuff the cavity in the bottle with twigs, and it was no trouble at all to imagine that you were hauling logs together and piling them in a "brow," as the men did.

The schoolhouse, midpoint in the long stretch of ledge and scrub that separated one part of the village from the other, was a mile from the nearest house; so we took our lunches. Lunch staples were bread, potatoes, molasses, and tea. Each family had its own molasses bottle on the window sill, and each took its weekly turn in providing tea for the general pot.

Around noon the stove was lined with tins of warming food, and almost every hand that shot up was to ask: "Please may I stir my hash?" Sometimes the onion was already in the mixture. Sometimes it was added on the spot.

If we had cake or some other tidbit our mothers were particularly proud of, we were told to share it with the teacher, now don't forget. We kept a steady eye on her as she ate these offerings, waiting for the little cluck of praise we'd be asked about when we got home—and she didn't dare refuse one of them, no matter how crammed she might become with boiled frosting or piccalilli, lest this be taken as a show of favoritism that would wound feelings beyond repair. It is a measure of her gallantry that she suffered this, day in and day out, without a flicker of dismay.

As for ourselves, we didn't know a vitamin from a split pea or a carbohydrate from an acorn; cleaned our teeth with ashes and soda; all drank from the pail of spring water with the same dipper—and were as healthy as horses.

School was something of all this—and yet more.

Whatever quirks in the way we were taught, we went there for studies alone. There was nothing of the later idea that school is for practicing the broad jump or turning out a nutpick on the workshop lathe: ours was for the mind. And, hit or miss, it did as good a job of training there as any I've met up with since.

Maybe it held something for the spirit too.

For who could forget how it was the morning the mote-thickened sunshine slanted through the open window and touched your morning slate with the year's first thumb of warmth and you saw that the sun had somehow marked the problem you were working on Right, and you thought in the same moment about the sap kettle in the cool green shadow, waiting to be emptied at noon?

Or the day the hot hum of the locust sounded in the still, pencil-tapping afternoon, though the summer was really over, and Grade Six was reading aloud about the brave boy dying smiling at Ratisbon, and the blurless glister of the blackberries was just outside the wall?

Or the day when school was really out, but you were all waiting for the men to come and see you safely home through the window-lashing bluster (with the "cloud" pulled up over your face and your breath warm and wool-smelling inside it), and the seats were all drawn up in a circle around the stove on the larrigan-blackened softwood floor, and as each gust in the chimney lighted each face with snugger and snugger excitement you knew you would never forget each other as long as you lived?

5 / Chords and Acres

GROWNUPS TOO HAD THEIR ISLANDS of fraternity. The pie sales. The tea meetings. The dances after the chopping frolics. The evenings of 45's . . . Which too are now seen as a decayed and threadbare vaudeville.

Perhaps that's all they ever were; perhaps it isn't.

I remember one pie sale that was got up specificially to buy a community bull. (It was prompted by the remark of an eighty-year-old spinster. "Things have come to a pretty how-do-you-do," she chided, "when there's no *animal* in the place!") Another to top out the schoolhouse chimney. Another to raise funds for the man laid up with a winter of boils.

Pies never varied. The raisin, with the latticed crust. The lemon, with the turrets of whipped egg white drawn up to as fine a thread as the twist of a baby's wet hair. The buttermilk, with the beads of pure flavor sparkling on its surface. The apple, with a whole vial of colored "showers" sprinkled over it. All encircled with wreaths of traveling ivy and geranium blossoms (there was always *some* good-natured woman in the place who would let her house plants be plundered)—or stockaded with brilliantly dyed matchsticks, each topped with a silver star of pressedout tea lead.

The auctioneer, surprising antic out of his sober workday self, swooped them precariously about on the tripod of his fingers and lashed the laggard bidding into a nimble frenzy.

Boys, who knew to a penny how much money they had in their pockets, would stop abruptly when that limit was reached; but there was always at least one young man whose tenacity tipped off the others that this pie was his girl's. Then would start the lively game of "running him up"—with the constant danger that, pushed too far, he might let chivalry go hang and "drop it on them."

All was good nature, however; and after the final disclosure of who had bought exactly whose, deals could always be struck and switches connived at, so that the right partners wound up together regardless.

A curious outcome of bidding that was truly blind happened once.

It turned out that Bob Withrow had bought Arch Tobin's wife's pie . . . and everyone rolled an eye toward the ceiling. What now? Though village feuds were almost unknown, Bob and Arch had clashed over which side of the line between them a cherry tree stood on and had matched stubbornness with stubbornness and silence with silence the whole month since. Bob hesitated a moment now, then walked over to Arch.

"Arch," he said, "I guess I bought your wife's pie."

"*That* so," Arch said, suddenly grinning. "Well, it ain't a cherry pie, I can tell you that. If it had a bin, there'd be some calculatin to do, wouldn't there!"

They never again crossed words.

The sessions of 45's had their own ritual and idiom.

Cards thought certain to take a "lift" were thumped down with a crack of the knuckles on the hardwood table—to be followed by a still more splitting crack if the next player ("I got just the paint for that one!") could top them. Players got up and walked around their chair three times to change a streak of bad luck. The dealer blew on the cards to ensure himself a good hand.

If a bluffing bidder got stuck with the contract he could take a further chance, throw away his hand and "go on the pussy," the four cards dealt face down in the center of the table. When asked to name the trump he would never name it simply. "Hearts are the good ones," he might say. Or: "Diamonds dearly bought for ladies."

If two partners, nearing the game mark, showed niggling caution they were taunted with "rotting out." The third-hand player, "sticking" the bidder with the Jack (next in value to the almighty "5"), invariably remarked: "That will take the roof!"

The dancing after the chopping frolics may have been a rite no less fixed—but it was as different from the somnambulant dancing of today (with that somehow masturbatory indraft about it even in its most frantic forms) as drink from drug.

All hands glowed with the cider that the spigot tender down cellar passed from one to another in the long-handled dipper. Yet they were not slewed away by it from the beam of pure pleasure that lit them as, tingling with willingness and anticipation, they pitched in to clear the dining room of all its furniture except the chair for the fiddler and the organ his wife played chords on. The swing of the "plain quadrille" mounted in a lightning spiral to boundlessness. It so romped in the blood and spiked it with sheer joy of limb and joy of neighbor that when you joined hands in the Big

Ring it was like a pledge of "this till death." When the youngest boy and the oldest woman "polkaed out" together, with everyone clapping, the whole company was of one age. Even the ticking of the big octagonal clock, with the long pendulum that swung the engraved butterfly and the reed it was forever lit on forever back and forth, seemed to catch the mood of it all. (Though the clock was scarcely to be looked at as the time grew late, with its reminder that pleasure too had its hour glass.)

And when you stepped outside to urinate sparklingly, parabolically, in the starlight, the very self-distancing of the sky seemed to melt and grant a concurring eye to the hub of zest and friendliness that echoed in the house behind you. In the greenest island of all.

There is another kind of island that waits for most people.

You look outside yourself and you see only the blindness of people moving no less blindly than things. The whole world is stonestruck because there is nothing listening to *all* of it at once. There is no brother look in any of it toward your chill at its strangeness. You look inside yourself and you see no brother-besiding self there either. Only the chalk-face of dismay holding its chalk-faced breath with never an exhalation. Pressing its fingers before its eyes to try to keep out the flat dead light of drilling is-ness, but forever failing.

Things turning the other way are turning away

from *you* without a backward glance. Things turning toward you bare their dead intent *at* you without a flicker of thought to what particular sentience you have. Things standing still cry out (though not to you) their deafness to themselves. Silence tortures. It is the loudness of yourself alone. Speech tortures. It is the husk of speech forever falling short of the wall that the voice crying beneath it knows it can never penetrate or reach over. Music tortures. It holds out to you the leap beyond yourself to where it promises to fuse all things, but lands you there to find nothing but its orchestration of your singleness. Living tortures. It will give you no clear space in its mirror where you can see both yourself defined for everyone and your self reflected out into all things. And because it will not stop.

This these people knew nothing of. Not then. The village seemed to be inside the day. The day's pulse was its pulse. Each fàce was written and readable in the same language as its neighbors'. A clear stream of well-being flowed through everyone. Unhappiness was only a parenthesis, as happiness is only a parenthesis now.

The heart, born solitary, must draw back a breath not its own or it stifles and, no longer recognizing itself, flaps on its hinges like a derelict gate. But theirs did not draw this breath from any planned amusements set like traps for it. What chiefly kept theirs live (and beating with the saving nextness to itself and the things around it) were its chance concordances with some texture of the day. Some texture that filled it full of meeting its likeness in the touch that aroused it, the way that light striking a field at a certain slant can suddenly emblazon it with a new and soaring self-description.

In the city you walk down the streets with their eyes put out, and noises without voice beat against each other without knowledge. Soulless light strikes daylight in the mouth. The effigies in the shop displays smile their wax smiles ceaselessly against the plate glass. Each face has its window to itself walled up, each with the small world behind it running like clockwork wound up and forgotten. They jostle each other, the eyes only a thing to steer them by. Headless subjects and predicates, no two ever joining to bloodstream a sentence. There is a bleaching yawn of distance between the closest things. The uncreated breaks from its grave at the core of objects and glitteringly prevails . . . And at the end of the day, something like the steady blows of those momentary landscapes glimpsed some stone-bruised dusk from a speeding train (and so brutally other for your having nothing you've both known in time past to touch them with) turns its soundless heel on your silenced heart.

Your morning self had had a sense of comforting two-ness; the one of it in mutual confidence and protection of the other. Now your very flesh splits, and these are separated beyond hand-reach. A draft of longing searches you. You burn with homesickness, the only flame that smokes its chimney white.

In Norstead it was not like that.

You walked down the road and it took the imprint of your footsteps. The field that bordered the road was all yours to the depths of the earth. It was friends with the road. Your family fields knew you thoroughly. They accepted you so thoroughly that when you were in them you need give no thought to how you looked or hew yourself to any dictate of another's gaze. Your dialogues with the field chimed below the surface of your mind like the tune of health.

But it was good sometimes to leave them and have a neighbor bring your consciousness up front. You stepped onto the road. You felt yourself stretch and widen with its welcome. There were no sounds that didn't come from a living thing or from the earth-sourced tasks of man or woman. You knew everyone you met. You talked to him, the talk as unplotted as breathing.

In the city street of strangers your voice becomes like a weight in your throat. You bear it along orphaned with disuse. Here it was light as air. There was scarcely a man but would leave his work in the fields and come to the roadside for an easy chat when you waved to him. You had all been so close and unchanging a cast in all the plays life thrusts people into—the lead, where the big capitaled feelings are centered, now falling to one of you, next time to another—that you knew each other's parts clear through.

In the city, the tight imperious mouths and the taut impervious eyes batter you until you feel a ghostliness inside you like the lettering on a discarded wrapper tumbled by a heedless wind. Here, it was not like that. Eyes drove no bargains with themselves or with the eyes of anyone else. When you walked down the road and talked to each other you made each other solid as places.

There are fashions in city faces. Each looks as if it had been bought off the racks in a shop that stocked only the prevalent masks. No two faces here were alike, but all persons were made one by the livelihoods and likelihoods they all shared. Angers between them were never as deep as the bedrock loyalty to kind. (You quarrel with a friend because he is worth a quarrel; the weapon is never scorn.) And there was always one man who would fight for you quicker than he'd fight for himself.

Even the old were not shunted aside. The sound of their lives had been so long a keynote in the family chord that it never ceased to resound.

Earth and sky were such a constant in the field of vision that it seemed as if they lived, no less directly than the images of kitchen chairs, within the eye itself. So that there was never a lonesome sunset, as in the city streets, to strike stone from stone into the heart.

Things (the teakettle, the sled tongue, the well curb) broke the seal of inanimacy, showed they could be made friends of, spoke the unspoken history of each occasion they had ever had a part in each time they were looked at. The consciousness was galleried with them, so that the spirit was never faced with the bare, unyielding glare of those dead-white walls of the self the city self cages itself into.

These people suffered all the pains there are, but nothing in them ever had to die alone.

And the acres a man's heart and strength made his world of (or the way each large event was named for the man most closely connected with it) would always keep his name alive. The "Bart Ramsay place" would always be the "Bart Ramsay place," however often it changed hands. The sharp twist in the road near Davy Langille's house would always be "Davy's Bend." The fire that plundered the forests for miles around when it escaped from George Rawding's pipe bowl the day the falling hemlock knocked the pipe from his mouth in the tinder August would always be known as "the George Rawding fire." The brook through Peter Herald's meadow would be "Pete's Brook" as long as water ran.

And as long as there was work for the hands, there was wealth for the senses.

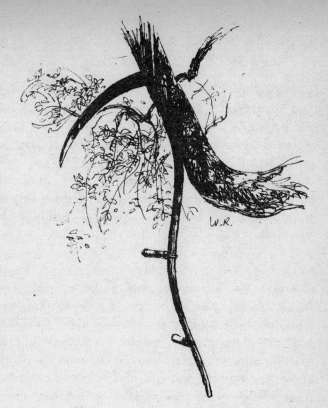

6 / Plow, Scythe, and Peavey

WORK, WOVEN WITH WEATHER, was the very grain of existence. Time was packed with it, atom against atom, with hardly a chink between.

It started at the brisk of dawn when you took the lantern from its hook in the cellarway, raised the globe with your thumb, put a match to the wick, and picked up the milk pails for the barn. It ended when you made your final trip to the barn that night, took the meal tubs from the oxen's mangers, rugged the horse, came back to the kitchen and blew the lantern out. There was a sun's length of labor with the ax or the scythe or the plow in between.

Some days it was *all* wealth, all anodyne. Others, it emblooded you and bled you almost equally. Days like these.

Perhaps you broached the morning with your hands on the plow. The air was fresh. The day was wide. The multiform leaves trembled with contentment in the noiseless breeze. They were a throng of friends. They gently crowned the nowness of everything, encircled you with it. The house was near. Your muscles had the knack of what they were doing built into them like a recitation. They pleasured themselves in steering the share just right to curl over the first ribbon of greensward without a break, in giving the reins looped about your neck just the right tug to keep the horse's path straight as a ruler from guide stick to guide stick. On the return path, they pleasured themselves still more in rolling the second sod so precisely edge to edge with the first that neither would topple the other back into the furrow.

Your body was just heavy enough to be pleasantly substantial. Your thoughts floated. Dappled as cleanly as the leaves were by their own shadows in the breeze, they lay composedly on everything they touched, without the slightest grip of shrillness.

Details mingled in the senses, in a song of themselves. The mesmeric rhythms of the turning sod as the plowed space grew broader and broader. The moist round rock dislodged clinking from its glistening socket. The knife creases the share made riding on its side across the grassy border at the end turns. The pencil line of sweat that frothed a little above the horse's britchen when the muscles of his powerful haunches sucked in against the rise. The horse smell, the grass smell, the loam smell, the sun smell . . .

But as the day wore on, your body began to have to carry itself a little. Little gray birds of weariness-memory settled in your muscles like scar ache. Your feet and hands had to be told what to do. The rhythm of the furrows became a gnaw. Your floating thoughts were squeezed together and looked straight down. Until they gave you back from whatever they touched only the stripped noun's name for it: rock, plow, horse, sod . . .

Or perhaps it was a day with your hands on the ax.

The winter sun came up behind the barn, silvering it, and creating a day more solid than any summer's. The white, stilling fact of snow in every direction gave to your lone movements a kingly validity, as if you carved them out of the bright hard air. The brilliant air went to your blood quicker than wine. It brought all your senses out, clear-eyed, to the edges

of yourself. A plenty beyond asking, they filled you
with such a glow of completeness that you felt like
giving everything a pat.

A knee braced against first one ox's warm mono-
lithic leg and then the other's, you drew the yoke
straps tight through the leather headpieces studded
with brass hearts, and cross-laced them firmly in the
grooves of the yoke pegs. You gave the oxen's muzzles
a pat.

With one hand you lifted the heavy double-sled
tongue, delighting in the sense of strength beyond
any challenge the morning could offer. With the other
you dropped in the backbolt that held the tongue to
the yoke. You broke the clench of frost that had
seized the sled runners to the ground with one surge
of the peavey, adjusted a link or two of the crossed
chains joining the sleds (so the sleds would track
fair), swiveled the front rocker straight on its bench,
placed the bag of straw on it for a seat, and spoke to
the oxen.

Acting on some ingrown memory of which their
slumbrous eyes showed not the faintest flicker (nor of
anything else) they headed of themselves toward the
log road without a moment's hesitation.

Inside the woods, the snow on the log road was
packed down so hard and smooth that at every dip in
it the hind sled slid up against the front. The road
glinted in the sun or was colored the lining of shells.
The silence had none of the loneliness in it of silences
that speak only of sounds elsewhere or of sounds gone

by. It was as if sound itself was wrapped warm and near beneath the snow, like a face you watch sleeping in the same room. You drew the tip of the whip handle in a steady runnel along the shelf of snow beside the road. The slow, measured pace of the oxen and the silencing sound of the bells set your thoughts lapping like windless waves against a peaceful shore.

In the hardwood chopping, you rugged the oxen and took the double-bitted ax from its leather fastener on the sled rocker.

The straight, leafless birches were each wrapped in its smooth silver bark as if with the very concision of the morning. The spaces between them were charged with cleanliness. You thought: There is nothing as beautiful as a stand of silver birches on a winter's day.

Your pleasantly sprawling thoughts sat up straight and took on an edge as keen as the ax's. As bright with purpose as wands, and with that clean, beautiful breathing space between them now like the spaces between the trees. By whatever miracle of translation, quicker than thought, quicker than light, your hands took their message from the brain. To swing the ax against the tree precisely where the eye said the first wedge-angled blows must be struck. As the chips fell shining from the wedges that deepened on either side, your shoulders sang. And when, held only by a thin splinter to its stump, the tree surrendered to a final shove of your palm, it gave up the morning's ghost in such a long sweeping sigh that your whole body seemed to breathe out with it. Your whole body glowed with the ozone of health.

(No slightest foreigner of dis-ease inside it yet, to keep drilling like a bedraggled raven its sullen message that no amount of heed can stop the repetition of—with its blunt hook always drawing back against the simple force of life that shoves you helplessly ahead.)

You scorned the niggling tricks of leverage and skids, grasping the butt ends of the fallen trees forthrightly in the circle of your arms and hoisting them on to the pile.

The pile grew. You could see the exact shape and weight of what you had done. For the great rock maples and the graven-hearted beeches that were like monuments of density you did use the oxen and the skid chain. But, as walking backward you tugged at the oxen's horns to guide them and saw the beeches' stun of fixedness yield to their living power, you felt as if the strength of the oxen was your own.

All morning long you had the steady feeling that your presence exactly filled the space that your eyes encompassed, with nothing stern or unrelated in any object it came up against or in any of your senses.

Then the bell of noonday made absolute the quiet woods' hush you had thought could be no quieter, and you boiled the noonday tea.

(Not for a moment did the tea beckon your mind to Ceylon or the flame to the rigid chemistry behind it.)

The snug warmth of your woolen clothing was

quite different from the bright leaves of heat the burning bark drew on the air, but you rejoiced in each alike.

You opened the dinner kettle and saw the food your wife had packed so neatly for you. And you were struck by the image, never so clear in her company as now in her absence, of how supportingly you were grained together. Even the tinge of sadness that goes with seeing *any*thing that plainly only added to your exaltation.

But later on, your lagging muscles one by one began to send their nullifying ether to your brain.

The afternoon began to sink. Not to the ground only, as in summer, but out of sounding beneath the eyeless white-faced snow. The snow closed over it like a sea over the upthrust arms of speechless drowners. The objects you now worked with were spiritless, like shells of themselves. It came to seem as if all your grasp met was the butt end of everything.

Your leaden weariness had to be harnessed tauter and tauter for the day's remaining work. The grime of it was like the grimy peas of snow that hubbled your mittens. There was a drawn-mouthed dishevelment in your thoughts like the tracked-over tracks of the morning's work that had mangled the smooth drifts.

When you loaded the wood you were taking home, the oxen started before you were quite ready. You shouted gritting oaths at their stupid lumbering bulks. They stopped, but not before one of the bottom birches, twisting under the binding chain, had thrust its point behind a standing tree. This so skewed the whole load that you had to undo the chain (with a vicious blow of the peavey that cracked the grab hook), let the sticks all topple to the ground, then reload them, piece by piece.

And then, five minutes later, the intersecting chains beneath the rockers wedged themselves so cleverly behind a stump that the load was stuck fast. There was no way to free it except to lie flat beneath the sleds, with no space to swing the ax, and hack at the stump in short crippled blows. Now hitting, now missing—and gapping the ax's blade on the iron runner. With your whole mind and body set in one rasping grimace . . .

Or perhaps the day was that best-natured of all: the perfect hay day.

A morning of light and air that splashed the open-doored kitchen with a kind of leaven, like the fresh-slept spirits of happy children. When even the dingy swamps were smiling with buttercups. The swaths of yesterday's mowing laced the square field next the house, lanes of a friendly maze leading squarely to its center.

(How summer-glad that first chatter of the mower, the one machine without a brutish voice, as you made the first cut through the standing grass, with the horse ducking his neck from time to time to snatch a few heads off the ripened timothy.)

The timothy smelled now of constancy. The clover of well springs. The browntop of ease. The hand scythe hung in the crotch of an apple tree, the grain of its wooden snath and the shine of its whetted blade catching the light like a spotless memory.

There had been no night dew. And now there was just enough breeze, with nothing of a wind's harshness in its touch, to dry the grass through and through. Even the thick bunches of clippings hand-mown where the machine couldn't reach: under the cherry tree and along the stone wall and close by the house and the borders of the garden.

(What satisfaction it had been to lay low these last blemishes on the field's shorn neatness with swipes of the scythe.)

The whole field now lay smooth and even. The untidy paths through the long, mauled grass to the garden were gone, and the messy cowlicks of clover that a driving rain had lodged. It beckoned your feet with the freedom to walk anywhere across it now.

You turned the swaths over with the pitchfork. At mid-morning they were dry enough to rake with the horse. The grass rustled like *hay* now.

(It gave you a special pleasure to remember other years when the air had hung so dead and humid that the grass would only wilt, not make at all. When rain would so verdigris the cut clover that it looked like those sickened leaves a block of wet wood has lain on. When the sun would never stay out long enough at one stretch so that you could get the hay into the barn without wondering if it would "heat" or rot.)

The bouncing comma-tines of the horse rake

spun the thousand crisscross strands it picked up into a tidy cylinder. And each time you tripped its load on to the straight, lengthening windrows the field seemed more than ever clean and emancipated. You felt no weariness at all: hay was such a light, fragrant thing to work with.

Noon held the day still for you, unhurrying, while you ate the midday meal in the child-hearted kitchen. Your wife had never seemed so wifely as when you watched her hands moving in and out of the leaf-shadow thrown against the pantry shelves by the white lilac outside the window. It seemed as if the light and the air were themselves at table with you, like fellow workers.

After you'd eaten you went out, commandingly, into the field again. The field was happy to be your dominion.

You felt the hay. It was just right to haul. You placed the tines of the long-handled fork into the end of the windrow and, thrusting forward on it almost at a trot, swept the hay, rod by rod, into bunches. Although these would only stand there for a few hours, you shaped each bunch into a neat cock.

When your wife saw you yoking the oxen to the hay wagon she came out into the field, to rake after. Somehow the scarecrow hat she wore and the old stockings drawn up over her arms against the blazing sun made your feeling for her stronger still. The children gleefully tramped the hay down into the wedge-shaped rack.

When the rack was level-full, a neighbor came across his field and volunteered to help you load the layers above. Your fork tines clinked against his as he took away the great shapeless forkfuls you passed up to him. He spread some of them evenly in the center; settled others with expert skill at the end points of the load, to keep his corners square.

"That hay's made good!" he kept exclaiming again and again. It was like a benediction.

A large patch of the field was now cleared and there wasn't a cloud in the sky to threaten the rest. In the barn the neighbor urged you to let him spell you a little. Let *him* pitch the load off and you stow away; that was easier work with the mow empty. You wouldn't listen to him. You spat on your hands and plunged the fork so deep into the tight-packed hay that the handle bent with each huge wig of it you lifted free. The sensual stir that always came from hay handled in a hot barn pleasantly stallioned your groin. And your limbs felt warm-eyed with a kind of praise as you put your hands on the oxen's horns and guided the empty wagon, with only inches to spare on either side, precisely back the length of the barn floor and down over the ramp of poles that broke the rise of the high sill.

But as the afternoon lengthened, the sun's light began to harden and smart.

Something ate slack sunken spaces between your muscles. They had to reach out and grip each other, to hold on. The burrowing hot iron light put weight into things as frost never could. The hay, as if changing substance, turned from feathery to leaden. The cocks of it did not wait peacefully for you, making light of themselves, as they had done at first; they stood mounded against your strength. There, and there, and there.

In the sweltering barn (where you'd driven in too close to the mow so that the hay on the load and the hay in the mow locked together) the mow was now so full that you had to pitch each forkful up over the big beam. Your neighbor could just manage to keep a small hole to receive it before stacking it higher than his head against the wall behind him. You strained to break the grip of the load's hay on itself and on the mow's hay it was jammed against. Your mind had nothing to hold to but the blind thought of when your fork tines would strike the rack and you'd know that the bulk of this load, anyway, had been overcome. Your eyes stung with sweat, your neck with chaff. Your blood (turned sickly white, it seemed) hammered in your ears.

And when you backed the empty wagon out into the remorseless sun again and looked at the hay still lying in the field, it seemed as if there would be load after load of it, with never a last one . . .

EARTH, GRASS, TREES. This was the trinity you spent the dollars of your strength on. But countless other things claimed its small coins as well.

The hardhacks, with the roots like the roots of wisdom teeth, to be kept back from the edges of the cleared land. New boards to be nailed on the bottom of the feed box where the oxen's rasplike tongues had hollowed out the old ones thin as paper. Winter potatoes to be sprouted of their white sapping quills. Yellow-eyed soldier beans to be threshed on the barn floor with the leather-jointed flail. The beech drag to be rolled up on to the saw horses, fixed there with the Z-shaped iron dogs, sawed into O-faced blocks by the W-shaped teeth of the crosscut; and then the stubborn blocks that no blow of the ax could divide to have their S-shaped sinews wrenched apart by the V-shaped wedge . . . Shingling to be patched, rafters reinforced, shop windows puttied, ladder rungs renewed . . .

Moments that might have been leisurely the cattle would disrupt.

One ox might knock the shell off his horn in a hooking match with the other. You'd have to smear the inside pith with tar, wrap it in cloth—and each time you turned him out again with his mate watch that their sparring did no further damage. Or maybe one of them, crazed by the sting of a gadfly, would gallop the pasture faster than a horse, ramming a low stub halfway up his pizzle. You'd have to shackle his hind legs, crawl under his belly, and take out the stub, splinter by splinter.

Another time, the cow would calve in a bitter midnight blizzard and the calf, shivering with first life and cold, would have to be dried and bedded down in the next manger, and the mother dosed with a quart of saltpeter and linseed oil to ward off milk fever . . .

When a neighbor, skilled with dynamite, kept urging you to blow the big rock between the house and the dooryard you told him, all right, bring his kit over the first slack day and you'd do it. He held the drill against the rock, revolving it between his hands, and you swung the sledge. Use had bashed the head of the drill into a rough circle with deep splits around the rim, so that it was hard to hit fair. It took two hundred blows to dent the rock the depth of an eye cup. The only pause you got was when he scooped the rock dust from the hole with a spill of wood whittled in the shape of a long-handled spoon. It took a thousand blows before the hole was deep enough to hold the sticks of dynamite. And then, before you lit the fuse, you had to carry brush enough to cover the rock two feet deep, so that it would fall harmlessly apart at the seams and not hurtle a fireworks of itself against the kitchen windows.

If there was urgent need of ready money—for county taxes or children's clothes—you worked off and on in the stave mill. Steaming the boiler with sawdust, or tending the haul-up, or wheeling out edgings. Or "on the roads," cutting alders along the ditches or spreading gravel where rains had gullied the hills.

Yes, ax, scythe, and peavey, each asking a different rhythm of your hands, were the three main task-masters. But they were not all. There were the hack, the grub hoe, the crowbar . . .

And the ground hornets stung you when you mowed into their papyrus nest. And the rocks scraped you. And the bushes scratched you. And the rain turned the peak of your cap into pulp. And the snow water grayed the toes of your larrigans. And the sun and the wind scored your skin . . .

Yet for all this, you stayed intact. You were never brought to the state when that dreadful stillness, like the stillness of the past, draws its face on the face of everything. The tide never went out to leave a rock pool of you drying up on the beach. Time was neither before you nor behind you: you were exactly opposite the present moment. It made a rushing sound that the sound of your consciousness was in total chorus with.

And there were all those times when, almost as with the children, the moment would suddenly petal back in a beatification of itself: so that being exactly as you were, at the very focus of it, would send the breath of life flashing through you like a shooting star.

These moments were only sentences, and scattered ones, in the book of your life—but added up, they formed its vital core.

7 / *Seed, Forges, and*
Rising Bread

E ACH MAN'S CORE OF LIGHT was different, but in most of them there were gleams like these.

You awoke before your wife and looked at her sleeping hand outside the quilt. Work-storied and curled slightly in on itself like a child of her, its empty palm slept somehow more defencelessly than her face. You tiptoed to the kitchen, so as not to rouse her before the fire had warmed their day selves back into things. And as the first flame sprang up there was something almost as clenching in the thought of her as if you were bringing her back from death.

Or you walked, Sunday-lulled, between the fresh-hoed garden rows in the Sunday sun. You looked at the clean brown earth hugging the enlivened plants that yesterday had been choked with blowsy weeds. The sound of the screen door closing aerated the voices of your children who came hopping across the rows, helter-skelter with zest but already respectful of things like gardens. And it seemed as if your whole life had been weeded of every uncertainty and sealed with endless summer . . .

These moments often struck through you for no reason you could decipher, or wished to. But you would always remember the occasion of them.

Once: A winter's night. The storm lashed at the windows and, advancing out of the woods it had captured and forced into its own camp, built trenches and battlements of snow all around the house. You looked through a frost niche in the frozen window-pane and saw a neighbor's light—while you watched your wife wrap first the white linen cloth and then the swaddling of old sweaters around the big round pan on the chair by the side of the stove that held the rising bread you had earned and she had made.

Once: Word came that a neighbor was failing fast. You went to see him. You looked at his face so out of its element in the hollow of the pillow in the April bedroom. It was washed whiter with mortal sickness than any water cupped in his hands from the sinkroom basin had ever washed it. And suddenly you thought of all the times when the man-mirroring of each in the other, as you'd worked with him in the fields and talked about the work together, had made the day into a steady hymn of you both.

Once: You were cutting hoop poles alone in the pasture, your consciousness spreading a little as always to fill the quiet. All around you was the living greenery in its infinite shapes. The saw-toothed edges of the sweet fern. The dancing-white stars of the blackberry blossoms. The pink pleating of the toad-stool's lining. The purple loops of the sheepkill. The miniature chalices of the ground moss. The green-needled hackmatack with the bright-red cones that were like solid flowers cross-petaled as intricately as a rose. The daisy with its tens of white tongues encircling the thousand grains of gold mounded at its center. Each speckling, or roundness, or pointedness, or wallpaper scrolling, or shading of color into color was as perfectly in pattern as if a draftsman's lifetime had gone into the making of it. There was not a pinpoint of earth where this infinite variety did not spring up side by side, yet not the smallest member of it without a purity of diagram to dumfound gods or worlds.

But this wasteful squandering of perfection on things so slight did not mock or stagger you then. You sat down for a few wide moments in the shade of the great landmark maple where the cows sometimes stood so still the clapper of their bells never touched against the sides.

Your arms and legs felt magnified with the gift of rich and skillful blood. And in the stretching heat you felt your cock there like a chieftain. One thrust of it into the woman's silken part, mounded always as if to pout against it but tapering downward to that point of seeming to beckon for it constantly—one thrust, and all the problems of the flesh (and of all else) dissolved. You rode this warm, lapping, drawing, lusty sea in the champion blend of coarse and fine that makes this feeling the emperor of all. Until you cracked the very door of godhood itself: knowing that taken one by one most things were hundreds of miles away from you but that you were never more than inches away from everything, in that sweet pit where all the marrows lay . . .

The gleam could be just as bright in the simple moments when you weighed your child on the beam scales. Each time you killed a pig you weighed the carcass on these scales suspended from the shop ceiling. Then it was the child's turn. He sat eagerly in the small rope sling you'd fashioned for him, holding his feet up from the floor. You watched his shining eyes watch you move the big "pea" from notch to notch until it reached the one where nothing dipped a fraction up or down. He looked as if he were balancing on a miracle, and you felt a shining too.

Or when you simply undid the top button of his

reefer to brush away the cold shoulder of snow that had slumped on him from a spruce bough grazed by the side posts of the trail sleds and, touching the warm artless flesh of his neck where it curved upward into his head, felt a sigh of tenderness that was so completely different from the gust in your blood whatever night you'd made him.

Or when you brought him safely down from the ladder he'd climbed to the top rung, to the very peak of the barn you'd carelessly left it standing against— and then clung there frozen with fright and trembling over the rocks below but not crying until he'd surrendered his grip on the rung to his grip on your arm . . .

And sometimes it was laughter that touched off the sudden bridges between each part of you and every other.

When you saw Matt LeCain (spinning with fury and then having to laugh himself) trying to dig his heels into the ground to curb the heifer he was leading and at the same time leapfrog the splashes she scattered behind her from her first day on new grass.

Or when you heard someone go over an old yarn about Hett Millburn and her sister Grace that happened to be quite new to you. Hett and Grace were an aging pair who'd lived devotedly together all their lives, though sometimes they "jarred." And when they did, there was an unspoken rule between them that each should hold her tongue for the next two days. This silent day, Hett was sitting at the kitchen window staring out over the fuchsia plants on the sill.

Grace was working with her back to the stove. Turning slightly, Hett noticed that Grace's apron strings were dangling in the open draft. They started to blaze up. "I ain't speakin," she said in a neutral voice, "but your ass's afire."

Quite differently charged was the moment when a neighbor came rushing blindly up the path to the house, his face in pieces, to tell you about Frank Copeland. The colt Frank was breaking had bolted, throwing him from the wagon on to the schoolhouse ledge, where they'd found him dead. Your breath toppled as if Frank's name had been holding it up (neighbors were that much like brothers then).

Your gaze met your wife's. The years you'd been as one with her had never been so lettered on the air of any room before, this living neighbor never so strangely bonded to you as now.

All at once, with the sudden wisdom of survivorship, you seemed to *understand* even the ravelings at his sweater cuff. For some reason there flashed into your mind a stopping picture of the way your wife had looked one morning from a distance, winnowing the blueberries into the dishpan, with some of them bouncing back on to the ground. And with this picture the surge of feeling that you should never leave her by herself again, never again with the unshielded consciousness of one who does a thing alone.

Quite different too was the hillside moment when you watched your wife kneeling to smooth the white lake sand on to the surfaces of the graves in the cemetery that the pine-girdled, pine-soughing lake ceaselessly communed with in the language that they alone shared. She smoothed the sand and you rooted out the hardhacks that were choking the wild rose-bushes around the ancient tombstones. This was the old, old cemetery where the pioneer church had once stood. These were the ancestral graves. Their dead had been dead so long that all the challenge had been sifted out of their silence. And the grave-statement here merely gentled the air, engraved it (and you) with such contentment it was like an unseen fleece cushioning the edges of the breeze.

Once every year the man with the long wallet bulging against its wide leather straps came round the country buying cattle. That day, when you'd sold him all the stock you wanted to turn off, you walked into the kitchen with six or seven big bills in your pocket. You gave them to your wife to count again. You let the children count them awesomely before they were put away into the old pewter teapot on the top pantry shelf. And it was like the moment when the last sod of fall banking had been placed against the house.

But richer still, the moment when the bills had long since been broken, nearly spent, and you stood with your wife and children in the store in town. You watched the strangers buying high-priced goods that none of you could ever hope to buy for each other. Yet this suddenly brought out so piercingly the tie among you all that something moved inside you like a banner in the sun.

And once in your lifetime you had acted with real bravery.

Walking ahead of the oxen down the mountain slope that day, with the neighbor (who'd swamped a road out while you chopped) riding on top the heavy pile of hemlock on the sleds, you heard him shout. The girdling chain had given way, pinning his foot between two shifting logs. If the whole load slid to the ground he would be crushed.

You stopped the team and grasped the peavey, bracing it against the side of the load with more strength than you'd ever known you had. You held it there, though the load threatened to topple on you too. Straining until your muscles began to tremble. Praying that if you could "whoa" the oxen calmly enough they would not start ahead. The arteries in your neck began to pound, dizziness to swim in your eyes—but somehow you held the peavey there until your neighbor had unlaced his heavy boot, drawn his foot out and jumped clear.

It was less pride in yourself you felt then than a kind of meekness. But when he put his arm around your shoulder and you saw that he was close to tears, that was a splendid moment too.

And another in the spring when a man came to ask if you would let him have some seed potatoes. To say yes was to spare yourself short for table use, but it did your heart good to part with them—knowing that when it was a question of *seed* there was no man in the place but would do the same.

And another (among a thousand others) in the shop where Gus Jordan kept his forge.

A group of you sat there talking lazily, watching Gus heat the ox shoes until they glowed pink, beat them into shape on the ringing anvil, then drop them hissing into a pail of cold water. A torrential rain sheeted down outside the open door. It exempted you from every task, from having to be in any other place. And with each of you the other's faithful chronicler, the shop became another fasthold of total fellowship snugly umbrellaed from the downpour of time and stamping itself on the tablet of forever . . .

And the thousand and first . . . when the thronging day was done and all your work in it rested in the gentle coffin of darkness. (Although, as it rested, whatever would be the ear of corn kept forming itself in the seed; whatever would be the field of buckwheat worked toward itself with the ground's help; whatever would be the rose put itself together in the bush's root—while all the nails you had driven in all the sheltering wood held steadfastly all the night.) The soft sound of the children's sleeping, afloat on their dreams, peopled all the bedrooms in the inner house of you. Your wife was like the flesh of everything that would be ghost if she were not lying at your side. A little while ago you had joined flesh with her. Now she bore the very gist of you inside her, given over to her safer keeping. You stretched your full length along the sweet redeeming bed and nothing on earth could be better than when sleep started to blow out the candles of your thought, one by one . . .

Nor were these moments that flashlit themselves all.

There were others that bespoke themselves with no such clearness, yet heightened nonetheless whatever inner weather made you notice certain things just then:

The nodding of the timothy in the August fields the afternoon someone lay dead in the house next yours.

The June evening drenched absolutely motionless with the sun's last light, with everything in it (the grass, the bushes, the trees) glossed the green of reconciliation from mountain to cathedral mountain—except for the houses that shone pale as bone with tales of themselves, the shard of glass that sparkled pure white, the strands of wire that the light silvered into cobwebs.

The blackening of the brook that of all things first felt night coming on and drew deep into its glassy core the night-sigh of the meadow it bewitched.

The glaring, staring shell ice gripping itself so hard that cold shivers of lightning-tracery crisscrossed its universal patterns, but collapsing under the sled runners like shattered china.

The whole season's gallery of "still lifes" that were the nouns for each unstated adjective floating within your consciousness . . .

The steeping, bated, flag-blazoned Indian Summer dusk when you heard the snapping of one twig and then another—and then, *yes*, another—and the ancient pulse of the hunter blotted out all other senses as your body became one great eye searching for the wild graceful deer that walked toward you with its death in its nostrils.

Your wife's hair that still preserved the girl in her, springing lightly back from the strokes of the brush in the evening of the day that you had seemed to glean every good thing the day held.

(And the bare rectangle of the sideboard drawer you pulled out on the day that seemed to have been gleaned of nothing, to search idly for a paper of pins. Opening idly the album of faded snapshots that lay beside the scraps of hoarded ribbon, the living face of the child who had not come home for supper that night so long ago because he was drowned in the millpond sprang at you—and you were gripped by a yawning moment of pure agony at the thought of all the things that had once breathed at the quick of you now lying in all the drawers of your heart in their dusting envelopes.)

The oxheart cherries seen to be ripening on the tree that shaded the ell kitchen on the morning so flawless it seemed rehearsed, with your own perfect health the oracle that gave you all the answers. (And the puddle scum on the shambled day when weariness blunted you with its peevish questions that flapped hingeless in the rain forests of your mind, finding no answers at all, and the stilt-legged flies fastened on the dead mouse beside the clump of violets in the cowpath.)

When each day was a train of quotes from the letter writing between sense and object. Each as different from the other as the painted maple burning its memories in the late October afternoon was from the gray lichened stone . . .

OF STILL ANOTHER KIND were all the things that stirred no reflectiveness, matched none, yet put a crown on the moment all their own:

The sound the last strippings of milk made in the froth that topped the brimming pail just short of spilling down the sides, and the warmth of the pail against your encompassing thighs.

Easing the long ladder to the ground when the last of the apple-smelling apples had been gathered into a barrel from the tree which had held its note of ripeness so long it had started to bear it, but which now stood spokenly concluded. The flames of the bonfire leveling the confusion of trash. Broken tool handles. Old boots that leaked. The lettering of the months and the numbering of the days on the calendar of the year that was past.

The feel of your feet not sinking into the hilled and valleyed drifts you snowshoed over . . .

A teeming multitude of sense-framings like that —from the sleepless green of the mountain hemlocks in the evening of the longest day to the confiding green of the mountain spruces, familied with the soon-coming of Christmas, in the evening of the shortest.

Simplest of all, but not least, was the host of things that spoke from no "text" whatever, were mere remarks of themselves. Nothing more than the plain which-ness of what was here and now. But they so stippled the backdrop of your notice (the city has nothing but strange faces and stone) that it never for an instant went white with the waxworking of monotony.

Trout circles widening in the still, evening lake. Bright orange poison lilies. Thorns. The thread tracks of tiny creatures between the midget pockets in the snow. Little circus tents of August dew. The white lace of sloughed-off snake skins. Raindrops round as worlds pocking the dust. Pea pods. Scarlet runners. The "chestnut" on the horse's hock; and the million scaled-down horseshoe markings on the horse chestnut tree, with every nail head in perfect place . . .

Hummingbirds' nests. Bears' dens in the caverns walled by ancient woods rocks. Volcanoes of the burrowing mole . . .

The glint-leoparding, never for two seconds the same, of ground and running water by light and shade striking on them through a canopy of moving leaves . . .

Blades of grass, blades of wind. Tines of fork, tines of sun . . .

Wings, paws, hoofs, beaks . . .

Beechnut pyramids, snail fortresses, spider webs . . .

Lion's paw and sheepkill. Ganders and horn-pouts. Sunrises and sunsets. Moonlight and microcosms . . .

And the man's knowing that for each saving instant that brimmed him whole his wife had one of her own.

8 / Wicks and Cups

WORK WAS THE WOMAN'S CLIMATE TOO. Her task-masters were needle and frying pan, flour barrel (on its swinging clamps beneath the pantry shelves) and scrub brush, washboard and creamers, bean crocks and jelly jars, mat hooks and baskets.

Each day of the week had its particular chore.

Tuesdays she cleaned the lamps, misting her breath inside the chimneys and polishing them until they shone, filled the bowls with fresh oil, spliced the short wicks with flannelette and trimmed them so that the flame (which always made her think of the bishop's miter) would have no "pooks" around the edges. Fridays she scoured the chamber mugs (raised lilies on their sides) with a twist of factory cotton wrapped around a kindling stick, swept the straw matting in the bedrooms, dusted the stops of the parlor organ with a hawk wing, and gave the window plants, the elephant's ear, and the Christmas cactus their waterings of cold tea . . .

Her hands moved from scissors to stove damper, banister rail to turnip bin, clock shelf to closet. Her tasks lacked the scope her husband's had to stretch themselves in. But that very limit was a pleasure in itself. She could keep the whole brood under her eye at once.

Sometimes her thoughts spread beyond her own tasks to a rallying concern for his—as afloat on the lake of her contentment she watched her knife uncoil the skin of one apple after another for the mincemeat, or whipped the seam of a garment stitch after stitch, or shelled the peas. But his was the decision when decisions must be made; she was royally screened from the rack of doubt by having his fist-mindedness stand between her and all the hard-eyed problems. Once he'd manned a course, whatever it might be, she had only to disciple it. He was her army and she was his flag.

A few women were gadders. ("I don't see how she ever accomplishes anything in the house, the way she beats the road!"); but for most the house was her principality. A snug citadel that drew its breath from the swarming outdoors it was partitioned from, yet warmed its blood at this very separation. Where her hands hummed in a key beyond sound the litany of their routine, and the tendrils of her imagination lifted and fell as if grazed by a commending breeze.

It was a sure domain, weatherproofed by the wing of man-and-wife and garrisoned by the ringing of children that enfurnished the furniture even in their absence. And when she worked in the fields with her husband she carried the stamp of this domain with her like an image inside an invisible locket.

In the fields, with him at the helm, her help was saddled with little more exaction than a visitor's. The visitor is always given the light end of a job and bound with no responsibility for it.

When they were on their knees together picking up drop apples and the heavy basket had to be emptied, he lifted it, and she held open the mouth of the bag. She raked the light scatterings of hay into a pile, but it was he who took the weight of the pile on his fork and carried it to the nearest windrow. She slipped the tugs on to the wagon shafts when he backed the horse between them, but he held the shafts up. While he sweated to raise the boulder out of its socket in the ground she merely dropped in the smaller stones to hold each gain of the pry.

Yet in all these tasks that two could do ten times as quickly as one, nothing gratified her more than to know that however small her part in them it was just as valuable as if her strength were on a par with his.

And in the pauses when she was left with nothing to do—while he rolled the boulder down the slope into the bushes, or whetted the mowing machine blade, or hammered out a twist in the rake tine that had hooked a root, or took the linchpins from the wagon wheels and greased each axle with daubs of lard, or undid all the straps on the ox yoke to relace them tighter—she luxuriated in the one reproachless ease. Resting in the shade of the wild pear tree at the edge of the field and summering in the shade of his muscle. Watching, with her sun hat in her lap, the horizon lazily circle round and round itself and the sky dome itself like a great indulgent thimble.

There was something of the same peculiar nearness between them when he, absurdly scaling down his strength, helped her with a woman's task. Berrying together, he would pick the ripe berries one by one (lacking her knack of thumbing out the leaves and green ones as he went) and she would have to smile (no smile more fostering) when she noticed that the bottom of his tin was scarcely covered while hers was half full.

And spaced along the plainsong of her daily work

she too had a choir of things that lifted up her spirit. If not always with the vividest brocade of joy, at least with the cambric of it.

The sound of rain starting, each testing footstep of it distinct on the leaves outside, when her dahlias needed rain.

The cat purr of sunlight striking through the parlor window on the mat she had just taken from the frames.

The even dozen jars of pickles cooling on the pantry shelf like a row of capital "A"s formed practice-perfect in the copybooks of her mind.

The wood warmth against her hands when, waifed with extra clothing, she came in from the clothesline with the basketful of garments frost-stiffened into effigies of themselves.

A yellowbird lighting in the syringa bush, its movements like the glances of a diamond (though the waddling crows riddled the beef's paunch thrown behind the barn).

The sharp smell of bobbin oil in the sewing machine drawer.

A bowl of cucumbers, sliced in vinegar, cooling the whole dog-day noon.

A cup—just that.

The thumbs of children's mittens drying on the zinc beneath the stove when the children were asleep.

A phrase from the Psalms turning up in her mind, not sought religiously, but like some alabastered surface she had touched in the dark.

The sudden reality, suddenly upper-cased, of the pepper she was seasoning the rich "poor soup" with.

And with it, the upper-casing of everything. Of Kindling Flame. Of Dustpan. Of Buttermilk and Distance. Of Spoons and Laughter. Of Firkin and Cloud . . .

THE HOUSE WAS her one escape from any atmosphere that went against her. Every object in it was grained with the handlight of the whole family. If this were a day for dwelling on things, each of them would cite to her some memory of this wovenness.

But as she worked, glimpses and foreglimpses of other pleasures skimmed through her mind like wing shadow.

Looking out the church window at fields solemnity could hush but never bruise, and listening to herself sing "I Love to Tell the Story" in a voice the organ seemed to smooth the motes from, in a hat she knew became her.

Standing back to look at the first strip of wallpaper (patterned with great urns that loops of crimson roses garlanded together) transforming the rough unplastered wall she'd "bagged" beforehand with meal sacks soaked in flour glue.

Gathering the sprays of silver beech leaves in the fall, her thoughts finding as firm a ground wherever they put a roving foot down as if she were knitting. (Yes, she would put the leaves beside the peacock feathers in the big milk-glass pitcher that stood on the center table in the parlor. The top of the center table had mother-of-pearl inlays at each corner. On the shelf beneath was the huge Concordance Bible with the gilded clasps. The leaves would look nice there, and they would last all winter long) . . .

Mostly, she steeped in the houselight. But sometimes her spirits drew livelier flashes from the thought of herself placed as if at the center of broad daylight by the flowering of some outside event.

Or in the lamplight when neighbors came of an evening to stitch the week's happenings together.

Or in the lanternlight her husband held out wide for her (himself never such a stalwart tower of himself as when she was blinded by the darkness they stepped into from the lamplight of another's kitchen) so that she could see the ditches on the side of the road home . . .

AND NOW AND THEN those arching moments when the spell of separateness that held things captive would suddenly be scattered. Then she would touch the very meaning of the thing itself that the word for it had always stood in front of. Her knots of inwardness suddenly unskeined, she would stand and stare exultantly at the riches of her own being. She would see herself indulged in everything she looked at. The whole day would turn a face toward her, friendlier to her than her own. The wick of living would take instant light inside her, flooding every murky niche, wiping it cleaner of shadow than a cloth . . .

When she drew up the bedroom blind in the morning or drew it down when it was time for sleep, and thought of every member in the household being well and strong.

When she saw the comb marks in the child's hair she'd just wetted and slicked back for the school recitation. When she laid out her husband's good suit for a trip to town.

When half-shocked (but half-laughing) she felt the straddle of her husband in the tumbling night . . .

A STRANGER GIVING their singsong appearances (man's *or* woman's) only a skimming glance would see none of this. None. But in some degree or other it was there.

9 / *Goose Grease, Death,*
and Parables

HANDS WORKING IN HEALTH at the same tasks
strengthened the ties between these people. So
did sickness, the common enemy: a Blind Pew that
could track down its victims even here.

And a dread enemy this "black spot" was. The
doctor in town was a good one: a gruff old giant

(with a giant kindness) who with only his reckoning eye and the stethoscope he carried in a pocket of his bearskin coat could spot your trouble at once. But he was sixteen horse-driven miles away, and his stock of medicines hardly more advanced than the bread poultices and mustard plasters of his patients.

Yet sickness here was not the bleak and bat-breathed thing it is for the city dweller suffering it alone.

There, it paints a kind of distant cloud-cold over every object and nails the dogged writ it carries to the backs of your eyes so that there's no escaping it even when the eyes are closed. It puts a cord around each outpost of the senses at the surface of the flesh and keeps a steady downward pull on them. It shoves you into a corner of yourself with the self it has tainted, so that the well can never maintain their image of you free from the coloring of this squalid company. Here, anyone's sickness was everyone's anxiety. Its burrowing gaze was thus splintered, the load of it lightened.

Here, there was a man who'd harness his horse at any hour of the day or night and go for the doctor "without a murmur." Another would leave his saw in the cut and spend a day hunting the scarce woodcock, the one morsel that was thought sure to tempt the sufferer's appetite when all else failed. Neighbors took turns "setting up" with the patient night after night, their first flush of good will never souring into a duty and then a grudging duty.

The man who was laid up in planting time need have no worry about his garden. Others would put it in for him. It would not be just "slapped in," either. It would be done exactly as he'd want it done. If he covered his potato seed with a hoe instead of the plow, they would be covered with a hoe, no matter what extra time that took. If he sowed his carrot seed thin and covered them by hand, they'd be sown thin and covered by hand.

The sick woman could rest content that her family lacked no care, that her house was being run exactly as she liked it run. If she always hung the white things in the wash on the end of the clothesline next to the Spy tree and the colored things on the end next the Nonpareil, that's the way they would be hung. If she turned her parlor fern every third day so that neither half of it would grow lopsidedly toward the windowlight, it would be turned every third day.

And those who were really "good in sickness" were better than all the apothecaries. Perhaps their cure-alls of goose grease, tansy root, and turpentine packs worked no wonders. But there was a kind of healing in their presence alone that goose grease (or, for that matter, streptomycin) could take a lesson from.

Not everyone was Spartan about sickness. A few were "spleeny as a cat" and "always doctorin," reading into the slightest twinge of pain a deadly threat to one main organ or another. "Information of the kidneys" was the thing most often hinted at—although over the quilting frames some curious imbalance spoken of as the "tilted womb" ran it a close second. Others made a roll call of symptoms ("The stuff I riz!") the backbone of all their conversation.

But even in such cases the twist of speech often redeemed a twice-told tale. What medical term is as dead-on as "that 'gone' feelin"? What better picture of a woman plagued with neuralgia than "She looks like a hen with an egg broke in her"? How better describe a man after a bout of quinsy than "He looks as if he'd been pulled through a knothole and beat with a sutt bag"?

And, generally, if someone drew a real Queen of Spades in the blind deal (the diabetic before insulin, the consumptive whose one thin hope lay in a syrup of balsam blisters), he played out his hand without shriek or whimper.

There was almost nothing that could be called mental sickness. Oddness to spare; but that was no more than each having the courage of his differences.

In fevers there was delirium. As one man reported his own case: "I was hilarious for three days." But, by and large, people didn't take out their minds (and paw them over) often enough to lose them. They were simply too *busy* with growing things, too purged by fresh air and friendship, to go crazy. Freud would have found lean pickings here and Oedipus no bird of his feather at all.

The same held for imaginary illness. Body and mind talked back and forth but they didn't nose around in each other's affairs. Once in a while a high-strung woman might work the "bad spell" a bit to gain some end. But if you had diarrhea it merely meant that you'd eaten too much cabbage kraut, not that you were symbolically casting out a hated parent. If you felt draggy and irritable all the time it was because you needed "iron," not because you'd leaned too heavily on the solace of the sugar teat at age two. Such twaddle would have been scoffed at. For they had a rare eye for the absurd, which focused on everything. This often held them back from change—they were too quick to spot the nonsense factor in anything new and judge it only on that—but it was also what kept them sane.

Turning a thing inside out with this jester's irreverence was known as "makin speeches" about it. Speeches were made about everything. Even Death had its comic lore.

Once upon a death years ago, it was told, the man with the lisp was laying out a huge old patriarch. As he strove with the skimpy underpants provided him he was heard (all the way downstairs) muttering to himself: "Theeth drawth wuth never built for theeth ballth!" And there were the funeral mice that shot out of a parlor organ at the first swell of its moldering bellows, scattering the women around the coffin like blackbirds.

But this did not mean that Death itself was ever mocked. When its great sabled presence came over the rim of Never and took back in its closed hand the breath of someone its hand would never open on again, it struck that stillness of stillnesses inside everyone. All hearts swallowed hard. Thought stumbled: Why did this conundrum that knew all the conundrums come down among the puzzled, yet not unriddle itself to them by as much as the sound of its voice? Flesh sought the nearness of other flesh, searching there for the one saving grip: a fellow mortality. Fields, immortal, changed. Lying in a kind of suspense, they stared as quietly as Death itself at their own immortality, yet gazed with a sudden speechful gaze into some great distance. Rocks lost their deafness in the kind of silence that was most like their own.

A man walking in the fields would glance at the windows of the house where the dead lay—windows that were like eyes dense to the weight of bone with the secret imposed on them—then stare back at the fields that seemed almost persuaded to yield up the mystery. But the fields did not. The eternals talk only to each other.

He would look at some handiwork of the dead still standing there, ghosted by the memory of its maker almost to utterance, but it too would just fail to gather its voice. And maybe then his sight would blur with that strangest of human answers, the globe of a tear. ("Tears," "stare," they have the same letters.) We cried for one another's deaths then, because each of them was a part of our own.

The ceremonial of death was as fixed as Sunday.

All worked stopped until the funeral was over. A man who took his team into the hayfield (however certainly rain threatened the made clover with ruin) would have felt his movements there as glaring as if he were an open thief. Women took cakes and pies to the eclipsed house, as if these might bear some witness of what they couldn't express. At the side of the coffin they murmured, "He looks as if he could speak." Men stood there, silent. Their gnarled hands looking as if, in this moment of mystery, they should disown the rude tasks their scorings spoke of; the simplest emphasis of their clothing as if, in this moment of muteness, it was somehow fraudulent or an imposture.

School was closed. But there was no thrust in the children's play. Even the morning air was bated with the hush of the night to come.

Three days later there was the precise moment at the grave when Now and Never went their separate ways. When for the space of a held breath each face lost its running total and collided with its own eyes.

And then the ritual was over. A kind of freedom welled up in everyone. Rocks and fields brought their gaze back from the eternal to the present. Faces could be summed again. Grieving no less, the family of the dead nevertheless came down from their pinnacle of grief; and their faces too could now be helped back to a running total. The flush of religion faded to the far edges of the mind, like a shadowy relative.

RELIGION, IN FACT, always sat lightly on them. It was never a vise, twisting the limbs of the spirit until they seized, parching to a stone-bed the robust human springs. Belief was without doubt ("Oh, Jesus is a rock in a weary land," they sang); but it didn't much dictate their daily lives. Except to back up what common decency held right.

Rites of worship were shown the respect of a sober face, but nobody pulled a sanctimonious one. No eye's geniality hardened into the fanatic glitter of the crank. A winter sunset or a hymn might set people half-musing on a Higher Power, but they were not crippled with God-*fearing*. The revivalist's hell-fire singed not a hair. God (when He crossed their mind) was neighborly. Heaven (when they thought of it) was the green starry pasture of the Heaven on the children's Sunday School cards. The Bible was less a books of sermons (though they knew all the parables by heart) than a great golden country they somehow had a stake in.

Passages of scripture were often quoted ("While the earth remaineth, seedtime and harvest will never cease"), but no more solemnly than saws. When a woman's work was done at night she might pick up her New Testament (bookmarked with pressed grave flowers at the pages where the funeral texts of friend or child had been ticked) and read a little; but the air around her would not stiffen as it does when someone makes a show of faith in anything beyond the everyday. She would pick it up as naturally as a sock to mend and put it as naturally by.

This ease with the unearthly did not go as deep as sacrilege. No matter how gruff the man (who might "swear in his common talk" and "never darken a church door"), real sacrilege would have struck his bones pale. Yet there was as healthy a cluster of "stories" about religions as about anything else.

One had to do with a couple at a prayer meeting. Garbled by nervousness, the wife's plea came out: "Thank God for the sick and the afflicted." A few minutes later she prodded her lagging husband to "testify." "Well," he began, hitching up his crotch as he stood, "the longer I set the harder it gits!"

Another had to do with a time the minister came to supper. This woman had thought to feast him with new-potato hash and crumb cake. For two days back she'd sorted out the smallest and tenderest potatoes from the family pot and placed them in a special bowl. The afternoon he was due she'd spent an hour preparing the "crumbs" that were to crown the cake, then gone to lie down. Her husband happened into the pantry to make a cot for his abscessed thumb from the finger of an old leather glove in the twine box. He saw the potatoes and the crumbs. Thinking the tiny potatoes were discards, he dumped them into the pig swill; and thinking the crumbs were for the birds, he scattered them on the field. And then turning up late for supper (a makeshift now of pancakes and gingersnaps) with more than a little woodsaw cider under his belt, he'd greeted each of the minister's watery jokes with claps of laughter so uproarious but so plainly false that the woman herself got the "laughing 'sterics" and had to be slapped roundly on both cheeks to bring her to.

As a rule, men left most religious observances to their wives, as if it were a kind of housekeeping. Few Baptist males "came forward," no matter how many choruses of "Why Not Now?" implored them to. Except for a sheepish "Amen," few Anglican males spoke the prayer-book responses. And if a minister making weekday calls tagged them about the fields for a chipper man-to-man talk as they raked the hay or turned the sod, they felt as awkward as moose.

Apart from a sprinkling of Methodists and Catholics, the congregations were about evenly split between Baptist and Anglican. But there were no sectarian feuds. You were born either a Baptist or an Anglican, just as you were born either blue-eyed or brown-eyed—and little more was made of the one difference than the other.

The Anglican might raise an eyebrow at the Baptist immersions in the millpond ("I'll do the talking over here!" a wrathy preacher once roared at some chattering youths on the bank, shaking his fist at them while the candidate's head was still under water.) The Baptist might smile at the way the Anglicans kept "hoppin up and down all the time in church." But that's as far as it went. Each group attended the other's services—and any minister who tried to poach converts from the other faith or spouted any bigotry in his sermons that might tread on the other's toes was severely reprimanded for it by his own flock.

In mixed marriages it was taken for granted that the wife would "go with her husband," and that was that. One Sunday School did for both persuasions. Often as not, the Anglican minister would borrow a Baptist sleigh if a sudden snowstorm clogged his wagon wheels as he started back to town; and often as not the Baptist minister would stable his horse in an Anglican barn.

Nor was there much of that "pull-haul-and-drag" *within* each group that religion often hatches in a self-contradiction to make wonder itself shake its head. One organist might sulk a mite if another was asked to "play." The man who brought nothing to the harvest festival but a huge pumpkin—showy, but not worth a hill of beans—might run into some rather un-Christian looks. But that was about the size of it.

"We are not di-vi-i-ded," they sang. "All one bod-y we." They were not far wrong.

10 / *Soft Soap and Drawknives*

POLITICS WERE AS PEACEABLE AS RELIGION—up to a point. Election time. This was the one month every four years when a ferment hardly to be believed riled the place from stem to stern. Compound fractures (though they'd knit again as quickly as they'd split) shattered the bonds of harmony in all directions like a pane of glass struck by a rock. Friends from birth could see nothing in each other (if their politics differed) but "rotten" Grit or "rotten" Tory. Excuses were found to call off the quiltings: who could control the needle in her hand or in her tongue in an atmosphere like that?

At church, the Tories sat together on one side of the aisle, the Grits on the other. (For the time being, a Baptist Tory felt much warmer toward an Anglican Tory than toward a Baptist Grit, and vice versa.) Such exchanges between them as couldn't be sidestepped going into church or coming out were limited to the weather, in a pattern as frozen as a gavotte. Day by day, standoffishness built up into bristling. And on Election Day itself the air around the polling booth was charged with a kind of knuckled politeness that the slightest friction might spark into blows.

More than this, all normal transactions were thrown completely out of joint.

Diehards of one party shunned the houses of the other like the plague, lest anyone think they'd "turned." If a Grit's wife and a Tory's wife had gone halves on a meat grinder (one using it one day, one another), there would be a stretch when the grinder ceased making its rounds altogether.

It was the same with the men. Before there was any talk of election, a Tory with several cows just freshened might be giving what skim milk he couldn't use to a Grit neighbor with none. The Grit would station a pail on the Tory's back porch to hold it.

Each night he'd come with a second pail to take the milk home in. But let word of election be sprung and *that* night he'd arrive without the second pail and carry away the first—a wordless signal both men would understand, that all such give-and-take was over until the campaign ended. On the other hand, two fellow Tories (or two fellow Grits), whatever their loggerheads in general, would suddenly be mulled as if with campfire glow at the mere sight of each other.

These were the diehards. After them came those who only "leaned" Grit or Tory. In the final showdown they rarely bolted the party of their bias, but very often came up with a "grievance" against it which had to be "sweetened" away. And last came a fairish band of fence-sitters who were quite open to canvass (or "courting," as each party scornfully referred to the methods of the other). The Grits got the name of being the more enterprising rustlers, the Tories of being more apt to huddle comfortably together "canvassing themselves."

No canvasser worth his salt paid the slightest mind to a candidate's platform. Why waste his breath on questions of tariff revision and the like, which would mean less than nothing to anyone here? The wedges to hammer at, whether pertinent or not, were those much closer home; and the approach a nice balance of barb and blarney.

"I know the Grits is givin everyone road work *now* that can lift a shovel," it might go, "but last fall when they was ditchin right in front of your *house*, did they take you on? . . . By God, George, that's a handsome sow there! You certainly got the knack o' raisin pigs!"

Or: "I ain't sayin a good Tory ain't as good as a good Grit, and I don't deny that Reg Kendall's tendin out on everyone this last fort'nit—but you watch how long that'll last after election. About as long as it takes you to turn that door knob . . . He*llo* there, Annie. Well, if that ain't the best-lookin bread I ever saw come out of an oven! You know, Annie, you and your husband here should go into the bakery business. You'd make a fortune!"

It was strange. Any other time these men would no more act like that than fly. To be "salvy" was the worst thing that could be said of anyone. And hard liquor was never thought of. But come election, even the most "candid" and temperate of them would mount a barrage of soft soap and rum without a qualm.

The chief dodge was to be first on hand with a drink for the wavering and "vote him" right away, while he was in the first flush of comradeship the drink kindled. Leave it too late and the other side might ply him with sweeter music and stronger wine. Or he, knowing a good thing when he saw one, might go on hedging, supping from both sides alike, until he could no more have aimed his cross at the right spot than he could have pinned the tail on the donkey—if, indeed, in this blissful state he could be bothered to try.

The next day he'd have his headaches, but they'd be nothing compared to those of the canvassers. One canvasser might awake to the bleak recollection that, carried away by party zeal, he'd promised to haul out Robie Wheeler's logs on the first good going, even if his own had to lie in the woods and rot. Another that he'd paid Fred Killam twice what they were worth for a pair of unbroken steers, thin as bread knives, which would only stand in his barn and eat their heads off, the price meal was now. Either recollection all the more galling if the canvasser's side had lost. (At the local poll, that is. How the country went at large no one cared beans about.)

In politics as in religion the wife "went with her husband"—but again with a difference. She often became quite "saucy" in her new loyalty. And tight-lipped, if not outright huffy, with even her own parents on Election Day.

One couple only, who lived at the far end of the settlement, stuck each to his original guns. They drove to the poll sitting aloof as ramrods from each other in the wagon, swapping not a word. She held the reins while he went in and voted Tory; he held the reins while she went in and killed his vote. Then they separated, he going to a Tory's house for dinner, she to a Grit's. After dinner they joined each other again in the wagon and drove as mutely away.

Dinner-watching was, in fact, one of the best means to gauge the tide of battle. Nearly every house had a spy post where members stood what amounted to regular shifts, checking who had dinner where and who drove by in whose wagon. The gentlest people sputtered without cease.

"Here comes Mel and his wife," a woman might report to her husband. "They're headin up at Tom's. I knew they'd vote right! . . . No, sir, they're goin *by* Tom's. They're goin into *Freem's!* Well, if I was you, I'd just march myself down to Mel's tomorrow and demand that three-inch auger o' yours he borrowed six months ago. He's just like his father before him. They say his father borrowed a horse one plantin time and didn't take it back for three years."

Or: "Ain't that Jim and Annie Calder gettin out of Al Bartlett's wagon? It is! And they'd like you to think they're votin for us! You know, I've as good a mind as ever I had to eat to say to Annie next time I see her, 'It's funny you ain't well enough to get out to church, but you're able to vote all right!' And you'll see how anxious Al'll be to drive em home once they've marked their ballots. Well, it won't worry me none if they have to stand around on one leg all day."

An eagle eye was also kept on who kept nodding with more than usual heartiness to whom and who kept his distance from whom.

Before the event, both parties made a great show of confidence. "You notice the postmaster's makin damn sure he don't offend no one," one canvasser might hearten another. "That shows they're scared." (Postmaster and road man, the only two people whose actual jobs were in jeopardy, faced a ticklish

gamble. If they didn't "work" and their party was re-
turned to power, they'd lose their job to someone
who'd put up a better fight. On the other hand, if they
did work and their party lost, the winners would
probably oust them like a shot.) Or, the word might
go around: "You know how hot Glenn always was.
Well, I hear he ain't gonna do a thing this year."

On the day itself, however, it was found that talk
of backsliding was nothing to go on. Old loyalties
might spring up ranker than ever and all comfortable
prophecies be undone.

The voting booth was a corner wedge of dining
room in some central house, curtained off by a pair of
bed sheets. Inside this wedge the window blind was
pulled down, and a small lamp on the writing stand
laced the air with fumes of kerosene. You marked
your ballot and brought it out to the returning officer,
who sat at the head of the dining-room table.

All the leaves of the table had been taken out
beforehand so that there'd be room at it for no one
but himself, his clerk, and the two scrutineers of his
party. Scrutineers of the opposite party were given
chairs well back toward the sideboard.

The returning officer was chosen not so much as
a party stalwart as for sleight of hand. No matter how
closely you watched his motions as he tore off the
counterfoil, you couldn't detect that lightning twist of
the ballot which gave him a peek at where you'd
placed your cross. He'd drop your ballot in the box,
then glance at his own scrutineers. If his eyeballs

tilted upward this meant: one for our side—and the scrutineers would put a plus sign beside your name on their copies of the voters' list. A downward tilt and you'd be marked with a minus. These lists were the scourges of anyone who thought he could pretend to have voted one way when actually he'd voted another. For those outside, the returning officer's countenance was the surest weather vane of the day. It was read like a bulletin whenever he left the room to relieve himself in the shop. If his opponents were piling up votes, he'd be black as a thundercloud. If his own party was running strong, he'd be pleasant as a basket of chips.

The atmosphere in the dining room was taut as a drum cover. Some voters stepped in sheepishly, some defiantly. But all were met with crisscross tensions hardly less than in a ring where bears and tigers may at any moment leap from their separate pedestals and send the fur flying. Who should speak to whom, and with what shade of warmth or coldness?

Here, that question landed the party representatives into a real predicament. Especially in those cases where the voter's stand was doubtful. Might not a chipper greeting be all that was needed to swing him your way? But what if you stuck out your honey like that and learned later that it hadn't swayed him one iota? You'd kick yourself.

To make choice harder still, there was often a whisper from some other part of the mind to add confusion. "What if he *does* vote against me?" it might say. "That time I had the shingles, didn't he set up all night with my sow when she farrowed, to watch she didn't roll on her young? When no one else had offered a hand?" . . . It was a problem that would have stumped Solomon.

Each voter, the gantlet run and his ballot cast, seemed duty-bound to toss out a small joke as he turned to leave. "Well," he'd say, "I guess I can't do no more damage here." Or, "I guess we'll still have to scratch for a livin how*ever* she goes, what?" But these self-conscious stabs at ice-breaking fell hollow as gourds on the airtight air.

The most explosive tactic was for either party to "swear" a certain enemy. That is, put him on oath that he was truly of voting age. Positive though the evidence might be that he was not ("I know as well as I want to know that Clint Langley ain't twenty-one, because his mother was still carryin him a month after my Gladys was born and Gladys ain't twenty-one till next Tuesday"), he was rarely challenged.

In the dying moments of the poll a challenge might pay off, but earlier in the day it could touch off a disastrous backfire. Perhaps some lukewarm Tories (or lukewarm Grits) had decided not to vote at all. But let the word get around that the Grits (or the Tories) were "swearin people" and these lukewarm Tories (or Grits) would come swarming out of their indifference like wasps.

Undoubtedly the person whose nerves took the sorest beating all day long was the lady of the house where the poll was held.

Her kitchen was a constant hive of prickly

neighbors waiting their turn to vote. Her spotless floor
became grimed with mud or snow. She had to "dinner"
half the faithful from far ends of the district, who
then loitered under her feet for hours to watch the
show from a ringside seat. And she, even more than
the officials, was tormented from moment to moment
with the problem of what face to put on. How did you
greet your best friend who this day was a sworn
enemy? How did you judge the right proportion of
warmth between the smile you gave her and the one
you gave the woman not half as well liked but who
today was your stoutest ally? To make everyone feel
at home in her house was something she'd always
prided herself on—but what worse pickle could a
hostess be in than to have a group of neighbors in her
kitchen who sat there looking daggers at each other?

Maybe the booth had been given to her and her
husband as a plum, but by four o'clock she'd have
traded it for a gooseberry.

As the afternoon wore on tension snowballed,
and guessing games among the bystanders who
lounged about the shop or perched on the woodpile
or the well curb kept pace with it.

What was Paul and Hattie hangin back for?
Someone'd seen Paul outside the house with his neck-
tie on way before noon. They'd figured he was just
waitin for Arth to drive him down. Paul'd been
workin in Arth's mill all along and everyone thought
Arth had him in his pocket. But someone else said
when Arth did call for them, Hattie'd peeled Arth for
fair!

If the Tories tried to "vote" Herb Dunn, who was eighty-seven and wandering in the mind, would the Grits try to "vote" Jud Stoddart again?

(Jud was ninety, and no one would forget the last time he went to the poll. His son was allowed to lead him into the dining room, where he was to vote "open," because of his failing sight. All week the family had been schooling him to name the Grit candidate as his choice, and each time they tested him— "Now who are you goin to vote for, Grampie?"—he'd got the answer letter-perfect. When the question was put to him by the returning officer, however, he came out with a booming "Wilfred Laurier!" "Now, Dad," the son wheedled, "you know that's not who . . ." "Dammit, boy," the old man flared up, "will you hold your tongue? I'm goin to vote for Laurier and"— brandishing his cane—"I'd like to see anyone here try and stop me. It's a free country, ain't it?" No one could convince him that the once Prime Minister Laurier had long, long since gone to his rest.)

The Tories had sent a team all the way to Clark's Cove, where Wilf Orde was scaling logs, to bring him home to vote; and the Grits had sent a team all the way to Four Finger Lake to bring Ned Armour off the drive. Would they make it back in time?

And what about Wes Hergett? Had he really tripped over some loose chicken wire, like his wife Florence said, and set his sciatica going so he couldn't move a muscle off the kitchen lounge? And was her own diarrhea really so bad she didn't dare budge three steps away from the commode? Or were these just excuses to steer clear of voting altogether?

Perhaps they were. For a man in Wes's circumstance, caught between at least four fires, it could be understood.

He was an Anglican Tory who'd married a Baptist Grit. Florence had gone with him both ways—but *her* family, not his, was the one that had always been first to help them out in a pinch. To keep voting Tory was to keep voting against them, and against the Anglican Grit who'd given him work on the roads when he needed it most, and against his favorite brother-in-law who had the post office. Yet to switch to Grit was to feel himself a turncoat and to shrivel inside when some other Tory, never dreaming he'd quit the fold, clapped him on the back and said, "Wes, boy, I think we *got* em this time!" He'd think about the Anglican Grit who'd risked his life, nearly, to help him unyoke the oxen when they broke through the lake ice, so they could keep their heads up and swim to shore. And then he'd think about the Baptist Tory who'd done the chores for him that whole month he'd had the blood poison in his heel . . .

So what simpler way out than to pretend that he and Florence weren't *able* to vote?

Was it maybe Wes then who'd voted for *both* candidates last time? But no, that wasn't like Wes. That was more like something Gil Henley would do.

Gil was an odd one. He always spoiled his ballot

one way or another, just for the light-hearted hell of it. Once, by his own account, he'd made his X for the Grit candidate and then (tempted by the thought of the returning officer's face between a shit and a sweat about what signal to flash his lieutenants when he peeked at *this* one), he'd built the thing up to read: $2 \times 2 = 4$. Another time (he denied that this was his work, but it could have been no one else's), he'd filled the whole space opposite the Tory candidate's name with X's and the whole space opposite the Grit's with O's—so that his ballot looked like a string of kisses for one and a string of hugs for the other.

The miracle was that for all these quirks in the local contest the result of it so often echoed the national pattern. If either party swept the country at large, it usually made the same sweep here. If it lost heavily here, the news was almost sure to follow that it had collapsed all over. You could only conclude that victory or defeat was not so much a matter of issues as something in the air, like influenza.

ELECTION NIGHT WAS STRANGELY QUIET. When the dining room door was opened and the winning candidate announced, a ragged cheer went up from his supporters; but that was all. The victors didn't crow, and there was no more backbiting. It almost seemed as if the election fever that had sown the germs of contention had at the same time scotched them. People looked almost equally shamefaced and purged.

It would be false to say that the welts of discord faded away within the hour. But within the week at most, the Grit's milk pail would be on the Tory's porch again and the meat grinder would again be shuttling back and forth. Within the fortnight, a Tory lady who had reason to doubt the manhood of her own Leghorn rooster would be dropping, as cosily as ever, into a Grit lady's kitchen to borrow a setting of fertile eggs. And the rotten Grit who'd been soaking his hoop poles in the brook so they'd be limber enough to bend around a barrel would ask again with the same old ease for the lend of the rotten Tory's draw-knife. No other knives were drawn until Election Day rolled around once more.

Even if the post office did change hands, there was little hard feeling. Everyone knew that where there's a contest there has to be a trophy. They bowed to this with extraordinary good humor and grace.

11 / Drop Mail and
Diplomats

Dᴵᴰ ᴛʜᴇ ᴍᴀɪʟ ɢᴏ?" was the first question asked
in a blizzard or on a day when spring thaw had
turned the road into a mire. If the answer was no,
spirits dipped. A day when no letter could possibly be
hoped for was a day with half its lights out.

This feeling we shared with people everywhere.

But otherwise our mail system (a combination of post office and rural route) was quite different from the common run. If it could be called a system at all. Rules and red tape got short shrift from everyone concerned.

Take the Time Bill, one of those nuisance forms the postmistress had to complete for headquarters. (The post office was always in her husband's name, but it was always she who managed it.) On this sheet she was supposed to keep a daily record of when the mail driver left her door for the round trip to town and when he got back, precise to the minute. It was designed to rule out any dawdling on his part. If he took longer than the scant time limit laid down, he'd be hauled over the coals.

But what was the sense in a regulation like that? When one trip his mare might be lame, another he might have to walk her all the way behind the oxen breaking a road through the drifts, or another be held up while he scoured the town for a left-handed nut that would fit the four-inch bolt someone had asked him to match up?

So she simply put down any figures that would keep him off the hook, headquarters be damned. These entries were often made well ahead of the dates they covered. Whenever she happened to have a free minute. "Now go outdoors and play," you might hear her say to a nagging child. "Can't you see I'm busy fillin out these Time Bills for next month?"

The mail driver himself was no stickler for rules

either. He could properly refuse "drop mail" from any box not of regulation make, but he didn't. Smoked-herring boxes perched in the crotch of a gateway tree, old creamers nailed lengthwise on the top of a fence post—they were all the same to him. Sometimes a boxholder, having no stamps, would put out a letter with three pennies wrapped in a twist of paper, and tied to it with yarn. He could have refused that too, but he didn't. That wouldn't have been "obliging." And, as we well knew, OBLIGING was the label he must earn above all.

If he was that, he could be forgiven anything else. He could rest easy that when his contract was up for renewal no one would tender against him. But let him become too "independent" or "show his author-ity" and this would no longer hold.

His official duties, in fact, must often take second place to his errandry. The packages he carried with-out postage far outweighed those in the mail bag.

It was he who took Nat's beaver pelts in to the man who bought furs. ("If he won't give you a decent price, bring em back. I'll burn em before I'll sacrifice em.") He picked up an order of onion sets that some-one had left for Jenny at the livery stable. There might be a pair of boots saddled across a mailbox by their laces, with a note saying: "Will you please get these boots half-soled if the cobbler thinks the uppers is worth it. Tell him I'll settle with him later." When anyone killed a pig he took the heart and kidneys in to the meat market. (Nobody here could "go" things like that.) In later years he took everyone's upper plate back to the dentist at least once, to ask him if he couldn't build it up a little there where—did he remember?—the suction never *was* too good. And when spring house cleaning came around, his wagon bristled like a porcupine with window blinds and curtain rods he'd been given the money to buy.

He must be a diplomat as well.

There was the winter's day one woman along the route entrusted a jar of urine to him, tagged for the doctor's. For purposes of disguise she'd put the jar inside a shoe box and (in case he might come early) slipped the package into the mailbox the night before. What happened was that the urine froze, split the jar, thawed again during a sudden change in the weather on the way to town, and gave the "drop letters" beside it such a drenching that their addresses were nearly washed out. This driver being a very bashful man (and she a very bashful woman), it took all the tact he could muster to break such news to her in a way that wouldn't leave them both blushing to the roots of their hair.

Passenger service was another of his sidelines. And this called for diplomacy too.

Since he could seat only one person, he was faced with many a ticklish judgment. Which should have first claim: the lady who must go as far as Lake La Forge with him today because her daughter there was "expecting" any minute, or the lady who could arrange no other time to take her "rolls" to the carding mill? If neither had had the foresight to "bespeak her chance" a week ahead, how could he take one without offending the other? And how could he best curb the passenger who insisted on "helping" him put mail into the boxes or take it out—so that he could discover who was writing to whom? Or best discourage those who tried to pump him about the correspondence of someone thought to be "after a pension" or to have some girl "on the string" in another settlement?

Through this passenger service he also got a closer look into other people's feelings than was granted anyone else. He saw them in so many of their unguarded moments. He was there at the gate, for instance, when the family said goodbye to one of their number leaving home for the first time, and there at the gate when they welcomed the prodigal back (with a suitcase of presents . . . or for a parent's funeral).

If the passenger in this case was a young girl leaving home he'd be peppered with questions. "Did she break down?" "Did her young man come down to the road when she went by? How did *he* seem to feel?"

If, in another case, she was a quick-tempered lady whose tiffs with her husband were common knowledge he might be asked: "Did she say what made up her mind to go down to her sister's in Roxdale so sudden? I was in there just after breakfast and she was gettin ready to wash!" Or: "Did she seem quiet? Did she mention Harry's name at all? Did she take *both* her hats?"

If he brought a visitor *into* the place, he'd face an

even more thorough quiz. "How old would you take her to be? Was she stuck up? Did she tell you how long she laid out to stay? And was that feathery thing she had around her neck real maribou?"

As long as it was merely good-natured "family" gossip like that, he'd give out what answers would harm no one—and feel like a seer.

The day he really came into his own, though, was the day he brought home the first soldier back from France. The school children all marched down the road to meet him and formed a guard of honor in front of the sleigh. He slowed the horse to a processional walk, and didn't even bother to drop the mail bag off at the post office until after the parade had seen the soldier to his very door. Naturally, he wouldn't take a cent of pay from this passenger.

Others were charged fifteen cents a trip, and his government salary was one hundred to one hundred twenty-five dollars a year. The postmistress got exactly fifty dollars a year—with no extras except the small "percentage" allowed her on postal notes sold, and what pin money she could pick up from the mail order houses for revising their local address lists.

Her job had as many unofficial offshoots as his, but its trappings were simple.

The "post office" was nothing more than a narrow wooden structure standing in a corner of the kitchen like a coffin on end. One of those that saw the longest service had started life as a pickle closet.

Its upper section was now partitioned off into

separate cubbyholes for each item of business: Incoming mail. Outgoing mail. The Registered-Letter Book. The postal notes. The date stamp (and the wooden honeycomb of type that had to be fished from their cells with tweezers). The postage-due stamps (not one of them ever used: could you charge a *neighbor* for a letter?). The weighing "ouncels." The file of dusty paraphernalia such as "Customs Declarations to be Affixed to Packages Destined for Brazil" or Notices of "change in rates, effective immediately, on uncured goat hides addressed to Valparaiso" . . .

The lower section was a wide-open storage space for the mail bags, the rock that was heated in winter for the driver's feet, and such odds and ends of household gear as these left room for. "*Where's* my stub rub*bers?*" a tired child would whine. "Why, they're where they always are, if you had any eyes," the mother would reply. "They're in the post office."

Not the strictest way to run things, maybe, but as long as no piece of mail ever went astray (and none ever did), what did it matter?

It didn't—provided the postmistress, like the mailman, was obliging. And she was. Though it wasn't always easy. She had her own trials.

Not *one* child from a family, but the whole six of them, might come for the mail an hour before it was due: letting swarms of flies through the kitchen door as they raced in and out, bouncing up and down on the aging couch springs. Office hours meant nothing: just when she was ready for bed someone would drop in for a twenty-cent postal note and sit there till she could hardly keep her eyes open. She'd have to take a chance that her bread wouldn't scorch in the oven while she hurried to the store to weigh a package heavier than her ouncels could cope with . . . But she, like the mailman, never grumbled. Not in public anyway.

And she, also, knew when common sense was a better guide than rule. If Jess asked someone else to get his mail and there was a "bank notice" for him she'd overlook that letter until Jess came himself. If Annie George's Christmas order arrived from Eaton's or Simpson's she wouldn't give it to the children, she'd sneak it down to Annie George after they'd gone to bed. If no one came for Clara's mail (because Clara's family almost never got any mail) and this day there *was* a letter, she'd make an excuse to borrow a pinch of sage from Clara and take it along.

She was a quite ordinary woman. The mail driver was a quite ordinary man. But when he carried the mail bag into her kitchen and she unlocked the lock that held the bar that threaded through the loops of metal tucked together at the top and emptied the mail bag onto the floor, there was something of the dream merchant about them.

Maybe there'd be only the bare "letter bill" inside. But maybe not. There *had* been letters for the storekeeper all the way from Lisbon. There had been letters from a British lawyer tracing the link between an earldom in his country and the descendants of an old settler family here. There had been the "bounty" of a hundred dollars (delayed for sixty years) to a veteran of the Fenian Raids . . . You could never tell what surprises might be in that bag. And "the ghost of a chance," as the saying went, "is the one ghost can dance."

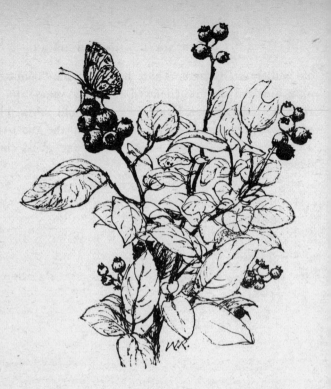

12 / As the Saying Went, or Slugs and Gluts

PEOPLE WHOSE SENSES graze always in the same pasture have a wordless intercourse circling among them without stop. So it was with these people. Their faces were steadily fluent with it, one to another.

The same did not always hold true of their speech. Much of that was the ticktock of empty rote.

The daily caller at another's house would say as many times as he opened the door: "Who comes often'r I do?" The reply was bound to be: "Them that comes twice to your once." A woman would repeat as often as the cucumbers "repeated" on her: "I like cucumbers, but they don't like *me*." If asked the age of a man who might be in his fifties, his sixties, you weren't sure which, you answered: "I don't know, but he must be crawlin along."

Berries were "just hangin" or "scatterin." Anyone with second sight was "as good as a witch"; the man crippled up with rheumatism was a "distressed-lookin creetur"; the woman who pointed out to him how lucky he was he didn't have it in his elbows too, like she'd had it all last fall right into Christmas, was a "Job's comforter"; and the man who never turned up anywhere on time was (in male talk, at least, where annoyance made short work of delicacy) "always behind like a boar's nuts."

Looks were judged "handsome as a dollar," "homely as a hedge fence," or (in the absence of a single "redeeming feature") "heenyus." A man who bought anything on time was "runnin his face." And ("Great scissors to grind and no one to turn!") many a "spin-it-out" would "hang her down" in your kitchen until the clock struck midnight before he "made a muster to go."

For the most part, words were tools as blunt and honest as the work tools of the field, not tatting shuttles. (It was not necessary for words to tat when the

silent crochet of presence with presence went on so
constantly.) Yet they could sometimes hit the mark
dead-on. What better retort to the touchy than "Now
don't fly off the handle and stick in the wall!"? How
better size up an alto fumbling for the right key than
"She sounds like a bee under a cup"?

Every conversation, whatever its threadbare pattern, was sprinkled with a few of these bull's-eyes;
and, as in all things, the more unbridled the vivider.
The women had little "rough talk" and the men seldom "bla'guarded" in their hearing. But when the
men were by themselves candor was curbed by no bit
whatsoever. Especially when the talk was of strangers.

"His face would fit into a sheep track," they said
of this one or that. Others might be simply "hard-
lookin skids." The wishy-washy reminded them of
"somethin that was sent for and couldn't come." A
visiting lady somewhat on the dowdy side looked
"like a hen that'd lay brown eggs." The minister who
dwelt too long on the merits of the dead in his funeral
remarks was "harrishin the mourners' feelins"; if once
in a while he rapped out a sermon that made everyone sit up and take notice he'd given them a "good
stave." A bald head was "bare as a bird's ass in fly
time."

Value judgments were strict. The brag (second
in disfavor only to the "two-faced" or "the treacherous") was "mouthy," "a blow": he should be "hooted."
The mean would "skin a louse for its hide and tallow."

The prankster was "smart where the skin's off." The gossip had a tongue that "hung in the middle and flapped on both ends." The surly was "determinedly damned to be opposite." As was the "jealous-minded."

In contrast to the "big-feelin" was anyone who "had no lugs about him." (These were not the same lugs the child was warned he'd get "thinned" if "his eyes were bigger than his belly" at a neighbor's groaning table.) The prim "wouldn't say shit for a shovelful," and the generous to a fault would "give away his nose and breathe through his ears." The truly jovial (or the truly cantankerous) was "as full of it as he can stick"; the coward had no "sand."

"Slugs" were what the sharp tongue "threw" at anyone it wanted to "grind." (But the man who came off best against these was the one who "never unsealed his lips.") A blanket criticism that cut too close to the listener's particular weakness without the speaker's knowing it was usually grinned away with: "Now you're startin to infringe on *my* patent." "Gluts" were what the comic "got off." The literal glutton "scoffed" his food, and the wasteful housekeeper was "extravagant." The hypocrite would, of course, "strain at a gnat and swallow a camel." The frank "told him right to his head."

Rote decreed that whenever food or drink was offered it was without exception "good for what ails ya." But ails themselves called on a wider range of terms.

If you were merely "draggy" and out of sorts you

were "dumpin around" and should "throw yourself down" somewhere. If you were really all in, you "didn't feel fit to carry guts to a bear." Diarrhea was "flying axe-handles"; the "low-spirited" were "blue as a whetstone." For rare cases when this dolefulness took graven shape inside the person's mind as a cloud no sun could scatter, one word was reserved: "melancholy." "He is melancholy," they said, placing him in as precise a pigeonhole as if they were saying: "He is forty-six."

Pregnancy being an airier thing, the bulging woman had plainly been "sleepin on her husband's shirttail" or "eatin dried apples." The shadow of death was "cold as the hinges of Newgate."

Names for the forceless ranged from "niddy-noddy" to "pilgarlic." The spongy fellow who didn't stand up for his own rights was a "sawney." One who had no mind of his own but agreed with everyone was "a chip in the porridge." The man who was forever interrupting you with some piddling concern just when you were busiest, or full of stuffy advice and solemn practicalities when some madcap frolic was in play, was a "stabfart." (Polonius would have been an "old stabfart.") The sentimental were "soft as a punkin"; the overexuberant "made a spectacle of themselves."

The short-tempered might cuss "until the air was blue," and the mimic who could "make a dog laugh" had a field day with their tantrums. Unless he "carried it to extremes." In which case, he was given a snub that made him "laugh on the other side of his face." "What are you *rhymin* about?" was the dig a chatterbox of any kind laid himself open to. The response to any kind of irritation was: "Well, wouldn't that rattle your slats!"

Money matters hatched a few sayings that were off the beaten path. The man with a small nest egg had saved up "quite a puckle." He with none should not, however, go around crying hard times. This was "pleadin poverty," "makin a poor mouth"—a whimper no one cared to hear. Any chronic drain on the purse (such as county taxes) was "quite a moth." If, on the other hand, you were lucky enough to have a gravel pit the road foreman would haul from whenever the government gave him a "commission" to "lay out," or a pasture slope with the sandy soil that blueberries thrived on (market price: five cents a quart), or the teacher to board, this was "quite an herb."

The root of most expressions was perfectly clear, the meaning perfectly plain. ("Love will go where it's sent, if it's only into a cow pad" needs no footnote.) Others could be puzzling.

"How's the state of your copperosity?" was a greeting heard every day. But how "copperosity" (if it was a word at all) came to double for "well-being" was a total mystery. "Defewgulty" rolled splendidly off the tongue; ("What's the defewgulty?"); but who invented the question "What's the defewgulty?" to improve on "What's the trouble?" "Sevaggirous" was another such word ("Every time he gets a chill he has this sevaggirous time with his waterworks too"); but how did it come to take the place of "wretched"? "Lazy as a Mahone soldier." What was a Mahone soldier? No one could have told you.

Or take the "Calithumpians," a word unknown to any dictionary. Were the Calithumpians supposed to be a mob, clowns, or what? No one could have told you that either.

And yet if the weary houewife, just drawing her first calm breath after a clean-up of the house from top to bottom on a blistering August day, were to look out and see a visitor coming up the path with her whole rambunctious brood in tow (one would be sure to head straight for the bric-a-brac, another's diaper certain to overflow on the settee), and were she to sigh, "Oh dear, here come the Calithumpians!" she would somehow have said exactly what she meant.

Prepositions were always ready to give each other a hand. If "unless" was overworked, "without" would take over. ("I'm not fussy about goin, without you are.") "E'er a" often did service for "either." (An elderly lady whose hearing had faded was once asked if her pullets were laying. "No," she answered, "I ain't got a tooth in e'er a jaw.")

In other liaisons, "go" and "go to work" often lent support to the main verb, whether the sentence had anything to do with movement or not. "Now what do you suppose would make him want to go and do that fer?" or "He went and put this notion into her head." Even: "I think he went and went back to the orchard," or "He went to work and 'popped the question' to her point blank." And there was a wealth of such tongue twisters as "He'd got so thin and rainicky, if I hadn'ta knowed him I wouldn'ta knowed it was him!"

A show of grief was "takin on." Making water was "drainin yer potatoes" or "squirtin yer pickle."

THEY SPOKE LIKE THAT, yes—but their talk was no measure of them. Laughable or weedy as it might be, it did not spatter *them* with its weediness.

For they talked another way too. And not the cheap way city people talk, with their scuffed or flinty tongues—or the way city people try to preen their minds into peacocks, forgetting that the mind can never be more than a pecking bantam. Another way still. Since birth they had seen the wind and heard the sun and touched the voice of the rain. They had learned from this the art of instant translation. From sense to sense. From self to self. So that half a dozen words from one man was all that was needed to set up the whole mirror of response in the other. "Come see the colt." "Yes, he died in the night." Words as simple as that could be charged with whole courts and zodiacs of meaning.

A man's qualities did not then war among themselves, to be the one to label him: the coarsest man could also be the tenderest, the sharpest-tongued the best-hearted. Yet each man knew who he was. Each knew who the other was. That was what talked between them. City people harden their hearts until the heart hardens. Here it was different. There were no angers or quarrels or differences between any two men that could not be smoothed out if one or the other of them were to sound the simple point: "John, this is *George*."

Gab they did, but it had nothing to do with this deeper kind of speech. "Talk is cheap," they said of words, knowing sound from substance.

In much the same way they knew sex from love.

13 / *Antics and After*

Who can deny that sex in general is the funniest thing in the world? (People with their mouths together like guppies', sprawled in the pose of grass-hoppers.) Perhaps the act is no funnier in itself than the twitch of an eyelid or a knee jerk. But to have had such a furtive mumbo jumbo founded on a simple physical condition no one can escape: there's the joke.

With their level eye so quick to pierce the sham and shirring that becloud and barnacle a thing's honest password, these villagers saw sex so.

True, it was never an open subject with them; but neither was it one so underground that it moldered or grew nightmares of itself. There was much sniggering about it, but little that was sidelong or septic. It was plain fun. They saw it clear: a blend of comedy and sheet lightning.

Sometimes the comedy was uppermost, sometimes the lightning.

As lightning, it was both find and fund. It was the one thread in the weave of life that was all quicksilver. Unlike beauty or any other lure it was the one thing that the flesh, drawn to, could totally possess— in an explosion that turned both people into stars and acmes of themselves.

It gave the flesh a crown nothing else could claim, because nothing but the flesh was given the tongue to say itself so completely. It blossomed and filled out the vocal hollows of the flesh that flesh itself couldn't fill. What could have taken its place in the nostrils of the boys when they felt the first stags strutting on the stages of their blood? In the girls' neck pits when the first flush of it wrote there the beckoning message of their entire bodies in the skin's miraculously smooth hand?

Men carried the modest ounces of it in their groins as quietly as knuckle hair; but when the clasp of women turned these physical ounces into force the basic natures of both man and woman were multiplied and steepled Time-high. Couples, finding sex in bed with them, took each other to the one place where the two of them could become one—and brought each other back from the journey farthest west from Death.

Old people who had never left their firesides had been around the world a thousand ways because they had traveled this one.

It was all this—and yet remained a simple shindig, a roaring clown.

And because it was not taken seriously it caused little serious trouble.

Men and boys talked about it in sturdy snorts, women and girls in grins behind their eyes; but there were few wanton scrapes. Hay mows had the odd secret, and the crumpled pasture brakes; but not a great many. The handsome must-eyed logger from "outside" who straddled the load upright as he maneuvered his gleaming span of matched and mettled blacks with the dash of a Ben Hur might flutter the girls' glances—but little more.

In flintier districts, many a girl had to "swear" her child on a lover who balked at marriage. Let a "slip" happen here and the wedding followed at once, without a thought on the groom's part of dodging the issue. And not here the rumor of men "running" each other's wives. Once couples were paired off they stayed that way.

If sex was comic, courtship was antic. Sometimes

as frozen to rule as the mating dance of the penguin. Sometimes way off key.

There was one young man who used to visit his girl of an evening, lay wait for some errand to take her into the pantry, then post his chair at the pantry door and playfully hold her captive there with the threat of a kindling stick. The day they were married he set off for the rectory in town with her in the sleigh beside him. Halfway along he suddenly remembered a bag of apples he'd planned to drop off at the cider press. Wedding day or not, he swung around and went back for it. Thinking the couple had already been joined together, everyone pelted the returning sleigh with a shower of diced catalogue covers and cracked corn—and the bride was still picking kernels from her hair when she reached the parson's on a second try.

I myself still blush to remember the time I bribed the kid brother of a girl I was sweet on (the girl and I were both thirteen) to pin a love note to his sister's pillow. I had copied it word for word from an ancient manual called "The Up-to-Date Letter Writer," which I'd come across one rainy day I was ranging through the attic. This sample was called Missive from a Gentleman to a Lady Offering Her His Hand.

It read: "It is now nearly a year and a half since I first had the great pleasure of being received at your house as a friend. During the greater part of that time there has been but one attraction (your personal charm) and one strong hope (the desire of winning your favor). Have I been successful? Has the deep faithful love that I felt for you met any response in your heart? I feel that my future happiness hangs on your answer. It is not the fleeting fancy of an hour, but the true abiding love that is founded on respect and admiration, which has been for months my dearest life dream. Your maidenly dignity has kept your heart so securely hidden that I scarcely venture to hope I have a place there. I feel that I cannot endure suspense any longer, so I write to win or lose all. Devotedly yours . . ."

Though I felt sheepish after the deed was done, I basked in the thought of all those fancy words at work on her. As it happened, her mother found the note first. And took it to the next mat hooking.

For a week after that just to walk along the road was torture. Someone was sure to straighten up from his weeding and call out: "Hi, there! Goin up to see her maidenly dignity?" The way "stories" stuck to people, a tag like that could haunt you for life.

Interest in girls started early. Just after pollywog nests had become an old story. But the first step was not to carry her books home from school. The first step was to shout some mild gibe at her. If she brought the books down on your head you knew she liked you too.

The courage for such advances could only be found, of course, if you were in a group. If one boy found himself alone with one girl this swagger wilted at once. ("Your father rowed up his garden yet?" "I don't know. I imagine. Yours?" "I don't know. I imagine.")

Later on, the byplay was standard. After a dance you sidled up to her while she was putting on her rubbers and mumbled, "Please may I see you home tonight?" Or if you were too nervous about the plunge to get that many words out, "Comp'ny?" would do. She either "gave you a look" or giggled.

If she gave you a look, you had got what was known as "the mitten." And it was talked about for days. ("Did you know that Bonnie give Ed the mitten Friday night? And Saturday night he bids on her pie just the same. I'd *see* myself.")

On the other hand, if she giggled and let you take her arm, that was not lost on anyone either. You were "teased" about her from that day on.

Though certainly nothing romantic took place on the way to her door. One merry grandmother used to tell about the first time *she* was seen home. Not a word was said until they reached her gate. Right then a bubble of gas made its long thunderous round of her escort's lower intestine. He turned to her in the pearly moonlight and made his one remark of the night: "Did you hear my guts a-rollin!"

The next move was to put on your good boots and your Sunday braces and drop into the girl's house of a weekday evening. The boots and braces were usually the only sign that you were calling on *her*. The talk was usually all with her father. ("Suppose hackmatack stakes'd peel now?" or "That Guernsey heifer o' yours looks like she'll make a good milker. I see she's springin bag already.")

Not until it was time to leave would you saunter over to pump yourself a drink and mutter behind the dipper handle, "You goin on the sleigh ride to Pender's Cove?"

She'd say, "I don't know. Is any of em goin from here?"

You'd say, "Some of em is, I guess. I am. You'd best make up your mind to go."

This zigzag manner lasted even when things had reached the stage of "setting up"—until two or three o'clock in the morning or until (as often happened) a warning tattoo was rapped out on the parents' chamber mug upstairs.

Sundays, you braided the mare's tail, hung scarlet tassels from her blinders, sneaked out the sewing machine throw for a laprobe, and took the girl for a drive. A good trotter gave you a slight edge on your rivals. If you happened to have a really showy *pacer* the battle was all but won.

Sometimes you just drove. Sometimes you went to the next settlement and had supper there. In the local eye this was taken as a pledge to each other almost as binding as a present.

Presents to the girl were always the same. The first, a pair of side combs. The next, a pendant. And the next (which meant you were actually engaged), a muff. Engagement *rings* were held to be costly nonsense and the girl who fished for one a poor risk.

('She'll keep *that* poor boy's nose to the grindstone all right!") Match watchers didn't spread the word by saying, "Did you know Elsie has her ring?"; they said, "Did you hear that Elsie got her muff?"

That is, if anyone knew about it. Secrecy was usually the keynote of the whole affair—from start to finish.

One boy waited for a pitch black night and left the side combs on a rock where he knew his girl always put down her pails and rested on her way back from the pasture spring. Another left the pendant in a barrel of scratch feed where his would come across it when she next fed the hens. And quite often the girl herself kept all her presents dark until after the wedding.

This was in line with the general stand expected of her. She mustn't show off her hold on a boy in any way. That would be "chasin him"—something nearly as frowned on as "shakin him" or "throwin him over her shoulder" after the muff stage.

Naturally, the wedding date itself was the most closely guarded secret of all. The only clues to it were what could be pumped from a child in the girl's household. Or if someone got wind of the boy's having been measured for a blue serge suit, or of his having buttonholed the minister some Sunday after church. Or—the real clincher—if someone surprised the dressmaker whisking a "shot silk" dress out of sight.

Shot silk dresses—trimmed with cylinder-shaped

glass beads of all colors that came in long vials, were strung on thread, and sewn all over the dress's front "panel" in shimmering scrolls that made ordinary wear look like a dust cloth—were for brides alone. If one of these was in the making we knew the wedding could not be far off.

And with the wedding day hush-hush ended. Salutings broke with a bang that split the night. Old muzzle loaders that hadn't known powder for years were brought out, clapboards were whacked with cudgels, and the din of bells could be heard for miles.

(One bride, so keyed up by this hullabaloo that it went to her bladder, sat down with such force on the chamber pot that it split in two, nicked her rump with its sharp edges—and the whole performance had to be held up until cobwebs were brought from the cellar beams to stanch the wound.)

When the couple finally "appeared" in the doorway, you filed past them, shying "Congratulations" at the groom and "Wish ya much joy" at the bride. That was the end of formalities. While the bride and groom were enthroned on the settee in the front room, even the most sedate of the company were already planning what they'd do to the marriage bed.

A favorite start was either to take out enough of the slats that the bed would fall down or to drape the slats with cowbells. (Once I offered our cow bells for this caper. That's the last we ever saw of them. Next morning the groom simply got up and put them on his own Jerseys.) And on or between the sheets was laid anything from an itch powder of finely scissored horse mane to a setting hen cuddling all her thirteen eggs.

Love (because they were tough enough to dare to be tender too) was abruptly different. It was not long-faced either, but it played no pranks, wore no finery—and in its thousand simple forms was more than sex the invisible breadstuff of the spirit.

It was what was there when the woman rubbed the warm liniment on the muscles of her husband's neck and knew that hers would be the only hands he'd want to bring him a glass of water even, if his muscles ever forsook him . . .

When the two of them talked things over (as he picked the apples from the top of the tree in the October afternoon and she picked the ones that could be reached from the ground), things they'd have had to *make* talk about if either had been another and they hadn't worked together at the same tasks all their lives . . .

There too when the child looked at his brother's foot bleeding from the spike, as if it was his fault not to have defended enough this flesh that was all at once closer than his own. Or when he saw his father's broad hands bend down on the blustery day to fasten the scarf snugger around his throat before he'd known himself (until he felt suddenly warmer) that he'd been cold . . . Or when the grandfather told the grandchild a story, with the child gazing straight into his face when he asked him questions, without seeing that his face was old . . .

Or when a man cried watching another man's barn burning . . .

Look at the lonely to know what it was: what it was, *not* to have it. The few who'd been left alone. The few who'd kept to themselves until it was too late to break from this shell that made them as if invisible. Only in the lack of it there was the true wealth of it seen.

Three steps before they turned the knob of the door into the empty house they heard the circling quiet of each wall and each chair ringing in its own deafness. Even their clothing was a stranger to them, with no echo of themselves to fill it with: none of the kind that only the daily eye of someone whose clothing has hung on the hook beside your own through the happy times and the sad can provide.

They had nothing beside them to color with its presence-blur (warmest of all colors) the gray of the sickness that sickened and sickened them (though with its face turned away) in the still, midnight bed. Or when one day age yawned as suddenly before them as the crater of a landslide under their feet. Nothing between them and the ear-ringing silence (not even their own faces, which mirrored no sign of having heard it) of their own brains going round and round with the tin, supperless thoughts of themselves. Nothing or no one that stood for more than all things else to stand between them and the sulphur of looking back not at the crippling mistakes they had made in folly or ignorance but at those they had *known* were mistakes when they were making them.

And those chance still lifes in the physical day that can be the very paintings of either gladness or melancholy were equal fires that burned the cold shaft of self deeper into their defenceless flesh.

These things were the scourges of the lonely. But for the others it was often these very things—even age, sickness, and blunders—that gave love an added strength. So that it turned weather and place and circumstance, whether dark or fair, to its own increase.

The stoning rain and the rat-toothed wind and the bitter boiling clouds no less than the sun on the meadows or the breeze in the pines. (For the roof was tight against the rain, and were they not tented closer than ever then, beneath the roofs of one another?) The dingy November fields where their strengths tired together under the careworn sky no less than the softwood square of dance floor when the harmonica sounded for the first figure of the Eights. The night watch at the child's fevered bed no less than the childrened Christmas . . .

It was doubled in the one by the hatred of what went against the other.

The night glow of the flames eating into the man's small timber lot where he had walked a hundred Sundays, tall with ownership, prizing it as a savings for his sons.

The crooked root that tripped the woman and

scattered into the underbrush the raspberries she had spent all morning picking one by one, when her eyes on the lost berries (without notice of her skinned arm) made her look like a child hurt on a cold day.

The sliver of iron off the splitting wedge that flew into the eye of the child who had been so proud all afternoon that his work was like a man's.

Any snubbing words (or words you speak as if to one of small account) spoken by a stranger to the woman, when the husband himself had not long ago spoken to her in just the same way.

The egg-white pallor at the temples of the old that no amount of youthful spirit could bring the youthful flush back into.

The heat, sometimes, and the frost . . .

IT WAS LOVE OF CHIMNEY SMOKE when the fall plow had folded the last strip of withered stubble back under the upturned earth just before the first snow came. And the smell of the snow when it came on the rekindled field.

Or the sound of the smiling stillness inside the yellow pumpkins.

Of the tender meat next to the wild duck's wishbone, tasting to the child of marvels.

Of the touch of the indwelling, one in another, that echoed and echoed: yes, yes . . .

It was sudden little combers of itself that the simplest things touched off.

The storm door that now closed tight as a drum when the warped sill had been replaced.

The light sworls, and the dark, of the Christmas marble cake the woman molded with the mixing spoon that glowed in the snug December light like altar wood.

The breath of the lilaced air the child breathed in as he rose higher and higher toward himself in the swing and was suddenly all of himself in the spreading moment before the swing arced downward again.

The pillow the morning you started to swing your drowsy legs from the bed to the floor and then remembered this was Sunday and the hay was all in, and you heard the drumming of the rain that would fill up the dry well.

The geranium transplants, not one of them wilted, that the woman saw when she looked up from her mending and saw the man tying the child's shoelace on their way to tap the sugar maples.

The tumbling waves of grass the boy looked at as his cock crowed when the girls went by on the road and saw him guiding the cutter bar like the captain of a sailing ship.

The woman's wedding ring (that was the signature somehow to all the years' ups and downs) as the two of them meshed their flesh so certainly this time, joking at the nervous way they had done it together that first night how many sighs ago.

The fresh water the one put into the teakettle and the match the other touched to the kindling in

the stove when the wind had shifted from the west to the
north on their way back from the January funeral . . .

AND WHEN IT IDLED just below the edge of feeling,
there were all the small things that could give it just
the nudge to set its pulses humming.

The sun (if it was not lonely) sunning itself on
the cabbage hearts.

The hummingbird in the throat of the nastur-
tium.

The scheminglessness of trees.

The hills that gave each other that cleansing look
in the moon-rising dusk.

The taste of the egg the man gave you from his
dinner kettle the day you blazed up the old uncertain
timber line between you, having been warned he'd try
to claim each doubtful rod but having found him
more than fair.

The wind telling its troubles to the eaves when
you were one untroubled step from sleep and one untroubled night away from being ten years old.

The feel of the sleek oats you let slide through
your fingers, and the thought of them busheled together out of the weathers they'd waved singly in all
season long.

The partnership of muscle as the group of you
strained (laughing when someone farted) at the rope
sling under a neighbor's horse that was "cast" in the
swamp.

The whiteness of wool brought to a foaming purity on the carding boards.

The shapes of everyone you had bonded ties with and of every headstone for yourself your life had pieced together seen in the mind's eye as you watched the endless play of shadow under the mapled arch in the hardwood grove.

Children, yours and your wife's, who looked like both of you, when they poured the water into the holes you'd dug for the windbreak hedge and held the seedling spruces straight as you tramped the earth in tight around their roots . . .

IT WAS WHAT PUT THE MAN at the core of all the green he looked at, what shielded him from all the grays—because it so mingled his presence with the woman's and the child's that each had the companion seeing of the other at the back of his own seeing eye.

It was what spared you the blenching of when it *isn't* there: when even the things you work with (no less than those far-off) know you are at their mercy and lash you with that speechlessness which will not accord the one alone a single word.

It was the final strength, the inmost sun.

It was what a house was, then.

14 / Houses

THE HOUSES THEN WERE BORN HOUSES, not mere
happenstances of board and mortar. They neither
strutted nor sat stunned, as the bloodless houses do
now. They didn't dwell on themselves, but they knew
themselves inside out. They were all big-boned, with
the timbers hewn from trees in the family woodlot,

and all plain-faced, as the square houses children draw, but each was distinct and as full of its own distinct communication as a person.

All of them had been born in, lived in, died in. Most of them had passed from father to son to grandson. And generations of memory were stored in that archival light that lit the sunlight on their walls or chairs or floors; that gently and invisibly stood and stood and stood in the doorways or the room spaces where what is gone is held so much more changelessly than in any chamber of the heart or mind. So that even the children seemed to sense (in some way least like thought) exactly what had made their lives what they were.

To know how totally the born house was an ark of all it had ever seen you had only to be left finally alone in it and have it loose the whole torrent of its memory on your flesh, crushing your breath tighter than if the very rafters had collapsed.

But few houses had anyone alone in them then. The currents of parent and child and grandparent mingled in them as in a shaded stream, kept us a bright and saving heedlessness away from what our passing moments were writing in the ink that dried on the air.

"House" has "he" in it, and "she." So had these. They had gentle manners and wristed strength. In rain they were patient. In sun they thanked. In storm they stood.

Some were well-kept (and showed their gratefulness by putting every object inside them at ease with every other, from the organ stool to the egg cup). Some were not (those of the "mussy" dishcloth and the tea grounds thrown from the back doorstep onto the spring slush). But whenever any man stepped in over his own threshold he stepped in over the threshold of himself.

Downstairs, the kitchen thronged with conduciveness. The other rooms were always a trifle on their best behavior; but here nothing withheld itself or was a wallflower.

In most meeting grounds of the day there is a touch of the courtroom. People and things are so blurred by the masks that others' expectations force on them that they can't quite be reached. Simple *place* challenges your attention, exacts it. The kitchen, with that unstudied acceptance of you that goes beyond mere loyalty, was the one place where there was none of this at all.

All things in it steeped contentedly in what they were and were for, feeling no slight if at times the only part they were asked to take was being there.

The pump at the sink stood willing with all its heart to bring you water from the well in the cellar, but it could be quiet without loudness. The Star stove, with the barrel-shaped oven on a short stout neck and the firebox beneath where two small doors opened on the coals of the hearth and a slice of bread could be speared with a fork and propped up to toast, gave out its heat like surges of generosity; but in between chip fires on a summer's day it could be cool without blunting. The comb box under the mirror (where the eyes looked at themselves looking at themselves, never seeing themselves strangers) was as satisfied to be only a comb box as the rocker was to be a rocker. The couch against the side wall rested itself, resting you. The softwood floor had never known the glass-eyed horror of linoleum. It rested the sunlight and the lamplight.

The table was queen of the room, as the stove was king. It stood with its leaves folded, ready (but not tiring with readiness) to be crowned with the steams and splendors of food that, however simple, was never starved—or to bear the school books of the children who gathered around the lamp, pushing aside the echoes of wind and sun in their minds to make place for pronouns and centimeters and the volcanoes of the earth and the dates of Hastings and Waterloo.

While the woman sat with the garment in her lap and fitted the patch on the rent, stitching it into place as her mind leisured; and the man, his muscles drowsing in the knitted silence, quietly savored all this roomful of living he had brought about.

From the row of hooks that stretched from the clock shelf (where the thread basket was home for every stray: the loose pins, the odd shoelace that had survived its mate, the scrap of chalk for marking hems, the keys without locks, the locks without keys, a few bright solitary beads . . .) to the back door where the roller towel hung, hung the coats and caps and sweaters, cheerfully ghosted with all their memories of outdoors and the weather of their wearers.

And the cellar door (the one door in the house that never frowned) did the listening for everyone, to the silent sound of fullness below. In bins, and jars, and earthenware crocks, and creamers standing in a tub of cool water while their sidegauges of isinglass showed a layer of marigold yellow growing thicker and thicker above the drift-white milk . . .

In the pantry, the room that breathed for all the rest, the summer yellow of egg yolks in a glass bowl and the milk-white drifts of flower in a sieve could give its grip back to any misty or musty day whose fortunes were at their lowest ebb.

Most rooms are a crowd. This one had one voice, one heart. In no other room were all of the objects each so singly themselves; yet here a strange harmony went round and round among them.

The sheet-sheathed ironing board behind the door, one long unwrinkled phrase of cleanliness, beguiled the odds and ends on the top shelf out of their disunity: the matches, the foot rule, the shot-shells, the worn-out shaving brush saved for none knew what, the tacks, the solder babbitt, the string, the shears for trimming graves, the nutmeg grater, the box of unmatched nuts and bolts, the Sunset dyes, the fishing line, the half-filled packages of seeds from last spring's planting, the hand plane, the scribbler of recipes ("Add the mixture slowly") written by the hand now dead, the yellowed sheaf of bills marked "Paid," the tobacco tin (Napoleon Plug) that might hold every red cent of ready money the family had to its name . . . The plump cheeks of kettles sent their good will to the medicines on the corner shelf: British Troop Liniment, alum, Friar's Balsam, wild strawberry extract, sweet spirits of niter—which took the compliment and passed theirs back.

Vanilla, for all its difference, was yet one with cinnamon and vinegar. The knife box and the cruet and the tureen interlocked their natures like the cub play of sun shadow on the brook where it runs over the white pebbles beneath the umbrella of umbrella ferns.

All weathers long the pantry hummed itself.

And in those days long before the cry spread that partitions between rooms must come down and the insides of houses be turned into ram pastures of wall-eyed space, halls were halls. Rooms, no less than people, dislike to be smack "up in each other's faces" day in and day out—and these were spared that discomfiture. With halls to open from, they had just the separateness they needed to be themselves without being moodily *by* themselves.

When the front door was swung wide the halls were a cool throat that brought in the poplared or the daisied or the Septembered breeze, gave the house its running current. Their simple lengthwiseness tamed the vastness of sun and air, made this strip of it the all of it. And the landings at the bottom of the stairs and at the top were the embarkation points for work or sleep that gave the foot its blessing.

Off the downstairs hall, the dining room held itself in constant preparedness for dining-room company, though this did not set the kitchen against it. It had a touch of pride in its calling that the kitchen was proud of.

Accents of linen and china (the butter dish with the cut-glass dome, the fragile old cups that had become really beautiful with lasting, the cake plates with the cake-plate flowers on them that had taken on a dusting of real delicacy as the years went by, the "good" napkins) tinctured the air with their mild graces even when the cupboard door was closed and the contents of the sideboard unseen. Objects on the mantelpiece—a sea shell with the symmetries so absolute that the eternal went round and round in it, or the spurious knickknack someone had given someone else in affection many years ago, thinking it was handsome—stood side by side in that special fellowship between the perfect and the kind-intentioned. And the room made lace of the sunshine.

The parlor made lace of the sunshine too, but a kind of vestment lace. The Morris chair and the wicker rocker and the settee with the cluster of grapes on its back sat a little like churches of themselves. The "enlarged pictures" of grandfather and grandmother in their gilt oval frames mused from the wall on the verities their sitters had never recognized in their lifetime. And if you listened to it alone, you could hear the organ holding its breath.

Yet when there was trouble or rejoicing or at Christmas this room threw itself in with the rest of the house as unstintingly as any other.

There was a single bedroom downstairs—for the sick. So that the one already othered by the inner landscape of pain should not also be a stairway away.

The upstairs bedrooms where the Sunday clothes hung votively in the closets were different. There the bureaus and the commodes and the quilts became totally verbs of themselves as single-mindedly as leaves leafed. These rooms were like branches from the tree trunk of the hall. And nowhere was the family so closely one as there, when its members swayed separately through the night stillness on the boughs of sleep.

The whole thing was that each object then, indoors or out, gave off the total sum and climate of what it embodied. Not, however, in any spectral way. However sobering sometimes, there was nothing doomful about it. It was not like the haunting of awesome spirits. (The storm clouds might terrify, but they were never god-terrible in the pagan sense.) It was the simple light of suchness.

A few real superstitions still held root. It was bad luck to set straight a stocking that had been put on inside out. If a pig was killed on the wane of the moon the pork would shrivel in the barrel. Cucumbers, to thrive, must be planted on the fourth day of June. It was bad luck to finish a task on Friday: women would leave a mat's last rag dangling and hook in the final loops Saturday morning.

There was nothing dark about these fancies either. You laughed at yourself in the very act of minding them. (As you laughed at the few ghost stories still told: a man known to be on his death bed had been clearly seen walking the road; a tree had been hung with balls of fire.) But the word for them *was* superstition.

The way that each and every thing gave off its "virtue" had no superstitious quality about it whatsoever. It was never spooky or forbidding. It was as open as ABC books.

The houses were furnished with few other books. None of the kind that are themselves houses. Or that read them*selves*, their pages giving to the room a kind of sound of rivers, as in a room where one of a couple mends something the other can't and the other writes letters for them both. The few there were lay effigied between their liver-spotted covers, writing "dead letters" to an air whose address they had lost.

But what was the lack? When everyone had read with his nerve ends the only great writers—earth, sky, rock, and tree (not *these* the petticoated little penmen mooning about doubt and heartburn)—and been strengthened by them. When familiar faces held all the texts that mattered (and all their upshots), available at a glance. When there were whole libraries in

the eyes of someone you'd been through all the
weathers with—the eyes which had themselves read
the only utterances (of sun and storm) that are without deceit, and the only records that are printed
without falsity (on field and kitchen), messages that
make words the mere chips and whittlings of feeling
entire.

When the most common things would suddenly
flash out with the statement of all things that could
not be said. The movement of the first leaf breaking
on a tree or of the last one clinging to it. Longitudes
of sun stripe, wondrous as zebras, sleepwalking the
blazoned meadow. The eddy of a running stream
around a rock . . .

When every once in a summer or a winter while
the moods of light and object would, in their indelible
shorthand, write on the sheet of your consciousness a
pure description of all the moods there were, which
you yourself could never describe.

Late one November day when the waterfall
sounded dark in the woods, as before rain, though
there would be no rain (and though you yourself
might not know that you were sad), you would look
from the cloud locked inside yourself to the muddy
water seeping pointlessly into the hollow of your
tracks and you would know all there was to know
about despair.

Some clear morning when you lowered the pail
into the deep well, tipping it on its side with the well
pole when it struck the surface of the water, and then

felt the weight of the cool secret water drawn up hand over hand to the level of the curb where the sun made silk of it, you would know all there was to be known about hope.

Who needed books—when all their plots and all their wisdoms might be had, for the looking, in a cloudburst or a smile?

Who needed books, when he had memory?

W.R.

15 / *More Memory, or*
The's and And's

THE NET OF MEMORY has a mesh all its own. Events the size of lives slip through it and are lost; yet it can catch and hold the merest fragments of occasion. Perhaps it is because only these fragments have voice in the wilderness of cause unrestingly, ear-stunningly, causing effect—and that only voice gives a thing true body.

The rusted hinge on the barn door that sways half-open—perhaps that is the voice of missing some-one so far away that the distance between you hums like wires. Perhaps the sound of the waking orchard has the voice of healthy flesh harboring the mind's flock . . .

In any case, it was a medley of fragments like these—of things, times, or spoken words—that with voice or not made up the remembered day in Nor-stead.

PATHS ACROSS THE FIELDS between houses—some straight, some winding, all foot-worn hard as faith by the passage of neighbors to borrow a drawing of tea or to tell of catastrophe.

A child's history book, patiently wakeful to tell him of kings, while he sleeps dreaming of flying squir-rels . . . Wheat blades, incalculably honest, breaking through the ground in the first warm shower.

TWO MEN STAND BACK and look at a hay rack fitted with all new rungs and crosspieces.

"There. That does it, what? All right now, Bart—how much do I owe you?"

"*Owe* me? Fer what?"

"Fer half yer afternoon, man! And the use o' yer tools! You know damn well how far I'da got with a job like that myself."

"That's all right. I didn't come over here lookin fer pay."

"I know ya didn't, I know ya didn't. But . . ."

"You don't owe me nothin. If a man can't do that much fer anyone without chargin, he better be dead."

WOOD BOXES. Candle molds. Afternoons of one creed or another . . .

"WHAT DID YOU SEE in town yesterday?"

"Not a thing. Just a bunch o' people with a jigger in their heel. Nothin."

EVERY KIND of face:

Children's faces swarming with innocence.

Men's faces, quantitied solid and square beneath their screen of unconcern by the ram's stroke of sex impacted in every feature.

Women's faces, blooming and *qualitied* somehow by the very nowhereness in them of what it is that makes the man's a quantity.

Faces, fulfilled by suppertimes, with no craters of dead yearning in the eyes—waking to work to be rejoiced in and rested after: and family faces so enlisted with each other that together they make up the one sure shield against the smiting breath of all things strange.

Faces, too, hewn scar-thatched out of their own shadowless flesh by the fine and sleepless edge of hidden pain or the cutting day's end with nothing accomplished, looking as if the heart's house with all its lifetime belongings had burned to the ground behind them—yet, no matter what the ruin, with some rooted flagpole of themselves still standing straight . . .

THE CHILD is six. The grandmother is eighty. When she was six she was in England.

"Gram, what makes so many cracks in your face?"

"Cracks ?"

"Yes. There's *more* . . . when you laugh like that."

"Yes, you can get them from laughing. I did laugh a lot. And you can get them from . . . I suppose I got some of them from the day the well your grandfather was rocking up caved in on him and I heard him scream just once for me to come help, but I couldn't see where he was . . . and from the day the forest fires were so thick around us the cinders were lighting on the roof, until some miracle sent the rain, and . . ."

"Do you get them from bein married?"

"Yes. But they're the best kind. The worst kind's the kind you get when you've got nothing to trouble you. Not a husband. Not a chick nor a child. When there's no one you can say 'What would *you* do?' to, when you're puzzled."

"Will I get them someday?"

"Yes, child. You likely will. But don't you worry. You'll have things happen to you, I can see. You'll make things happen. You'll have the best kind of wrinkles in your face."

"I didn't mean I didn't like your face, Gram."

"I know, child."

"When we have something special for supper you slip some offa your plate onto mine, don't you."

"Sometimes."

"And when I want to do something they can't see why I want to do it, you know why, the very first one, don't you. And when it's too cold to say my prayers on the floor, you let me say them in bed, don't you. And when I tore the whole seat outa my pants slidin down the shop roof into the big drift, you just laughed, didn't you."

"Yes."

"I didn't mean I didn't like your face, Gram."

"I know, child, I know."

"You laughed, didn't you. We can always make each other laugh, can't we."

YES, AND ICICLES fringing an eave, with each freezing drop pointing a dagger nearer the window ledge the way the mind's cold white blood of uncertainty daggers down toward the pulse.

Barn-warmth lazily furnaced by the church-eyed cows.

A flock of blackbirds gusting the air and sprinkling the wild rose bush.

A strength of log chains hanging from a nail . . . A clench of warping-bars . . .

Curb bits greened with the horse's slaver. Dunghills (with the snakes' nests inside them) steaming in the February thaw.

A joy of brooks. A sigh of hemlocks. A grief of stones . . .

TWO MEN STAND beside a gateway.

"Now don't you be in no hurry bringin them horse clippers back till you're all through with em, Arth. I won't be needin em. I don't suppose you'd have a minute to walk down and see that new oat field I cleared beyond the swale there?"

"Why, sure. Things ain't very rushin today." They go to the field. "Well, by God, ain't that a pretty sight! And a year ago that was just alders and hardhacks!"

"Yeah. Hardhacks mostly."

"Man, that musta meant some bone labor! And look at the way them oats's headin out . . . and not a swath of em lodged! By God, Arth, that's somethin to be proud of!"

"Oh, I don't know as it's anything to be proud of, but . . . as long as a man has his strength, I don't know any work that makes him feel better. And o'course I had help. The kids picked off most o' the small rock, and the wife she liked to come down evenins and help me burn the roots. Did you get a mate fer that steer?"

"Yeah. I got one from Cale. Come on over to the barn and see what you think of em."

"All right." They go to Arth's barn. "Well, by God, ain't them a pair o' beauties!"

"They ain't too bad a match, are they. Get up, Spark. Lion."

"Match? You'd swear they was twins! Are they broke yet?"

"Not altogether. But just about. The young fulla there—Hal—he yokes em up every night after school. They crowded a little at first, or hauled off, but he's got em now so they're startin to pull together like an old team."

"That's a smart boy o' yours, Arth! He kin do anything. A few more years and he'll be a damn big help to ya."

"Well, yes . . . Hal ain't a bad boy. You know, we all got pretty good kids, Freem—so I guess we shouldn't complain."

A WOMAN PULLING THE SLATS out lengthwise from their bracket on the kitchen wall to air the ironing on (while the son with the strawberry birthmark on his left shoulder who'd come in from the hayfield that day to pump himself a drink, saying he'd decided to enlist, bleeds the drop that is next to the last drop that is round with all forgetting, at Vimy).

A man putting the dipper of clear sap to his mouth in the maple grove in the morning dew alert as a partridge (while all over the world the ink rusts on the paper).

Mixing bowls, cheerful as stars. Barrel hoops, secure as a month. Roosters, regal as noon.

Roads leading the uneasied eye to their point of disappearance, in the last storybook light of December days when the days first start to stretch out longer . . .

ONE WOMAN GOES to the kitchen door to greet another. It is five o'clock.

"Why, Clara. Come in. You're just in time."

"Oh. You're gettin supper." Clara steps inside. "I never thought. We don't most gen'lly eat till six when Steve's in the woods. I thought Jim was in the woods too."

"He was. But the kids wanted their snowshoes fixed, so he only made two turns this afternoon. Now take off your things and have a bite with us."

"Well . . . you know how good it is to taste someone else's cookin for a change. But I'd have to eat and run. And—no!—this is an imposition."

"It's nothin of the kind. Johnnie, you skip down cellars and get a bottle o' quince preserve. You like quince, don't you, Clara?"

"It's my favorite. And our tree died last year. Now, don't you go to any extry trouble, Martha. Don't you put on a tablecloth for me."

"I ain't goin to any extry trouble. I most always put on a cloth."

"So do I. Most always. It don't cost nothin, and I always think the food *tastes* better somehow."

"Mum, can *I* light the lamp tonight? Johnnie lit it *last* night."

"I don't know why these two get into such a glee over lightin the lamp. You'd think it was some kind of a . . ."

"I know. Mine's the same."

A VASE OF RIBBON GRASS on the organ rest.

The great red honeycomb bell at the center of the Christmas ceiling.

Gam-spread pigs hanging head down from a beam in the shop, gleaming whiter than ghosts in the dusk-chill that stiffens the one long thread of blood at the tip of their snout.

Monarch butterflies mainsailing the honeyed clover. Shepherd's purse and lady's slippers.

Knobbled conches (from what fathomless sea?) pink as women and as satin-smooth where their hollow curves inward and certain as numbers where the wing flares out, lying beside a verandah post, to be blown like trumpets for dinnertime or death . . .

AND SOME DAYS, at four o'clock, the sleep-walking snow comes down again on the stubble in the fields. The sky sheds it straight downward like a brimming of its own white calm. Only against the darkness of an open door can any slant at all be seen in its direction.

The old watch it and feel a strange reprieve. There is activity in all the air, something wide and universal is happening, and they stir from their own happenless weather to happen with it. Feeling at the same time cosy and protected. It is snowing, snowing is the day's whole fact and concern, the day is too busy with its snowing to notice *them*—to single them out and deliver their years' reckoning.

It snows and snows. And then it stops.

The old feel naked again, as if a truce had ended.

Then, in the night, the wind revives. The old, sleeping so lightly, awaken and are cold: this raging lawlessness is nothing like the truce of before.

The wind blows and blows. All night and all the next day until dusk. And then it stops.

The old stare out at the small lakes of hard blue ice the wind has scoured bare in the fields. They sigh twice-deep for faces gone—then, with a third and deeper sigh, fasten what grip they can again upon their living blood . . .

A CLUSTER OF BOYS mills about in the road. They speak so quickly, one after another, that the talk is a cat's cradle.

"What'll we do?"

"Let's all go down to the Baptizin pool and dam up the narrows there and make a raft. Or ketch perch."

"No. Let's go back and climb trees and get some spruce gum."

"Hey! Looka the toad! Get some timothy straws

and you kin tickle him and make him hop any way you want."

"I got a turtle I found, in the wash tub. Let's get him and race him against the toad up to the church."

"Toads'll give you warts."

"They will not."

"*I* know. Let's go climb the stagin on Wilf's barn."

"All right. We kin cut across the field."

"No. We don't wanta waller his grass down."

" 'Git outa my grass or I'll . . . leather you ass!' "

"Let's rassle."

"Let's make out we're . . . Hey! Looka the crows on the churchyard fence. One crow sorrow, two crows joy, three crows a wedding, four crows a boy, five crows silver, six crows gold. Six crows gold!"

"If I had a lotta gold . . . I wouldn't care if I had a cold."

"Aw, *How*ie!"

"Gus Jordan's got a new rowboat. It's a real piss-cutter!"

"Who said?"

"I said."

"Let's go see it."

"Here comes Lennie. Hi, Lennie. What'll we do?"

"I don't know. Anything."

"Whatta you got in your blouse . . . you louse?"

"Yeah, what's stickin yer blouse out?"

"Lennie's got a hard-on!"

"Shut up! It's apples. Our Astrakans is just gettin

ripe. Here. There's lots. We kin all have a good feed. Where's Jack?"

"Yeah! Where's Jack?"

"There he is. Down by their woodpile."

"Hey! Jack! Come. On. Over. We're. Gonna. Do. Somethin."

"He heard ya. He's comin. Hurry up, Jack. Come on!"

"Hi, Jack. Here's some apples. Whatta you want to do?"

" 'My son Thom-as/ Went to a circass / Ridin on a jackass / Come home bare-ass / Wasn't that gloriass / My son Thom-as!' "

"Howie, if you don't stop that . . . we'll take yer dink out! What *do* you want to do, Jack?"

"I don't know. Let's just go down the road. Let's just walk down through the woods to that place the woman was killed that Charlie Spence made up the verses about."

"Ain't that a long ways?"

"We got all afternoon."

"All right. We kin set on the Big Rock down there and eat our apples."

"No. Let's set on Little Tim's Bridge and eat em."

"All right. Come on."

"Let's roll down the hill."

"If you roll down the hill . . . you'll turn into a pill."

[207

"Awwww, How*ieeeeee!*"
"Come on, come on . . ."

Green signing itself on every twig like kings on postage stamps. Deer tracks neat as an inch. Ox silence solid as a pound. Carrion jays conceited as dukes. Leaves and loaves . . .

It is time to light the kitchen lamp and the oil is below the wick. A child takes the oil can to the store for a half-gallon of kerosene.

He hears the first frogs in those black spots in the fields where the water lies. He thinks: How do the frogs get there? How do they keep alive in the winter? Where is the raft we made last summer? His pace picks up, the oil can swinging.

He goes out to Ben's back shop, where the oil puncheon is raised above the floor on two wooden blocks. The back shop smells of molasses and dry goods. He watches with fascination as Ben turns on the spigot with a gush and then, at the end, cuts down its flow to such short, skillful jets that the quart measure is filled precisely to the brim without a drop spilling over. Ben empties the measure into the oil can without the loss of a drop there either. Twice this feat is brought off.

He gives Ben a quarter. There are two cents change. He can buy two paper cylinders of "Long

Tom" popcorn. They have prizes in them. Mostly it's a whistle, but once in a great, great while it's a ring.

Which colors will he pick? He thinks and thinks. Once yellow had had a ring. But you couldn't tell. They switched them around. He takes a red and a green.

He waits until he is by himself to open them. Which will he open first? He can't decide.. He says, "Eeny, meeny, miney, mo . . ." It comes green.

He opens the green, his hands trembling. It's a ring!

STONE-DRAGS and organ rests. Pike poles and red ocher. Door sills, lanterns of themselves, gently shining in the falling night. Pine groves, Easters of themselves the whole year round. Church windows, jurors of themselves when the sun goes down.

All objects abstracts and sermons of themselves when the weather stares . . .

THIS DAY, light comes first, sending shafts of itself up and down the sides of things like ribbons of sunlight bisecting the sea. Then warmth, friends with light again after the long winter when they did not speak to each other, comes calling: light's guest.

It wakens all things with its touch, makes them neighbors, and then sits down with them to hear their story and fulfill their prophecies. The green strawberry at the road's edge dots itself with the first pin-points of red. Kernels of corn sprout their cobbed and tasseled future. Bean seeds, muscled like Atlas, feel the weight of the earth they struggle up through suddenly give way. Minnows in the brook dart quicker; and horizon trees, uncles of the forest, smile to themselves. Beech leaves, students of the sun, expand their just-discovered shapes millimeter by millimeter, keeping the tiny leaf with all its serrated points always in perfect scale with the map of the finished one held before them in the hands of the warmth—and the leaves of the cherry tree, quickest learners of all, knowing exactly in each rim cell when completeness has been reached, stop there and bask in their accomplished goal like theorems.

The sun reads the earth's palm. The day is all hand, making a gift of itself that has everyone's name on it.

Cows that have lain all night in the pasture like hippopotamuses of contentment, heaving great sighs of fullness as they shifted their cuds, lunge to their feet. They stretch, and begin to crop the grass, their heads thrusting from bite to bite like joyful bobbins. The horse goes down on his knees and begins to roll—once, twice, on his back with his legs flailing in the air, and at the third try completely over—then rises, shivers the daylights out of every slack muscle and, flashing his nostrils into the sun, gallops the paddock, his belly sounding ga-*flump*, ga-*flump*, and his mane flying.

Latches, hooks, and door buttons, entrusted to hold against the night, lighten their grip. Bugling gathers in the rooster's throat and the hen cackles cosily at her smooth egg. The lake wakes innocently from dreams of drowning and the tombstones grandfather the slopes of distance.

Children, awaking in the same bed, puzzle the self-echo in each other's faces for a split second, then leap into their clothes.

Old people, waking in rooms by themselves, slowly watch the bands of sunlight circuit the walls. For the length of a sigh they feel the pluck of the question, vivid as any at nineteen: Where did I go to? Then, familied and more and more their own familiars, they lie there content to be museums of themselves.

A man in his prime, stirring before his wife, sits on the edge of the bed for a moment, meshing himself into the day. He glances down at his body's morning impudence. It stands up saucy and autonomous. He gives it the brief chuckling touch of comradeship. The earth of him shifts. He is not in his head or in his heart: he is there. Bunched there to throbbing. He stands up (glimpsing himself twice standing in the bureau mirror, himself and this rousing description of himself) and steps to the window.

His wife opens her eyes. She raises herself on one elbow. A stroke of she-ness comes from her flesh in that instant before the last tousle of sleep has been shaken from it.

He looks out the window at the day. And then, his senses mazed by the teeming lexicon of warmth and light, he goes back to the bed and (he is sure of it) consummately sows a son . . .

"IS YER LEGS gettin tired?" a father asks.

"No!" the boy says.

"I guess we shouldn't a follered that moose track so far. But I thought we might come onto their yard."

"No! I wanted to! I seen the track first, didn't I!"

"Yes. You didn't get your feet wet crossin that slough hole, did you?"

"No. Well, a little. But that don't hurt."

"Are they cold?"

"No."

"Maybe we better take the shortcut over the barrens here. The snow's a little deeper, but it'll get us home before dark."

"You never get lost in the woods, do you! You always know right where you are!"

"Well, I never bin lost yet. You ain't tired?"

"No! Yes. A little. Carry me, Dad?"

"THE" POINTS to something particular. "And" connects two things that are different. In the city, so much is alike that only a few "the"s are found, no more than a handful of "and"s is needed to couple them. Here the "the"s were numberless, the "and"s infinite.

The air bladder and the Leonardo fins keeping each movement of the rainbow trout as precise as Archimedes, and the discs of color confettied on its glistening sides.

The ashes bringing in clover and the sun bleaching the splintered bone-dent in an ox skull where the sledge hammer fell.

The hammock of sunken earth on the grave tops when the rough box collapsed beneath.

Two women exchanging petunia slips in the gentle casket light of Indian summer.

Two men (a circlet of hair sweated to their scalps where the perimeter of their caps has snugged it like the headbands of Roman emperors) brothered by the brawling meadow heat that stretches their balls as they pass their thumbs testing along the edges of the scythes they've just whetted and, putting down their scythes, pass from one to another the jug of spring water they'd hung in the cool of the running brook.

Empty worm cans (sage tins, By Appointment to His Majesty) rusting beside the stillwater; and knotholes in the barn siding where pencils of light prism through.

"Rescue the perishing, care for the dying/Snatch (the boys giggle) them in pity from sin and the grave . . ."

"HOW WAS THE BIRTHDAY PARTY?" a man asks his wife.

"I think it was the best yet. All the women said so. You know, we've been havin this little party for Mattie ever since she turned eighty, and I swear she gets younger every year. And we had one good laugh. She stooped down to pick up a piece of ribbon she'd dropped when she opened her presents and all of a sudden her puckerin string broke. No one knew which way to look for a minute. And then El said, 'Mattie, if you broke where you cracked you'd be short!' Well, you know Mattie—she's eighty-seven years old, but you have to get up early in the mornin to get ahead of her. 'Well,' she said, 'it's gone. And I can't get it back. And I wouldn't if I could.'"

A WOMAN STANDING on the pole floor of the shop tiering up the huge armfuls of winter wood, each a three hours' warmth, that the man carries in and drops at her feet.

A man watching a boy child eat bread, his own hands gladdening that this bread of their work is being made flesh; touching a girl child's hair and marveling where from the field quartz of himself this silver has come.

Grindstones and curtain stretchers.

Goldthread and pleurisy root.

Buttercups the children hold under each other's chins to see who likes butter best—and the wafered sunflower seed, thin as the host, that the child draws into his windpipe, choking to death on it, while his mother, her eyes screeching, strikes him the blows between the shoulders that his screeching eyes will never understand.

The handwriting on a faded letter, most living of ghosts; and the blades of shadow under the October beech aching that repentance can never be answer enough.

Spool beds and spring skates.

"Just a song at twilight / When the lights are low . . ."

"Who told you about the fracas?" one man asks another.

"No one. I was there! I was settin right beside em. You know that fulla I'm talkin about, dontcha? I've seen him at the dances before. He comes from outside somewheres, and I guess he thinks we don't know anything around here. He's kind of a sneer, and I guess he thought he'd have some fun with App. He kept askin him these foolish questions. One after another. Well, you know App. You'd think nothin could rile him, but you just touch him right and . . . All of a sudden App opened on him! He just grabbed the sonofabitch by the scruff o' the neck and lifted him about two feet offa the floor—and, by God, by the time he was through with him, he brought him to the ringbolt and don't you think he didn't!"

Kraut knives and brace bits. Earwigs and compasses. Linchpins and patchwork holders. "It's a long way to

Tipperary/ It's a long way to go . . ." Wheel ruts sad as a holiday, and crisscross branch-light stirring as your own name.

Yes, and the grinning man who cuts the calf making as if to sling the bloody mess at one of the others who hold the trembling calf beneath his knife, its eyes winking with pain. And the same man winnowing chaff from the linter floor for the snow birds . . .

A man and his wife are looking through the wall-paper catalogue.

"Which pattrun do you like best?" she says.

"I don't know," he says. "They're all pretty. Which do you?"

"I like this one with all the fern sprays through it." She holds the pattern up against the wall. "There. Don't it look good on the wall? Of course you can't tell from this little sample in the book, but . . ."

"Well, send fer it then."

"And it ain't too dear, neither. It's only fifteen cents a double roll."

"Well, send fer it then."

"Or I don't know . . . Maybe the walls could go another year. You've had that expense with the shinglin and . . . But this paper that's on now has bin on since that spring you was laid up with the pleurisy —do you remember?"

"Yes. That's goin on three years."

"And it *is* pretty dingy behind the stove there.

And, I don't know, somehow a little new wallpaper seems to . . . Maybe there's other things we need, but I don't waste *too* much on frills, do I."

"No. Some women's got to have somethin new every time they turn around. Now you take that order sheet and go to work and send fer it right now."

She takes the order sheet and starts to copy down the catalogue number and then its matching price from the page at the back of the book. Her face falls.

"Oh. I *thought* there must be somethin . . . I've been lookin at the wrong number all the time. This pattrun I like is *thirty* cents a double roll."

"Oh. Well . . . what's the odds? Send fer it, just the same."

"Oh, I couldn't. With the border and all, that'd bring it up around . . . You work too hard for what you get for me to . . ."

"If you want new paper, and that's the pattrun you like, you send fer it! A little extry ain't gonna kill us. We'll live. We always have."

AND SOMETIMES, as if by a borrowing from something unearthly, the sudden enormity of the plainest object or its leopardry stops the mind, as when you see pictures of an elephant or a python or a secretary bird and the mind is stopped by the fantastic made suddenly more real than anything plausible.

AND ALL THE COLORS that stood beside the colors that

came from the ends of the earth, or partook of them.

The Turkey red of the summer dawn and the Chinese white of the frozen cheek. The Indian yellow of the wind-wild flames and the hen's-foot yellow of the dead hand. "Grasshopper, grasshopper, grasshopper gray / Give me some molasses or I'll kill you today." The Persian blue of the child's hair ribbon and the plums of purple blood where the wounded deer pants in the thicket . . .

There is a voice outside the house.

"App!" the woman says. "Wake up! There's someone calling under the window!"

"What?" He is half-asleep. "What time is it?"

"It's the middle of the night." She calls. "Who's there?"

"It's me. Paul. The baby's taken worse. He seemed to be all better when we went to bed, but Hattie thinks his fever's gone way up agin now. She's afraid o' convulsions. I think he'll be all right in the mornin, but Hattie's gettin kinda stericky."

"I know. Sickness always seems worse in the night."

"She said she thought you had some sweet spirits o' niter."

"Yes. I have. You tell her I'll be right over."

"No, no . . . she don't expect you to do that. It's bad enough to wake you outa yer sleep. I'll just take the niter and . . ."

"Now it ain't no hardship at all for me to come over . . . and, anything like this, don't you ever hesitate. What did you say, App? . . . App says, you go back to Hattie, and we'll be over as soon as we get our things on."

THE BLACK FRIDAY BLACK of the ink the sick man signs his will with and the humming black of the kitchen stove.

And the ocelot freckling on the foxglove blossom, and the tortoiseshell of the winking coals, and the mackerel sky, and the Joseph's coat of the Sunday lake that mirrors the October hill . . .

A MAN WALKS down the woods trail in the dusk that comes out of the trees and hardens the packed snow to blue night-iron under his larrigans. His thoughts that have circled outside his head all day like deliciously blurred warranties of him while his muscles sang full-throated with the ax are now nested inside his head for sleep. At noon he took the bread and tea, sacrament of his wife, on a fallen log. The last crumbs he shook out of his lunch box on to the ground. The birds ate them and changed them into wing gloss that will catch the sun as they sing tomorrow on the tombstones.

It is almost dark when he comes out on to the main road. He crosses the bridge. He does not look at the initials he cut into the rail the August day the boys were all as darting and eternal as the current. A hawk that will never lay its head down until it dies flies across the road. It clenches its feet around its bed of a branch. Everything stands out sharp and separate in the chill, the line of itself drawn around itself. The dusk is silvered and slivered with all the "the"s in the world. He breathes deep of it and its clean fingers run through his lungs and his blood.

He climbs the hill. He has never been sick a day in his life. Then, between one step and the next, one breath and the next, through some niche so slight in the Here where it touches the Nowhere that he feels not the slightest change as he stoops to tie his lace, comes the faceless smoke of mortality. A traitor cell unlocks itself and death is inside him. "Death" that has "the" in it. All the "the"s. And "had." All the "had"s. And "eat" in the middle.

Slowly it will eat the day of the initials on the bridge and the day he tasted the first ripe apple from the tree his wife had helped him plant and the night they shook the bed so the moon shook and all the "the"s in the world became one THE. It will eat all the "the"s. And all the "had"s. But it will not eat the look of him in the eyes of the sons of the sons of the sons forever of the son they made the night they shook the moon . . . Or the grain of richness he gave to the earth his hands worked in . . . Or his hands that will change back into earth . . .

AND ALWAYS ALL THE SOUNDS, woven into the quintet of all the always senses . . .

The whisper of the scythes in the tall marsh grass after the rain, and the cracked voice of hinges.

The murmur of acres and the peal of children.

The ringing tap of the hammer on the wheel rim and the flump of groin against groin.

"When the trumpet of the Lord shall sound / And Time shall be no more . . ."

A GROUP OF MEN have gathered to help another lay a new sill under his barn.

"Hadn't I better hitch up the team and snig her closer the foundation there?" he says. "I don't want you fullas to come over here and lift yer guts out."

"Hell, no. There's six of us here. If we can't raft a sill that size into place, we ain't fit to pick shit with the hens. Come on, boys. Come *on* there, Willis. You only bin married two days, yer back can't be *that* weak!"

THE TICK OF SUNDAY EVENING, and the moose call that sounds instinct with the whole animal darkness.

The boom of the ice when the clench of cold splits it the length of the lake, and the quiet of wool.

The thunder of runaway horses, and the riffle of the pillowcase when it's torn up for bandages.

Wind harps of mountain spruce and choirs of hop vine . . .

"IT TOOK US SO LONG to ketch that damned horse of ours in the pasture," a visitor says, "we was afraid you'd be all locked up for the night before we got here!"

"No. As a matter o' fact, we never think o' lockin a door. Nobody does around here. Not even the storekeeper. And he's never lost as much as a nutmeg."

And all the sounds of silences:

The silence of another, who is your other, sleeping on the couch in the kitchen while the second hand of your consciousness suddenly has her for its clockface.

Of the bottoms of ponds when the surface blackens with its own absolute thereness.

Of stakes holding themselves straight in the ground . . . and ropes a child could lift stretching stronger than Samson between ton weights at either end . . . and rocks the size of whales bearing their centers of gravity on their shoulders without a whimper day or night . . .

"Bill, when I was down to the old mill bed yesterday I seen some fresh deer signs. All through the snow everywheres. Right there by the brook. I'd say it was the big buck and them two does you seen last fall. I guess when the season was open they got scared way back, and now they're comin out agin. What do you say we take a run down after dinner and see if we can't land one? A little deer steak would go good now, wouldn't it?"

"Nothin better. But how'll we . . . ? Suppose it's

all right to walk down the road with our guns in plain sight?"

"Hell, yes. No one around here'd inform on us."

THE SILENCE BETWEEN THE AX swung back and the ax descending, between the finger testing the pulse and the finger taken away, between the news and the scream, between the italics of the departing face and its first afterimage . . . . . .

The ethers of silence that come out of stumps and Bible covers and the bone handles of straight razors and rubber balls lost in the tall grass . . . And the back-to silences that come out of the pewter sugar bowl without a handle, lying in the shambled trash pile at the edge of the swamp . . . and out of the faded tintype and the flotsam caught in the windfall across the brook . . . and out of the North and the South and the East and the West when you open the door of the empty house after the silence of the grave . . .

A MAN COMES GRINNING into the kitchen, holding out his wallet.

"Angus! You found it!"

"Yeah. It was on the seat I'd rigged up on the buckboard, pushed back under the buffalo. I never thought o' lookin there. I was sure I musta lost it before I left town."

"Is the money all there?"

"Yes. There was five dollars fer the cider apples and nineteen dollars fer the pig. It's all there."

"Well, thank Heavens! Alec, you run down and tell Eva Woodworth your father found his wallet. She was as exercised over it as we was."

"Mrs. Woodworth, Dad found his wallet!"

"You don't mean it! Where? I must call to Frank. Frank? Can you hear me? Angus found his wallet!"

"Bob," Frank calls, "Angus found his wallet!"

"Fanny," Bob calls, "Angus found his wallet!"

"Ned," Fanny calls, "Angus found his wallet!" . . .

AND THE GREAT SILENCING SILENCES that come like godfathers out of the standstill afternoon when the sun and the fields and the breeze that shunts gently against your temples suddenly know you and multiply you until, mused with the sense of self and peace, you become the equal and duplicate of everything . . .

"JOHN, COME OVER HERE by the sink window. Ain't Matt's big barn doors blowed open?"

"Yeah. Yeah, I guess they have."

"You should go over and tell him. If he's in the back o' the house he can't see em."

"Like hell I'll go tell him! If he wanted to get mad over nothin, I'll be goddamned if *I*'ll be the first one to knuckle."

"But won't they blow off in this gale? Maybe the roof'll blow off."

"Let it blow. I got my own to worry about." He goes outside.

The child comes in. "Mum, after Dad braced our own doors, he went over to Matt's. I thought we didn't go there."

"Now never you mind. You go back out and play."

"All right."

A little later, the child comes in again. "Dad's back, Mum. He's out in the shop. And you oughta hear the way he's whistlin. I didn't know he could whistle as good as that. Did you?"

"Now don't you *mention* that to him, hear me? You just go back out and play. Or if you wanta go over to the orchard and pick me up a pail o' them Tallman Sweets's blew off, maybe I could find you five cents."

"All right."

John comes into the kitchen. "Man, this *is* a gale! But I think it's lettin up some now."

"What'd he say, John? Matt."

"Oh, I dunno. Nothin much. Only he said, why didn't I turn my horses out in his back field, the fall feed there was just goin to waste. I dunno . . . maybe . . . that other . . . maybe it was as much my fault as . . . And here's some, I don't know what she called em, 'hermits' or some damn thing, that Esther just took outa the oven. She said to tell you it was a new receipt. I'll say this for Matt, there's one fulla'd never fleece ya. I'd trust him with money uncounted. Man, that stew smells good! A raw day like today, that'll really hit the spot."

"John! Stop! Now you get your hands right down!"

"Yeah? Well, what're you gigglin about then?"

"John! Now you stop! If anyone was goin by the window, what'd they think?"

"I don't give a damn what they'd think. A man feels as good as I do right now, he's gotta . . . have a little . . ."

And the silences behind the sound of all the silences that line the heart like muslins or give it its ballast:

. . . of the heartbeat that itself can't hear; of pain (the one thing deaf and blind to all parley) thrown out by some defender deep inside you that you'd never known of . . .

. . . of all that's inexpressible: of the loyalty of roofs and supper plates and eyes your eyes have a home behind and the scales that give you honest weight in the trade of strength for bread . . .

A woman walks back the twisting cow path in the pasture, searching for blueberries. The afternoon is locked solidly in place by the steady sun.

She passes the bushes where others have picked: there is no pleasure in spots that have been picked over. She goes beyond sight of the house. And then, just at the point of turning back, she sees a kind of cove that the pasture fire licked into two years ago. The bushes there are loaded with berries that have never been touched. The ground is blue with them, and she sees beds of the luscious black ones twice the size of the blue and with the sheen of a black horse.

She kneels beside a cradle hill and begins to pick, expertly stripping the stems that are almost solid with fruit and with scarcely a green one, her mind supremely at peace. Her contentment grows as the sweet-grass basket fills. It is almost level full when she steps on something hard. A small tin cup, half-buried in the ground and rusted with years and rain. She loosens it and holds it in her hand. It was Owen's. Too young for his own basket, he used to "pick and pour in."

She remembers the day he put this cup down as a marker when he came to tell her about the ground linnet's nest he'd happened on. But when he led her back with him to see the nest, they could find neither cup nor nest again.

They planned to search for his cup the next morning, but the next morning it rained. And the next day she was too busy. And the next. And the next day the raging fever of meningitis killed him.

She stares at the cup. Sometimes things speak to her like oracles. But the only thing she hears now is that you can bear more than you can bear. And did that leave a desert patch in you where nothing would ever grow again?

For a moment she is sickened: and then she is dismayed that the sickening passes.

Owen! She tries to keep her mind on him. But the day is too real.

She puts the cup gently into her apron pocket, and stoops to pick again. She rounds her basket up to a crown. It is beautiful. She has no other container, but she cannot bear to leave. She takes off her wide straw hat and lines its deep crown with ferns and begins to pick in that . . .

YES, AND ALL THE SMELLS—with the voice of them more forcible, more stamping, less to be escaped, than any message (which it sometimes counters) to the eye or ear:

Of auger shavings and cranberry bogs. Of lavender and mint in the hollow where the old house once stood. Of horse lather and Canterbury bells. Of gun oil and currant wine. Of pear drops and the eelgrass that winds itself around an oar . . .

"I GUESS I SHOULDN'T BRING THIS UP, Amy, I don't want to talk about my neighbors, but . . . what did you think o' the way Sade took over yesterday at the mat-hookin?"

"Well, didn't she get on a strain! I thought it was altogether uncalled-for. But that's Sade. She gets her tongue onto somethin, she never knows when to stop."

"Still . . . she's *good*."

"Good as gold."

"And I wouldn't want anything I said to get back to her for the world—but I know what I say to you won't go no further."

"No. Heavens, no. And I know that anything I say to *you* . . . Ain't it nice to have someone you can speak your mind to and know it won't go no further!"

"And what did you think of Maggie's tam?"

"Wasn't that! Look, I didn't dare look at you or I'da snorted!"

"It wouldn't a looked so heenyus if she hadn't hauled it down over her ears like that, but . . . Oh, ain't this awful! Poor Maggie can't help her looks. But we don't mean no harm, do we?"

"No. We gotta have a little laugh once in a while. And I suppose people says the same things about us sometimes. But I don't care, do you?"

"Not a particle. Not a particle."

"Well, I guess I should go back and tackle that glory-hole up over the ell kitchen. I didn't get it cleaned out *last* spring."

"Oh, set still. The work'll keep. I got a thousand things I should be at, myself, and I've been workin in a bushel basket all mornin—but there'll be other days. Set still and talk a while."

AND WITH THE PEAR DROPS and the eelgrass, the smell of:

Onion sets and scarlet fever. Boneset and the red plush lining of collection plates. Groin sweat and juniper. Burlap and poplin. Sweet William and attic trunks. Cow's breath and honeysuckle. Woman's hair and man's hair. Trinket boxes and thunder showers. And the pure ringing smell of sun and sky . . .

And having the taste that was half smell:

The first crust off the warm loaf of rusk with the raisins on top, and the steaming doughboys of the partridge stew warming you back to yourself when you'd thought you were too tired to eat. Johnnycake and mushroom gravy. The skins of Early Rose potatoes dug by rite on the first Sunday in August and baked out of sensibleness into good humor . . .

"Karl, *where* have you *been?* We've had our dinner long ago. And do you think I want to keep a fire this hot afternoon? Your plate's in the oven there, but if it's cold you'll have to put up with it. I should make you go without, by rights."

"I didn't know it was so late, Mum, honest. You know how Ben's got everything piled up on top of everything else in his store. We had to rummage all through the back shop before we . . ."

"What was you doin down to the store? If I *wanted* you to go to the store for me . . ."

"I was gettin somethin for Dad. You said it was his birthday. Look! I got this screwdriver. It was twenty cents and I only had eighteen cents, but Ben let me have it just the same. What's wrong, Mum? Gosh, you don't have to look so funny just because I forgot you had dinner ready, do you?"

AND WITH THE DOUGHBOYS and the mushrooms, the taste of:

Headcheese and chives. Duck eggs and goose-berries. The taste of the supper fork when you'd had words with a neighbor and the taste of the Golden Russet when you'd made up with him. The taste of the Christmas ribbon candy, and the fleeting taste of the good-luck thimble and the birthday wedge of Washington pie. Winesaps bitten into more from thirst than from hunger, and dandelion greens. The taste of alum on the cold sore and the taste of your own blood in your mouth when the staging on the barn gave way. The taste of beer and of tears . . .

And the touch (king of the senses) of chestnuts smoother than onyx in the chill fallen leaves, and of the breeze that flickered at the hollow of your throat when the whole world was saying July. Of the chisel you fashioned the wheel hub of your child's cart with when health sang in you without a faulty note, and of the stones you filled the well with after he'd been drowned in it. Of dry clothes after wet, and of enamel doorknobs when you come home from school with 100 in history. The touch of bottom under your feet again the day you'd swum out farther than you'd thought, and the new and wondrous touch of every-thing the day you first surprised a girl's nakedness . . .

"I THOUGHT Mary washed yesterday," one woman says to another, "but I see she's got another line out this mornin."

"She probably had some straggler overnight. She's never turned anyone away from the door in her life, it don't matter who. And Joe's just the same. They're a great couple. Even poor old Abe Pine—do you remember old Abe Pine, that used to tramp the roads with that pack on his back?—he always headed up there. He wasn't none too clean, either, but she wouldn't just give him a woods blanket on the kitchen lounge. She'd make up a bed for him and wash after him half the next day. If that woman don't have stars in her crown!" . . .

THE TOUCH TOO of paths in the morning and paths at dusk. Of scrub brushes and corn silk. Hymnals and wickerwork. Rain and rein. Of grandfather's hands when you were ten and grandson's hands when you were seventy, hands of like texture by reason of a lifetime in the same house. The touch of pond ice beneath your first skates, and of the first dollar bill of your own, which you placed beside the tarnished watch fob and someone's old lenses in the mustache cup on the top shelf of the china closet. Of your own hands and your own handiwork . . .

And all the shapes:

The perpendiculars of bulrush and crane leg. The triangles of deer track and trowel. Pears and wombs. Scrota and walnut shells. Cloud-shaped rocks and rock-shaped clouds. The rectangles of door and grave. The cornucopias of Morning Glory and gramophone horn. Fox hearts the shape of strawberries. Cones of hackmatack and the cones that sand makes in the road when the child sifts it between his palms in the spellbound afternoon . . .

And the circles of sun, and moon, and breakfast plate, and clothing eyelet, and date stamp on the treasured letter . . . and the pupil within the eye that sees them all . . .

AND MEN. And women. And children. Of every description.

16 / A Man

CALL THE MAN JOSEPH. Call his son Mark. Two
scars had bracketed Mark's left eye since he
was twelve. But they were periods, not brackets, in
the punctuation of his life. The reason had to do with
his father.

Joseph had none of the stiffness that goes with
rock strength. He was one of those men who cast the

broadest shadow, without there being any darkness in them at all. Yet there was always a curious awkwardness between him and his son. In a neighbor's house of a Sunday afternoon Mark might stand nearer to him than to anyone else; but he never got onto his lap like the other kids got onto their fathers' laps. Joseph never teased him. He never made him any of those small-scale replicas of farm gear that the other men made their sons: tiny ox carts or trail sleds.

In any case, that kind of fussy workmanship was not his province. His instrument was the plow.

One day he came across Mark poking seeds between the potato plants.

"What's them?" he said.

Mark could dodge anyone else's questions; he could never answer his father with less than the whole truth.

"They're orange seeds," he said.

He'd saved them from the Christmas before. Oranges were such a seldom thing then that it was as if he was planting a mystery.

"They won't grow here," Joseph said.

Mark felt suddenly ridiculous, as he so often did when his father came upon anything fanciful he was doing: as if he had to shift himself to the sober footing of common sense. He dug the seeds out and planted them, secretly, behind the barn.

THE NIGHT OF THE ACCIDENT was one of those cold, drizzly nights in early summer when animals in the pasture huddle like forlorn statues. The sort of night when the cows never come.

School had ended that very day. This was the third year Mark had graded twice and he was very excited. All the time his mother washed the supper dishes he kept prattling on about the kings and queens of England he'd have in his studies next term. He felt two feet taller than the "kid" he'd been yesterday.

His father took no part in the conversation, but he was not for that reason outside it—and everything Mark said was for his benefit too.

Joseph was waiting to milk. "Ain't it about time you got after the cows?" he said at last. He never ordered Mark. It would have caused the strangest sort of embarrassment if he ever had.

Cows! Mark winced. Right when he could almost *see* the boy Plantagenet robed in ermine and wearing the jeweled crown!

"They'll come, won't they?" he said. (He knew better.) "They come last night."

He never used good speech when his father was around. He'd have felt like a girl. (Though Joseph was a far wiser, far better educated man in the true sense than Mark would ever be.)

"They won't come a night like this," Joseph said. "They're likely holed up in a spruce thicket somewheres, outa the rain."

"I'll see if I can hear the bell," Mark said.

He went out on the porch steps and listened. There wasn't a sound.

"It's no use to wait for the bell," Joseph called. "They won't budge a hair tonight."

"Well, if they ain't got sense enough to come themselves a night like this," Mark said, as near as he'd ever come to sputtering at his father, "why can't they just stay out?"

"I'd never get em back to their milk for a week," Joseph said.

Mark went then, but, as Joseph couldn't help seeing, grudgingly.

He sat on the bars of the pasture gate and called. "*Co*-boss, *co*-boss . . ." But there wasn't the tinkle of a bell.

He loved to be out in a good honest rain, but this was different. He picked his steps down the pasture lane to avoid the clammy drops that showered from every bush or fern he touched.

He came to the first clearing, where Joseph had planted the burntland potatoes last year. The cows were nowhere to be seen. But Pedro, the horse, was there—hunched up and gloomy-looking in the drizzle. Mark couldn't bear to see him so downcast and not try to soothe him.

He went close and patted his rump. Pedro moved just far enough ahead to shake off his touch. It was the kind of night when the touch of anything sent a shivery feeling all through you.

He should have known that the horse wanted to be left alone. But he kept at it. He'd touch him, the horse would move ahead, he'd follow behind and touch him again. The horse laid back his ears.

And then, in a flash, Mark saw the big black haunch rear up and the hoof, like a sudden devouring jaw, right in front of his left eye. The horse wasn't shod or Mark would have been killed.

He was stunned. But in a minute he got to his feet again. He put his hand to his face. It came away all blood. He began to scream and run for home.

Joseph could hear him crying before he came in sight. He started to meet him. When Mark came through the alder thicket below the barn and Joseph saw he was holding his hand up to his face, he broke into a run. Before he got to the bars he could see the blood.

He didn't stop to let down a single bar. He leapt them. Mark had never seen him move like that in his life before. He grabbed Mark up and raced back to the house.

Within minutes the house was a hubbub of neighbors. Mark gloried in the breathless attention that everyone bent on him. He asked Joseph to hold him up to the mirror over the sink. "No, no, Joseph, don't . . ." his mother pleaded, but Joseph obeyed him. His face was a mass of cuts and bruises. He felt like a Plantagenet borne off the field with royal wounds.

Afterward, he remembered all the head-shakings: "That biggest cut there don't look too good to me. Pretty deep . . ."

And the offers of help: "I got some b'racit acit for washin out cuts, down home. I could git it in a minute . . ."

And the warnings: "No, *don't* let him lay down. Anyone's had a blow on the head, always keep em movin around . . ."

And he remembered his mother beseeching him over and over: "Can you see all right? Are you sure you can see all right?"

He didn't remember his father doing or saying anything flustered, unusual. But Joseph would be the one who'd quietly put the extra leaves in the dining-room table so they could lay him on it when the doctor came at last, to have the stitches taken. And when the doctor put him to sleep (though he confessed that this was risky, with Mark's weak heart) it would be Joseph's hand that held the chloroform cone without a tremor.

The doctor said that Mark must stay in bed for two whole weeks. Joseph came in to see him once each day and again just before bedtime. Mark's eye was now swollen shut and the color of thunder sunsets. Maybe he'd have the mirror in his hand, admiring his eye, when he heard his father coming. He'd thrust the mirror in under the bedclothes. They exchanged the same awkward sentences each time. Joseph was the sort of man who looks helplessly out of place in a bedroom. He never sat down.

The first morning Mark was allowed outdoors again he had planned to walk; but Joseph picked him up without a word and carried him.

He didn't protest. But this time there was no tumult of excitement as before to leave him mindless of his father's arms about him; now the unaccustomed feel of them seemed to make him aware of every ounce of his own weight. And yet, though it was merely an ordinary fine summer's morning, it struck him as the freshest, greenest, sunniest he had ever seen.

The moment they left the house it was plain to him that this wasn't just an aimless jaunt. His father was taking him somewhere.

Joseph carried him straight across the house field and down the slope beyond—to where he'd stuck the orange seeds in the ground.

Mark saw what they were headed for before they got there. But he couldn't speak. If he had tried to, he'd have cried.

Joseph set him down beside a miniature garden.

Miniature, but with the rows as perfectly in line as washboard ribs. This had been no rough job for the plow. It had been the painstaking work of fork and spade and then the careful molding by his hands. He must have started it right after the accident, because the seeds were already through the ground. And he hadn't mentioned it to a soul.

"This can be yours," he said to Mark.

"Oh, Father," Mark began, "it's . . ." But how could he tell him what it was? He bent down to examine the sprouts. "What's them?" he said, touching the strange plants in the outside row.

"Melons," Joseph said, pointing, "and red peppers and citron."

He must have got them from the wealthy man who had the big glass hothouse in town. Things almost as fanciful as orange seeds.

"You never know," he said. "They might grow here."

Mark could not speak. But his face must have shown the bright amazement that raced behind it, or else what Joseph said next would never have broken out.

"You don't think I'da made you go for them cows if I'd a knowed you was gonna get hurt, do you?" he said. Almost savagely. "I wouldn'ta cared if they'd a never give another drop o' milk as long as they lived!"

Mark gave him a crazy answer, but it didn't seem crazy to either of them then, because of a sudden something that seemed to bridge all the gaps of speech.

"You jumped right over the bars when you saw I was hurt, didn't you!" he said. "You never even took the top one down. You just jumped right clear over em!"

His father turned his face away, and it looked as if his shoulders were taking a long deep breath.

Joseph let him walk back to the house.

When they went into the kitchen, Mark's sister said, "Where did you go?"

For no reason he could explain Mark felt another sudden compact with his father, that this should be some sort of secret.

"Just out," he said.

"Just out around," Joseph echoed.

And Mark knew that never again would he have to . . . shift . . . himself at the sound of his father's footsteps. Not ever.

17 / *A Woman*

CALL HER KATE.
    She was a good woman—but entirely without the brand of "goodness" people shy away from. An entirely natural person whose warmth-wide spirit everyone else felt enlarged by.

    The stamp of generosity was all over her. "Now

there's somebody!" she'd say of a neighbor, saluting worth wherever she saw it and sad that it couldn't be recognized far and wide. It never crossed her mind that she herself was somebody. As much as if the whole world had known her.

In her shoes another might have grown up warped and sour. When she was five her father was drowned on the drive. The men rolled him over a barrel to get the water from his lungs, but they couldn't bring the air back into them. There was no way her mother could support the family of six. The family was broken up and most of Kate's childhood was spent "pillar to post" in the household of one relative or another.

Times were hard. On the day of the single winter her grandfather had been able to buy a whole barrel of flour at once neighbors came with pillowcases, to borrow—until the barrel was down to its third hoop before his own wife could dip into it. The summer she was ten she and her grandfather carried the entire hay crop into the barn on poles. And at Christmas there was seldom anything in the way of presents but a bag of peppermints on the breakfast plate.

Times were hard; but she never made a sniveler's account of them. These people had all been kind, dividing with her what little they had—and it wasn't the gray moments but the green that colored her memory. The Christmas she did get two boughten handkerchiefs, a tin bluebird that climbed a wire, and a top. Or the day an uncle's blessing of the noonday meal got sidetracked by his glimpse of a strapping passerby. "Lord," he said, "bless this food to our use— Moses and Aaron, what a tall man!—and make us thankful." Or the day the most resounding boy in the place asked her to marry him.

They said she had "a heart as big as an ox." Most times there was very little to "do with," but somehow she could stretch it out like loaves and fishes.

Scarcely a Sunday went by that she didn't set the dining-room table twice, there'd be so much company. Her staggering helpings were a byword with the men who sometimes helped her husband in the fields. And the wood saw would scarcely have made the first cut again after one of these noonday spreads before she'd be out with milk and doughnuts. "I hate to see men working with nothing in their stomachs."

In sickness she was the first one sent for. More for the great bolster of her company than for the nursing anyone else could give as well. And she always went. Often on snowshoes, if the blizzard was so thick a horse couldn't follow the road. She hadn't the slightest fear of "catching" anything—or the slightest fear that what she did from her heart would be taken as a bid for praise. Yet when she was thanked she never simpered. She knew that the best thanks for thanks is to admit they're due.

She could "turn her hand at anything." Each stitch in a quilt she made showed as neat on the underside as on the top—and she could lay shingles as straight as her husband. With the burnt end of a matchstick she could freehand a rug design no one could fault—and she could stook the oat bundles into pyramids that the fiercest winds couldn't tear apart. She knew exactly the simple touch of decoration that would turn the barely useful into a thing of grace. Children brought their toys to her, to mend, and people their troubles. And with it all she had the poet's eye and awe for what the eye could never see. (And the clap of amusement ever to hear herself spoken of like that.)

Her life had many darknesses in it. In the third year of marriage she lost a child to cholera. She and her husband were like root and branch. He died when "they'd just got where they could live." She never had many of the things or went many of the places her brisk imagination must have told her she'd enjoy. But what she couldn't have in no way spoiled for her the life within reach.

She always put people ahead of work, and she could hit it off instantly with anyone, old or young. (The young could be more freely themselves with her than under the rein they kept on each other.)

Not that she lacked fire. She had plenty of that too. Tread on her loyalty to a friend and you'd feel it. "Let Hannah be what she will," she once stuck up for a wayward neighbor, "she's got more charity in her little finger than you've got in your whole carcass." And anyone who poked pity at the villagers in her hearing got as good as he sent. "But what do you ever find to talk about . . . to *think* about . . . all the long winters?" a city woman once asked her. "We think about you poor creatures droning your lives away in the cities," she answered.

She had no patience with stuffiness of any kind. "We got stuck with another of Bessie's endless recitations at the meeting today. I'd sooner hear a dog whistle The Doxology through a comb." And she could spot sham a mile away.

But she was not the kind of person who collects others' flaws and keeps a peevish file of them in his mind. Her mind had no room for baggage like that. She would "overlook" almost any shortcoming, as long as it had nothing mean or sanctimonious about it.

She could fit in with the company wherever she was. Late in her life (when the idea of "college" had come to be understood here, though it was still a word for something so remote as to be hardly real) she was determined her grandson should go to college. The whole family skimped and saved to send him. She went to see him graduate. He was afraid she would feel lost. He introduced her to his history professor, a scholar of such note that nearly everyone was ill at ease with him.

"I've always thought," the professor said to her, "that farming must be a well-nigh . . . holy . . . kind of life."

"It is," she said. "Did you ever notice how little it would take to change 'acres' into 'sacred'?"

The professor perked up his ears, and soon the

two of them were laughing and chatting away like old cronies. He said he'd be in her part of the province the next month and asked if he could drop in to see her.

He came for two or three days, summer after summer. They walked about the fields and talked about everything under the sun. Half the words he used might be strange to her, but somehow she always knew exactly what he meant and gave him an answer that made him think.

The first trip, he was of two minds whether or not to bring out the bottle of brandy in his suitcase—and could he dare ask her to have a swig with him? "Why not?" she said, when his hints became clear. "I've heard it's good for the circulation and—who knows?—maybe after I've had one I can think up a good excuse to have another." He'd heard enough old ladies make "naughty" remarks to be sick of them; he was delighted with Kate's.

He coaxed her for more and more tales of the life she'd seen and could bring alive again with just the right detail.

"The way you can fix on a thing's eye," he told her, "*you* should be the historian."

"No," she said, "I'd rather knit a sock than unravel one."

When she was past eighty, he told her he knew a brilliant eye surgeon—in the city hospital—who might save her rapidly closing sight. By that time the city hospital was not the world away it had once been; but hospital was still a dread word, especially to the old, and such surgery still a great gamble. No one thought she'd consent to it. But she did.

And so far from suffering the hospital stay in loneliness and terror, she turned it into the time and adventure of her life. Doctors and nurses immediately became her friends, shedding their professional masks exactly as the professor had done. They gathered in her room as if it were a little court.

The operation was a complete success. The day the surgeon took off the bandages there was a copy of the morning's newspaper on her bedside table. He propped it up and held a trial lens in front of her eye. "Can you see that word?" he asked, pointing to the date. "Yes," she said. "It's Saturday. And I never saw a happier day in my life!"

Later, he said to her, "Now for a few weeks certain things may look as if they had a ring of light around them. But that will clear up."

"I know what you mean," she said, nudging her own remark with just the right joking smile to cut the slush out of it yet let it stand, "I can see a sort of halo round your head this minute . . . But that will never go away."

SHE LIVED FOR EIGHT YEARS MORE; and they tell the story that light was shed on her twice again.

The gray December noon she died a blizzard thick as night was piling down outside the window.

Her mind had begun to wander. But even so she seemed to conquer. For in her last look at the day it wasn't the snow she saw. "What a lovely evening!" she said, the once she spoke. "I've never seen the glimmer of the sunset last so long!"

The day she was buried, in the old graveyard by the lake, the afternoon was dark and cold. The lake was frozen and the hillside ringed with deep woods and drifted snow. But at the very instant when the last hush fell the sun broke like banners through the clouds and changed the whole setting into a still life so radiant the people marveled.

"The sun knew . . ." a neighbor said. "I tell ya, it *knew!*"

And then he added: "But can't ya just hear Kate laugh if she heard anyone say that!"

18 / Another Man

CALL HIM SYD WRIGHT. He was the odd one.

"Old Man Wright," the children called him. He
wasn't old. No older than their fathers, but he lived
alone.

He knew the name they had for him—he'd heard
Lennie himself use it that very Friday night. But it

had never bothered him in the least, and didn't then.

Friday night was Halloween. He was sitting close to the table lamp, reading the Almanac, when he heard the smothered giggles of the boys outside. He pretended not to notice. There was nothing to worry about. No turnips still in the field for them to root out and scatter, no odds and ends lying about in plain sight. Nothing to tempt their deviltry as there might be around the other houses. The way Syd planned his work, all the straggle of summer was as neatly wound up and tucked away on October thirty-first as if that was the date of Judgment. He liked winter better than summer. It was so much tidier.

He never got mad at the children Halloween night. He'd wait until they put a tic-tac on the window. Then he'd go to the door and say, "Come in, come in, what's the hold-up?" As if he was a member of the fun too.

The children would sit inside for a few minutes, jostling together uneasily on the hard lounge, while he passed around the candy and cookies he'd bought to treat them with. None of them ever took more than one cookie, though, or more than one piece of candy; and soon they'd begin to nudge each other when his back was turned and shape an exaggerated "*Let's . . . go*" with their lips. Then they'd leave—cramming through the doorway on each other's heels and, as soon as they were outside again, letting loose a few wild yells as if they'd been unmuzzled.

This year it was a little different. Syd sat waiting for them. He heard their stealthy footsteps. And then, just as he moved to the door, he heard Lennie say, "Aw, let's not stop here!" Lennie didn't even bother to keep his voice down. "We don't wanta go into that old place! Ya can't even *tease* Old Man Wright."

"All right," Cale Wilson's boy said. "Let's go back to our place. Dad always gets rory-eyed!"

Syd stood at the door and listened, smiling to himself. They'd already forgotten him.

"Let's take Glenn's bain wagon apart," another boy suggested. "He never puts it under cover."

"No, he's got that big dog."

"Hey!"—another voice—"Listen what Mark says. Let's tie Herb's pump handle straight up in the air and hang two turnips underneath, like it's . . ."

"No," Lennie said, "I tell ya, fullas—listen, fullas, *listen*—after we go back to Cale's, let's come back this way to Wilf's and put his feed boxes up on the head scaffold. His barn doors's wide open."

One of them threw a head of somebody's cabbage against the side of the house, but it was only a mechanical gesture. When Syd opened the door they'd already moved away.

He closed the door and sat down again with the Almanac. He picked out a few soft pieces from the bag of candy and ate them himself.

Then he brought his billfold out from the pantry shelf, with the saucer of change and the small black scribbler he kept his accounts in. Any day he earned anything or spent anything he made a record of it in the scribbler. On the last day of each month he added up the totals and checked their balance with the actual cash. The cash and the figures had always tallied to the cent, and did now.

He was in bed, asleep, when the boys went back up the road on their way to Wilf's.

"Turn out!" they called automatically, but they didn't stop.

He awakened and again he smiled to himself. The long peaceful winter had begun.

AN HOUR LATER, the night cracked open and nightmare rushed out at the seams. There was not a breath of air, but the dark tossed like wind. Lights, never unsure of their path, lost their path in it. The window frames of light that came on one after another in houses that had been dark with sleep . . . the bobbing light of lanterns that the men with the news running inside them carried running . . . all had a core of trembling like horses in a fire. Eyes and mouth became unanchored in the face.

But Syd knew nothing of this. No one had come to rouse him. He'd slept straight through.

He heard the news next morning at the store. By then light was sure of itself again, the night had closed its seams, eyes and mouth were back at anchor: it was afterwards.

Lennie, they said, had slipped from Wilf's scaffold in the dark and pitched headlong to the barn floor. He'd lain there without a sound. The other boys had thought he was clowning. But he wasn't clowning. He was dead. Chris and Ellen were taking it hard, they said.

Syd was struck still. A sadness real as anyone else's brushed him in stroke after stroke: he had never been a hard-hearted man. And if anyone, himself nearly crying, had been watching him to see if he might be nearly crying too, tears might have come.

But nobody looked at him like that, and he took his sadness home like a parcel, to be opened and examined in—"comfort" was nearly the word. The fact that Lennie was Ellen's child didn't affect him in any special way. The part with Ellen had been so long ago.

In the kitchen the sadness stayed with him, but it was almost like reading a sad book. The sadness itself made common cause with him; it didn't come at him from anything. The familiar household objects did not go strange. They were more like friends silenced by your own troubled silence, and so all the closer and more shielding.

He moved about methodically. His mind was full of what he'd heard, but filled as a sun stripe in a still room is filled with the whorls and tendrils of a puff of smoke blown against it, each shape dissolving so instantly into a different one that never for an instant is the pattern fixed.

In this nearly thoughtless study, he took from his

pocket the change the storekeeper had given him and put it in the saucer on the pantry shelf.

And then he thought: how much did them things I bought this mornin come to? He couldn't remember. He knew he'd paid the storekeeper with a two-dollar bill, but exactly how much change had he got back? He hadn't counted it, either at the time or when he'd put it away, and now it was scattered among the rest of the silver in the saucer. What entry then would he make in the scribbler?

He felt a sudden stitch of uneasiness he couldn't help. He'd never been in this quandary before. It wasn't the money itself, he'd never been one to watch the penny that way. It was just the need of a lifetime to keep his reckonings absolutely straight.

And then the answer came to him. The monthly balance in the scribbler would tell him how much cash was in the house last night, and if he subtracted the amount of cash he had now from the amount he'd had then . . .

He took the scribbler and the money to the kitchen table and worked it out. $1.08. Yes, yes, that was exactly right, he remembered now. He ruled up the scribbler sheets for the new month and entered this figure on the debit side.

He felt a little glow of release that in the same moment carried over to the sadness, releasing it too to its full nature so that he could join with it more wholeheartedly.

THAT WAS SATURDAY. The funeral was on Monday, at three. As the hour came near, Syd felt grave. And quiet with himself. Nothing more.

Except that he dreaded the funeral. In a group, at a time like this, he always felt exposed—as if he'd lost all solid sight of himself and yet was the mark of every other eye. He knew there was no ground for this, and yet it crowded out every other feeling.

He kept a close watch on the clock. He didn't want to be conspicuously early or conspicuously late.

At twenty minutes to three he went upstairs to dress. He took off his work clothes and folded them carefully on the bedside chair. He put on a clean gray shirt and got into his good blue suit. The cloth was like new, though the cut was old, and it still fitted him; but it had the lifeless look of all clothing that has never taken on its wearer's speech under the coupling eye of a wife or anyone else. His hair, once so quick to join his face in any shifting mood, looked as if it didn't know it was on his head. He combed it before the bureau glass, but the keyless eyes in the face made no search for the lockless eyes in the mirror.

He thought about the raspberry canes. They'd been on his mind all last week. Other years, he'd covered their roots with sawdust long before this. But the best time to bank them was if you could catch a day when the ground was frozen and the first snow sure to follow right away—and this fall had been so open he'd had to hang off. There'd been a hard freeze last night, though. And it looked like snow this afternoon. He'd cover them after the funeral. He took great pride in his raspberry canes. They were the only cultivated ones in the place.

He went downstairs, and looked all around to make certain everything was shipshape. Then he raked what coals were left in the kitchen stove carefully through the grate into the ash pan. The clock said seven minutes to three. He waited exactly two minutes more, and then he put on his hat and coat, to go down the road.

He got no farther than the door. From one corner of his eye he saw the hearse go past, and from the other the cabbage that had been tossed against the wall on Halloween. By Lennie himself maybe, without as much as a backward glance.

The cabbage lay beside the woodbox. Its outside leaves were beginning to turn brown. It was the trifle that can suddenly daze a man with the news of his whole life.

The whorls and tendrils of his thoughts vanished like smoke and a moteless beam of truth about himself pierced him like a nail: No one even *bothers* me. Not even the children. Not even on Halloween. I am not like anyone else . . . When anything happens no one ever comes to tell me first. I am never in on anything at the time. The afterwards is all I ever know.

The nail went deeper, second by second, and the news frightened him more and more.

He took himself back to the rocker in front of the stove as if he was leading a sick man, and sat down. He couldn't go to the funeral now. He couldn't.

The clock ticked on, past three o'clock. The stove turned strange. Every object in the room drew a line of blindness around its shape. But with every tick of the clock his vision became more mercilessly clear.

He saw the whole scene down the road. The kitchen tidied up by neighbors' wives to the last sink cloth, the last clutter on the windowsills. Things stiffening in the spots where they'd been misplaced. The way people moved, as if their very weight must be whispered. The heavy look on Chris's and Ellen's lips . . .

He had gone with Ellen before she ever met Chris. The school teases used to cross his name out with hers when they were in Grade Three, as far back as that. "Friendship, courtship, love, hatred, indifference, marriage . . ." He'd never mentioned marriage to her, he was waiting until he had a hundred dollars saved up. Then Chris had come here with a lumbering crew. Chris was always laughing or ready to laugh; and Friday nights at the dance in the schoolhouse he'd sometimes give the fiddler every cent he had in his pocket to play an extra hour. Children were crazy over him.

The first night Ellen told him Chris had coaxed her for her picture, he hadn't said a word. Had she been testing him? What if he had spoken up then? What good did that hundred dollars do him now?

They said that Chris and Ellen hadn't got along too well late years—but Syd saw how she would look at him now when someone nodded to the carriers it was time to come into the parlor. A woman will never look at me like that, he thought. Brad Ruggles was one of the carriers. He'd had a little trouble with Chris over some breachy cattle, but Syd saw how the two men would look at each other when Brad put his hand on Chris's shoulder—Brad had sons of his own. A man will never look at me like that . . . No one will notice that I'm not at the funeral—until afterwards. And then they won't wonder why not . . .

He wrenched his eyes away from the funeral to the objects around him. The clock on the shelf, with the alarm that was set for five o'clock even on Sundays. The stove that was never filled to the top, even on the coldest nights, because that might warp the grates. The row of tin cans on the sink-room shelf with the used nails in them, each nail straightened with the hammer after he'd drawn it from the rotted board and all of them sorted out so that no can held two of a different length . . .

Fury seized him. That was the way the hours of his life had gone by . . . while the other men were leaning against the barns, laughing together . . . or mending the rake bows their children had broken . . . or looking through the catalogue with their wives the weeks before Christmas . . .

He opened and closed his fists. Fool . . . fool . . .

fool . . . And there was no one, no one, he could confess this to. The others always let the normal feelings spend themselves at the normal time. They wouldn't understand a word of this. There was no one he could tell *any*thing to . . .

He hadn't taken off his coat. His cap was still on his head, the ear tabs still down. He had lost all awareness of them.

But as the chill in the fireless kitchen grew until it became a voice, the flesh of his hands and face and of his legs where they were covered only by the thinness of his good suit was forced to listen. He put some bark and kindling in the stove and went to the pantry for a match.

He saw the scribbler lying next to the match box. That thing! That's what had betrayed him! He grabbed it up and crammed it into the stove. He thought about the raspberry canes and the sawdust.

"They can *go*," he shouted. "They can *go* . . ."

And then he said in a whisper, "Ellen . . . Lennie . . . What if you'd been *our* son?"

And then he sat down again in the rocker, and he cried. But he wasn't crying for Ellen. Or Lennie. Or for anyone else. His were the awful tears of a man who cries for himself—not because he has been hurt, but because he has never been hurt at all.

The clock ticked on past four o'clock, past the grave, and the snow began to come down.

THE MEN GATHERED as usual in the store that night. Each time someone new joined the group they went over the happenings of the day once more. Alf Fowler was sitting by the window.

"What's that lantern over in Syd's orchard?" he asked suddenly. "Surely to God he ain't prunin this time o' night."

"No," Gus said, coming to the window, "he's got his fall prunin all done. And that ain't the orchard. That's more where his raspberry canes are."

"But what would he be doin there?"

"God knows," Gus said. "He's a conundrum."

Alf chuckled. "He's that, all right. I should think he'd go crazy livin up there all be himself."

"*You* would and *I* would," Fred said. "But, no, I think he loves it."

A little later Syd came into the store himself. There was nothing unfriendly in the greeting they gave him, but he sensed a halt in their conversation that told him he'd been the subject of it. And when talk sprouted up again it was no longer group talk: two men compared larrigans, two others spoke about the snow. They didn't mention the funeral to him. And as he walked past them to the counter he knew that every ear was cocked to hear what his errand was. He almost never came to the store of an evening.

"Ben," he said to the storekeeper, and hesitated— nervously conscious of their listening, thinking ahead to going past them on the way out, knowing they'd be chuckling at his oddities again as soon as he had left.

"Ben," he said, "have you got any more o' them little black scribblers? Like . . . do you mind the one I got here last spring?"

19 / Like Spaces, Other Cases

Y ES, THERE WERE SOME ODD ONES, some sorry figures, some cruelty. No one could pretend that
every Norsteader was a blood ruby, or holy with that
holiness of the unperjurable that bread baked by a
wood fire has, or gold. Yet the thing was that even the
ore they were flawed with was as purely itself as a

member of the Table of Elements. Neither the good in them nor the bad in them was counterfeit. And their senses were always I-to-I with everything around them. (All sinkings of the heart spelled out to them in the waving of the long black skull moss on the brook rocks, beneath the current it no longer feels. All faithfulness in the stones that chock the wagon wheels, all jets of buoyancy in the wild pear blossoms . . .) By and large, they were as large as life.

What made them so? It was hard to say. Certainly not the single fact that they were villagers. There were other villages (and not a few, solidly alike) whose people were smaller than life in every way. Their senses were deaf as adders to the voice of the eternal around them; their spirits the width of rulers and the depth of thimbles; their hearts so pocked with pettiness, so cramped with caution, that they never set a foot ahead until they'd peeked first.

To look at them and their like was to see better what Norsteaders and *their* like were not.

These walked blindered through their skimpy lives, their eyes seeing only the paper husk a thing's name wraps it in or the brass penny directly in front of them. Their talk was the dry, dry raisins of the grapes of talk. There was no real fellowship among them—they spoke of each other not as the neighborly do, with love or rage, but as eyes eat that have never eaten anything but the pinched fare of self and what they can gather sidelong with their curtains just barely drawn back. Each was his own gospel, never shaped by the other's. Never explosions of themselves, they were nothing but their own dry bread.

The women were iron-maidened inside a primness as stifling as their own stifling parlors, where the stone-dead sentences of conversation on a Sunday afternoon when they had visitors of their own stripe striped the air like the lines on blank foolscap. Religion they claimed as their staff, but it parched and puckered them like chokecherry juice. They spouted the letter of it and acted the pose of it, but it was no more a real limb of them than the churchy hats they wore to the church that even when they (thinly) sang the hymns was a muster of everything that was hollow.

Their thin, certain suppers, even with company at the table, tasted of their thin hands and paper hearts. They laughed when rule said: Laugh—but their laughter sounded like sandpaper on glass.

The men sat and sucked their teeth, thinking nothing, tasting their own mouths. That, or they were as gross and stupid as pigweed, their senses of the same grain as body hair or spit, their eyes widening only when their groins slobbered at the woman's trough. That, or they were simply outlandish.

Their houses were of two kinds. One as narrow-eyed as themselves, with every unspeaking object in it (from the kitchen dustpan to the pincushion on the bureau) so blindly intent in being merely in its *place* that together they added up to the final bareness. The other as squalid as the splotches on the rust-pitted stove front where the man who lay on the rumpled couch through the drizzly afternoon had missed the ash box with his squirts of tobacco juice; cheerless as the undressed doll sprawled beside the rusted tin can on the windowsill that held the geranium dying for water behind the grimy curtains; slovenly as the hair in the gravy, or the urine-scalded legs of the children with the neglected diapers.

And, strangely enough, the nearer to the towns the truer this held.

A Norstead man had once lived in such a settlement—call it Claymore. He had a fine sense of sense and nonsense, and the tales he and his bubbling wife told of Claymore went like this.

THE OLDER WOMEN, particularly, were forever locking horns over church affairs, their paper sanctity reaching into everything but the heart.

Chief bone of contention was the Testament Band. As often as it collapsed there'd be plans to revive it—and endless sermonizing. ("It's not enough that we make our lives an example for the young. If we don't explain the Word to them as well, what can we expect of them when they grow up?") But the moment it came to choosing teachers someone was sure to feel "slighted" and scuttle the whole undertaking in a huff. ("I knew the minute Maud and Ethel come into the church together—when they've hardly looked sideways at each other since that fracas their husbands had over the horse trade—I knew right then they'd got their heads together about somethin. And sure enough. Didn't they both pipe up for Bertha to lead the Senior Class! Now I ain't sayin that should have been my job, but if I don't know more about the Scripture than Bertha Gaul . . . ! Well, if Maud and Ethel . . . if just *two people*'s goin to run the whole shebang, let em! I said to Ethel, comin out, 'How many horses did your good man winter *this* year?' She barely grunted, so I know she *took* it.")

When someone died it was always hotly argued whether or not two dollars should be taken from the Mite Box fund to buy a funeral wreath. ("Gertie was a peaceable soul and all that, and I hope she's in Heaven—but *you* know as well as *I* do she never done much for the church, herself.") When an evangelical rally was planned, there was always a squabble over which of them would "take the devotional." Feelings ran higher still over who should bring sponge cakes and who should bring "squares" for the refreshments afterward.

And there was never a food and apron sale (to raise ten dollars toward conversion of the Hindu) that didn't end with two or three of them at swords' points. ("I'd love to know what made Cora mark her aprons twelve cents more than mine, when mine had ric-rac braid all around the pockets even and hers wasn't even gingham—just the cheapest factory cotton she could lay her hands on.")

At least one of these clashes wound up in pitched battle. Two women had brought oatmeal parkins on cake plates that were exactly alike. One of the plates got chipped in the washing up, and each woman claimed that the *other* plate was hers. The spat finally died down, but only for the time being. That summer all the wells went dry and water had to be carried from a boiling spring at the edge of the woods. A month later, these women met there head-on, the tongue-lashing started up again, and the abler of the two unloosed the other's long black braids and tied her to a cat spruce with them.

As for the men:

There was Enoch, so fixed in his ways that lightning itself couldn't budge him. One night it set the barn he was milking in ablaze, but did he let that sway him? No, sir. He stuck to his stool until every cow had been stripped of her last drop before turning them out to night pasture, though the flames were already licking at the stanchions.

He was so *damn* stubborn that—well, there was the case of the pumpkin and the kitchen clock. The pumpkin had strayed on its vine across the border between his field and his brother's. The clock had been a gift from the brother's wife to his. He and his brother had words over which of them the roaming pumpkin belonged to and, though Enoch didn't banish the clock from the mantelpiece, he bought himself another to put beside it—so that he wouldn't be beholden to *any*thing his brother might have had a hand in for even the time of day.

Another time, in the winter, a daughter and her

husband came to visit. Thinking to please the old man with a good deed, the son-in-law hitched up the horses one morning when Enoch was back chopping and hauled out the barn manure on to the plowed land, unloading it in a heap at the center. Most men did it that way. The "going" was easier on the frozen ground, and the heap could be broadcast at planting time.

But that was not the way Enoch had always done it. He always waited until spring. When he came home, he didn't say a word, but he never touched the mound ever. Each spring plowing after that he circled the rows around it, so that they all had a huge bulge fair in the middle. The mound was still rotting there the day he died.

He always started to pick his Russets on the tenth of October and not one day before, no matter how surely frost might threaten them with ruin. If he piled on a rackful of cordwood that proved too heavy for his sleds to bear he wouldn't lighten it by one kindling stick, however the rockers might be in splinters when he got home and the harness in tatters from the horses' straining to "hold the load back" down the hills. He wasn't really quarrelsome, but he was certainly gruff. Once when he found his favorite church pew blocked by the legs of a young man sprawled in the aisle seat he roared at him, "Mister, would you mind haulin back your crotch?," in a voice that shook the pulpit.

Once when he suspected trespassers were raiding his back orchard he set a beaver trap for them and caught his old-maid cousin out for dilberries. He wouldn't put away his pipe, as everyone else did, when he went into a straw loft, his own or anyone else's—and once when he mowed into a ground-hornets' nest on the marsh he stuck to his guns until he'd burnt the nest to a cinder, though he was stung from head to foot and the rearing horses he'd tied to a fence stake were kicking the whiffletree to bits.

When his champion Jersey heifer, who promised to break all milking records after she'd had a few more calves, swiped him about the ears one night with a dung-sludged tail, he "dried her off" then and there, simply to deny her the *pleasure* of a bull ever again.

There was also the man who had lost one testicle to a hay fork—and gone on to have ten more children. The ruined testicle, taken out and pickled, was displayed in a self-sealer on the parlor organ rest.

And the man who raised young pigs for a single market: the party chief who "handled the money" at election time and bought them from him to barter for votes.

And the man who used to roar at his sons: "You'll sink the house with your goddam swearin!"

And the woman so hipped on temperance that she was bound the minister would substitute strained cranberry juice for the sacramental wine.

And the man who wore a circlet of brass around every appendage (arms, legs *and* dangler) to ward off sciatica.

And the woman who chipped in a dozen empty

thread spools and a doll's empty nursing bottle—
nothing else—to an auction sale for schoolhouse
needs.

And such, our neighbors said, only scratched the
surface.

They remembered the choir leader whose lust
sometimes took the form of chasing his wife up and
down between the rows of corn and boarding her beneath their overhang. The woman of seventy-five who
insisted she was pregnant, citing Sarah. The man who
ate fried bullfrogs to deepen his voice; and the man
who ordered two jars of "Hemorrhoid Balm" from the
catalogue, thinking it was a remedy for nosebleed.

There was the carpenter who had no arithmetic
whatever but always made a great show of calcula-
tion when you asked him for an estimate. ("Ought
times ought is oughty-ought. Eight from five ya can't
take . . . Oh hell, I'll do it fer six dollars!") And the
fence viewer who called his oxen not "Bright and
Brown" or "Spark and Lion," as was the rigid custom,
but "Willie and Solomon." The woman who boxed her
hens' ears when they didn't lay, swearing that this
discipline sent them back to the nest without fail. The
man who, at steady odds with his wife whenever she
cleaned house, could be heard shaking the mats outside the porch and timing each vicious flap he gave
them to the spoken rhythm: "*Hell! Hell!* Hell and
Dam*nation!*"

When another was told by a Crown Land sur-
veyor that the granting of wood lots was "out of my

jurisdiction," he replied: "What the hell has George Dixon got to do with it?" George Dixon was a local grouch.

Another kept a codfish in his well.

And another never answered his children's questions but one way, aiming a clout at their ears whether the question annoyed him or not. "Dad, can I have a new bookbag?" "I'll give ya new bookbags!" "Dad, can we throw them crabapples in to the pig?" "I'll give ya throwin crabapples in to the pig!" They never knew whether he meant yes or no.

And after these came the cattle reeve who kept the pound and gave the same stern lecture (written out and memorized) to each vagrant heifer he arrested. The wheelwright who worked out a special tool for his every task, down to a kind of comb (put together from the quill ends of feathers) for scraping potato bugs off the vines into a can of kerosene. The man who smoked his bacon in the outhouse, with a smudge pot on each seat cover. The woman who saved all seeds from the gutted cucumbers at pickling time, dried them, and strung them in long portieres to the bottom of her handbag.

There was the man who moved to his new house while it was still unfinished and in the next few months pared so many strips of kindling off the bare beams that the whole structure began to sag like a hammock; and the woman who wore "rats" of horsehair in her "psyche" knot.

The man who had the normal count of teeth, but

every one of them a molar; and the woman who, winter or summer, sealed off the parlor with old umbrella ribs wedged in the cracks around the door whenever she dusted down the stairs.

The man who tried to breed eels in the rain barrel and the woman who gave up pork hocks for Lent . . .

Along with these were the outright freaks:

The man who worked off his fits of energy by leaping onto the sow's back, locking his legs under her snout, clutching her tail, and galloping her around the pen like a drunken jockey.

The bashful soul who held his hands over a sister-in-law's ears while she read out loud to him a love letter he couldn't puzzle out himself—so that she couldn't hear what she was saying.

The man who often mailed letters to the King—stressing that many times when he was a soldier in the Great War he'd dined at Windsor Castle and found the whole Royal bunch "as plain as an old sock."

There was also the tale (hard to believe, our neighbor admitted, yet sworn to by dozens) of the graybeard who died and was buried in mid-September. At the first stiff frosts his sons dug him up and put on his woolen underwear.

And if you didn't believe that story, our neighbor said, there were scores like it that he could vouch for himself. How about the couple who kept their tasks and their money strictly separate, one charging the other for any help given, even in bed? If a romp there was his idea, he paid her. If it was hers, she paid him. Or the two who hadn't spoken for a solid fifteen years but had had three sets of twins in the meantime and . . .? He could go on for hours.

W.R.

20 / *A to Z*

WITH FEW EXCEPTIONS, Norstead could claim no such "characters" as either the whited sepulchers or the outlandish of Claymore. Each of its people (from App to Zeb) was equally one of a kind—but their watermarks were less glaring by far. Beneath their surface quirks (which resembled those in Claymore on occasion only) the apartness of village life seemed to act on them in a quite different way.

It didn't warp, curdle, ossify, or capsize their minds. It was more like a steady ventilation. Solitude seemed to clear a calm spot at the center of them where the self stood known—not blurred from its own eyes, as the city man's is, by the ceaseless dust of strangeness shuffling past. Imperfect as all men and not to be represented as saints of any kind, they yet had something in them that never held its hand back from any honest thing which went to them with its hand out.

And if their speech was sometimes halting and out of joint, it was nothing more to snicker at than the little air-bubbling of the learned that, for all its ease and slickness, ranks them with people who can fart at will.

They were independent to the core—proud to own what they owned "without a cent agin it"—but never so stiff with this as to look the other way if someone needed help. Whenever a man did do something laughable, he was the first to tell it on himself— and to have his own grin twice warmed by the others' each time they twitted him about it. A man's words might be lead, but his word was sterling. (If he promised to lend you a hand on a certain morning you need have no more worry about his showing up than of the sun's rising.)

They "sputtered" about each other, but anything like an ugly quarrel was so rare that if there ever was one the very place of it seemed to take on a kind of shocking blood stain which seemed to brand the day itself.

Mostly, they were as one-in-all as if one's name was the other's nickname. Gathered at each other's tables, the springing round of nextness made the very house robust and young again, coved it from the steel-level eye of anything outside. A man would pause, his hoe suspended midway in its move toward the plant, troubled by a neighbor's troubles. Whenever loss or bad luck struck, they didn't ask, "Is there anything we can do?": they came and did it. And when they showed joy or grief or kindness or generosity you knew they weren't "makin it."

None of them was great, but when one died he was greatly remembered. If strangely. It was often the most trifling context that first came to mind whenever his name was mentioned—one that seemed to bring him back in fuller flesh than any tablet of deed or worth. Perhaps that is the true mark of the best-remembered.

Anyway, there were these:

App. So small when he was born that his mother could put a cup over his head and her wedding ring up to his elbow. She had to fasten his clothing to a pillow with safety pins to carry him about. At twenty-one his hair turned snow-white, he was powerful enough to throw a steer, and had all the girls sighing for him.

He could split a deer's skull (and this narrow target was all he ever aimed at) with a Mauser bullet at five hundred yards, but when the moment came to stick a pig he'd always make an excuse to check the scraping knives.

He could whet a scythe so that it sliced through the bluejoint like singing.

He was a born storyteller (underlining each explosive "but" with a fling of one knee over the other), and when his own story moved him he'd "choke up" without the least embarrassment.

He could cut a rafter precisely the right length by eye alone; and he built a miniature castle for his children, down to the tiny workable chains for the tiny workable drawbridge, inside a vinegar bottle. He carved a clockface out of apple tree wood, with the twelve letters of his wife's name in place of numerals.

The most even-tempered of men, one thing only, the sound of a dropped dish, would unsettle him like a charge of lightning. "That's you!" he'd roar at the startled offender, even if it was the minister's wife there for tea, his great fists clenched as if to strike.

Getting out of bed one night in the dark of the bedroom, his leg went down the heat hole over the kitchen stove and wedged there almost to the thigh. His wife (who was a somehow regal woman with a magnificent laugh) lit the lamp, then flurried around him. "Well," he said, pointing down there, "latch onto it—it's never bit you yet, has it?—and give me a hoist outa here!" She laughed until she was weak. It was so unlike him to say anything like that, that whenever he did she "got foolish."

He wrote a handsome hand, and on skates could trace out his signature as handsomely on the meadow ice. One Christmas Eve, describing perfect figure eights around a celebration bonfire on the flooded meadow, he tripped on an air hole in the ice and punctured an ankle with the point of his skate. Gangrene set in and he died of it.

Guy was fat. The only fat man in the place. He ate slices of fat pork for breakfast.

He was unshakably good-natured, humming snatches of song between the joints of conversation in the way that other men took out their jackknives and whittled a silence away. You could hear him singing, all by himself, as his horse drank from the stream in the hollow where you could rein your team off the road and go straight through the shoals, to wash the wagon wheels.

He had a fiery colt called "Rowdy" that no one else dared harness. He could back him into the shafts with a single light grip on his mane.

He was a born persuader. He could take the pulse of every current (and undercurrent) around him and steer it with a well-timed joke. Even his monkeyshines were taken in good part. The groom in whose wedding bed he hid a mouse trap was the first to confirm that it had nipped him exactly where Guy had planned it might.

He was lucky in everything. His hay never got

rained on. If when he went to buy a pig the litter had all been sold except the stunted "teatman" which no one wanted, that "teatman" would grow for him into the finest hog around.

He never worked long hours or until he sweated. But he always had everything he wanted—and savings besides, in the cigar box with the nautch girls on the cover. Men would leave their own work to help with his, because he made them feel (blarney or not) such splendid Samaritans. On the other hand, no one could return a favor with readier heart or better grace. When he was mail driver (any job he wanted he got) he'd scour the whole town to find which storekeeper would give him the best deal on a box of dried apples a neighbor had asked him to trade for groceries.

His fields were as neat as a parlor floor: in haying time he'd have the whole family out "raking after," to catch the last slovenly straw.

He had a great tall fiery son, who, as often as they disagreed on a plan of work, would sling his tools to the ground and storm off, to leave home. Halfway to the house he'd hesitate, look back at his father, and they'd both roar with laughter.

Each Christmas his wife made a handsome Della Robbia out of pasture greenery and the wax fruit off old hats.

He used to tease her for crawling behind the flour barrel when she was scared of thunder. One summer afternoon he'd landed the last load of hay safely under cover just before the storm broke. As he stepped out of the barn with a pitchfork over his shoulder, the first bolt of lightning struck the tines and killed him.

DAN WAS NAMED after Daniel Hay, Champlain's apothecary. Once, on the track of a bear that led him deep into a backwoods stretch of ledge and scrub that looked the same in all directions he was lost for two days and two nights. This spot was known as "Dan's Barrens" forever after.

A great word with his wife was "charmin." To her most everything was "charmin"—from a crazy quilt to a cup of tea. She had a way of taking people out of themselves and their worries the moment she spoke their name. Her name was Diadem. One Sunday at a Harvest Festival, Uncle Billy-Rippy-Tippy, who was as full as a tick, took it into his head to reword the hymn they were singing. "Bri-ing forth the royal di-i-i-a-dem," it went, "A-and crown Him lo-o-ord of all." "Bri-ing forth the royal Di-i-i-a-dem," Uncle Billy roared out, "A-and crown her Queen this very fall." When these lines came up again in the next verse, the whole congregation chimed in with him.

JAKE HAD NEVER GONE TO SCHOOL a day in his life, but he could spot the hidden mechanics of an object with one glance. A log so big that no three men could load it on to the sleds he could load alone, knowing to an inch where to lever the skids, where the peavey, where the chain. To outwit a task's opposing forces in this way came to be known as "Jaking" it. Men came to him to learn how to "Jake" a heavy twelve-foot cross into place on the church roof, a leaning shed into position again; where to elbow a stovepipe so it would draw best; even how to balance a weather vane just right.

He was so powerful he could drive a stake three feet into hard ground with one blow of the mall.

He whittled small statues of people that looked more like them than their tintypes in the parlor album.

When his wife went to spend the day with a neighbor's wife she always wore his Sunday cap, stuck through with two great hatpins headed with amber glass. She once had a letter from Australia.

He had never studied arithmetic but he could add a column of lumber tally three figures wide as fast as his fingers moved up it. He was drowned in Lily Lake.

Bernie had the talents of a born actor. He could mimic to the life any voice he'd ever heard and turn his face into any face he'd ever seen. With one gesture he could change from young to old; to half his size or twice it. He made up songs. No one for miles around could come within a mile of his stepdancing: he could stepdance across a boom of logs swaying and bobbing in the water, and never miss a beat.

He had an answer for everyone. "The hens's eatin their eggs," his wife said to him once. "They must need somethin." "They do," he said. "Eggs."

He was a cooper.

Stella had bottomless black eyes, and jet black hair she could sit on. She always dressed in green and had green feathers in her hat. She'd have been a real beauty anywhere. She puzzled people.

At times she seemed to be all flesh, at times all spirit. Which was the real woman? Was it music of the Psalms that moved her so (she learned them by heart, propping the Bible over the wash tub as she scrubbed the clothes) or the wide shoulders of the young preacher? She loved an earthy joke and no laugh was louder than hers when the women swapped them among themselves. In the next breath she might be making a burning prayer.

She was as full of big schemes for the village as a crusader; always searching for new ideas. Her parlor had the first folding doors.

She could pick up live coals that dropped from the stove grate on to the kitchen floor and never scorch her delicate fingers.

Once she lost her wedding ring while she was feeding the cattle at noon. She never dreamed of finding it again; but when her husband beefed a steer that fall, there it was, lodged in the "Bible" tripe. She believed she'd been singled out for a small manifestation.

Her husband would never drive his team through a hopscotch pattern children had drawn in the dust of the road and were playing at, no matter how deep the ditch he must take to, to spare it.

He had a quarry on his land, where with only a hand drill but the skill of a diamond cutter he split out the great slabs of granite rock that went into the walls of every cellar that was dug.

Hewing ship spars was his passion. He would roam the wood lots for days, looking for the giant tree (scarce as leap years) that was tall enough and straight enough and round enough for his purpose, and pay the owner almost anything he asked for it.

He was so conscientious that when he measured out a cord of wood for sale he'd pile it so tight that not a chink of daylight showed through—then add some extra pieces to take care of the chips he'd struck from the odd stick to be sure it was sound from end to end. He made ox yokes and checkerboards.

On a frosty October morning Hugh could call a bull moose across the bog to within a rod of where he was hidden.

His wife Molly was a big, easygoing, tender-hearted woman who did a man's work beside him.

They had a small up-and-down mill. Hugh loaded the blocks on to the carriage, she sawed, and the son "took away" from the saw. Nothing about the mill was ever in safe condition. Scarcely a week went by that some of it didn't fly apart; once the saw shot clean through the roof, grazing the brim of Molly's sou'wester. But little things like that didn't faze them in the least. They'd patch the pieces together again and go right on; and, by a miracle, none of them was ever hurt.

Instead of buying sounder gear for the mill, they bought a phonograph. It was the wonder of the district, and they shared it with everyone.

Their house was "a great place to go." The young people gathered there almost every evening. You could dance or sing or romp through games that shook the ceiling, anything you liked: they didn't care if you "tore the house down." Or you could listen to Hugh's hunting stories. He never lied, but he "enlarged on things" in a way he knew the hearers loved.

He and Molly would give you the last crust of bread in the house, and often did. No one ever got away, day or night, without food of some kind. If a visitor's children polished off the whole evening's mess of milk and still showed signs of wanting more, Hugh would light the lantern and milk the cow a second time.

Their son went overseas. On leave from the trenches, he went to see Scotland, the home of his ancestors. The first night, not knowing, he blew out the gaslight in the hotel bedroom, as you would a lamp. In the morning he was dead.

The afternoon the news was brought to his father

and mother they were in the schoolhouse, watching a performance of the traveling medicine man. He showed magic lantern slides and pulled teeth.

They walked home, but they didn't go into the house first. They went into the mill (though its roof was all but gone now) and stood for a long time where their son had stood taking the fragrant pine boards from the saw. They gave the phonograph away.

EM HAD DIZZY SPELLS. So severe that she rarely set foot outside her own house.

She would be hilarious one minute and gloomy the next, but she was the kind of person who could make even her gloom funny. She could make her own *children* laugh, like no one else. Her husband, a mild and very sober man, almost never laughed. They would laugh at his not laughing at their laughing, and then he'd grin at their laughing at his not laughing.

It was a house where odd, laughable things were continually happening. No one had ever heard tell of a jug of molasses exploding in the night. It did there. Once when the flue was burning out, Em, in a sudden frantic urge to do *some*thing, aimed a bucket of water at the kitchen stovepipe. The water missed the pipe altogether, looping neatly over it and down on to her husband, who was sitting calmly on the other side, drenching him to the skin.

Once an ox buyer spent the night with them. He

snored so thunderously that no one else could sleep.
Em draped a blanket across his door to muffle the
sound, intending to take it away before he stirred in
the morning. He had a call of nature long before
dawn, however, and when he tiptoed out to the hall
the blanket fell around his ears like a ruffian's sack.

One day she and her husband were crossing a
sidehill ditch on a teetery plank. He stepped on the
high end while she was still on the low and sent her
flying in the air. Her head struck the ground, stunning
her for a moment, but (whatever the blow did) she
never had a dizzy spell again.

CARRIE WAS A DRESSMAKER. She used no pattern, and
when she poised her scissors for the first bold cut into a
length of Shantung the customer would gasp, but she
never made a miss.

Spring and fall, relatives in the States sent her "a
barrel." When word went around that Carrie had "got
a barrel," everyone flocked to see. It was always
packed with the most unpredictable assortment—
anything from long-stemmed goblets (hardly chipped at
all) to handkerchiefs of crepe de Chine. Everyone was
given a present from it, and everything was put to use.
(She covered wooden buttons with the crepe de Chine.)

She was wild about color. She said a bobbinful of
colored thread made her think of the Ascension. She
whitewashed the inside walls of the hen pen and
painted sunflowers all over them.

FORREST HAD A LONG WHITE BEARD. Strangers, seeing him at a distance, thought of Moses. It gave them the oddest start when he came close and raised his extraordinary eyes, younger than a boy's, younger than Christ's. He lived to be a hundred and three.

IT WAS TORTURE for Sam to sit still. Every movement he made was so darting that when there were guests for supper and he passed around the sugar cookies your hand had to be quicker than a snake's tongue to nail one before the plate whisked by.

He loved work (done right) as some men rejoice in music. If he came to help you with a job, he drove himself—and you—harder than if it was an undertaking of his own. Without there being the slightest bossiness about this, as there would have been in another man.

"I know it's easier to dump this oat straw in the bay there," he might say at threshing time. "But you'll curse it in the spring when you want to get at that old beddin. We'd best pitch it up onto the head scaffold, what?"

Or, if it was haying: "I'll swallow my bite while you're puttin out the team. And then I'll toss out them two damp windrows while you're eatin yours, so the whole cut'll be dry when we come to haul in."

Or, hauling out manure: "Well, that's a good job done! I always like to see the shed cleaned out slick like that, don't you? Where's your hoe? Now them sills's bare, you'll never have a better chance to scrape em off, so they don't rot . . . But ain't it a shame we didn't have enough to cover that last little corner be the orchard! Half a dozen forkfuls woulda done it. *I* tell ya. Take the team over to *my* shed and throw on a few forkfuls there. Then we can finish her out proper."

Or, hauling out wood: "Y'know, when we unloaded that first jag we got the butt ends facin wrong fer sawin, didn't we. We'd best turn em end fer end before we go fer any more. It won't take long."

Or, with the hack: "Now, that's what ya call somethin *like*, what? Good diggin like that and a crop o' potatoes like that! But I wouldn't leave em there in the rows tonight, Joe. Maybe it's too cloudy fer frost, but . . . Why don't I get my kids and you get yours, and we'll pick em up after supper and raft em into the cellar? It'd be a crime to let anything happen to em."

You couldn't find a friendlier man, but he never took the time to be less than blunt: you always knew exactly where you were with him. And sometimes his thoughts sprang into speech with so little preconsideration that the words played strange tricks on him. To his seven-year-old son: "No, you're not gonna have that chisel! I hid it behind the work bench." To a neighbor: "Why didn't ya tell me ya didn't know Bill'd bought the old Wentworth place? I'd a told ya!"

When his house burned down he searched and searched the ashes for the tin box that for years his wife had saved the fancy buttons in from all the Sunday dresses she'd outworn.

ZEB WAS SO TALL he had to bend for the doorways.

As soon as a child of his was old enough to ride on his shoulders he would carry him around that way while he sowed the first grain of the year—his great strides pacing strips off the field as evenly as if he was following a marker, the seed fanning out from his hand so evenly that when it came up there was never a thick patch or a thin.

He would lend you anything but his spirit level. This, with the little bean-shaped bubble that trembled in its cavity of liquid beneath the glass panel in the wood, had shown him the skewed from the true when he was building his house, and he guarded it like treasure. He demonstrated to his children how the bubble never ceased its watchfulness, as if it was a miracle. And when he stored the level on a cupboard shelf he made sure it lay so straight that even when it wasn't being used the bubble would be balanced perfectly at the center.

He could judge a beef's weight almost to the pound. The first wildflower he saw in the April woods he made a wish on, for his wife.

When she died the women asked him if they should take off her locket before the coffin was closed. He said no. He put some silks of wheat tassel inside it . . .

THESE ARE BUT A FEW. There are many more like them —in being so unlike each other.

And there were all the boys and girls, one so different from the next, yet so all the same in that their brilliant flesh was forever bringing the good news of itself to itself, and without a thistledown's heaviness yet in the blood's eyelids.

21 / *Fireflies and Freedom*

IT IS AN AUGUST AFTERNOON. Every year has a day
like this, before the season tips toward fall. Time
seems held and motionless, in a trance of benignity.
Things, luxuriously idle, come out of themselves and
touch each other. The fatherly sun and the brotherly
air are their interpreters. The hay is cut. There is no
task that clamors.

My father walks over the golden oat stubble, taking pleasure in the thick green clover that is beginning to spring up from the seed that was sowed with the oats in the spring. His eye marks out the lines the fence will take when he turns the cows in here next month, but he is not working. He will not sharpen a stake or drive one until tomorrow. Tomorrow is time enough for everything. He walks through the garden where a fullness of growing sates the air, but there is nothing quite ready to be harvested yet.

He is young and strong. My mother is young and pretty. She has washed her long brown hair. She is sitting outside drying it in the sun. In her lap is the basket of yarn. She sorts through it. There are balls and skeins of all colors, left over from other years. She holds one skein against another to see which colors will go together best, but she is not working. It is not time to start knitting yet.

This is the day so secure in ease that we are more closely joined together than ever before, yet freed of each other, freed from having to keep each other under a protective eye. The day does that. It is a day to wander . . . with the day's full sanction. With no spoiling sense of tasks sulking at your neglect of them, none that this idling is not quite earned.

I go back the cow lane to the pasture. Everywhere the earth is firm and dry. All the low-lying patches I have to skirt around when they are miry or puddled in the damp seasons are now solid as stone. It is a delight to walk straight over them.

The cows are sprawled under the giant maple, their eyes lakes of satisfaction. I kneel beside each one, stroking her great side. I feel the rumble of fixity in them. The horse is by himself. He never feeds in with the cows. I smell the groinish horse smell. I put my hand beneath his mane where the electric muscles of his neck twitch once, then ripple. I feel the speed in him.

I leave the clearing and go down the log road. I am in the woods. Some kind of valve seals the pasture off completely. I am in the very depths of the afternoon. The afternoon and I are Now's all. I look up at the great rugged trees on the side of the road. I see the heroism in them.

The road leads to the hardwood hill. I see the certainty in it. My bare feet touch the shadows where the trees overhang. I feel the acceptance in them. It is so still that not even the pines whisper among themselves. I smell them, though, and I hear the chording of their silence with the heat. Brilliantly cosy in my own skin, I feel the verses of blood circling in my own flesh.

Off the road there is a great flat-topped rock. I see the everlasting in it. I leave the road and scramble up it. A popple grows behind it, bent over it like an umbrella. The popple rustles its leaves softer than silence. It is like a tree of answers. I lie on my back on the rock and look at the sky through the leaves. My eyes follow the sky's single cloud, the shape of a wing. I see creation in it. I don't move. I see a squirrel moving on the ground. A partridge. A snail. There is no one there to see them but me. I have created them.

I close my eyes. The rock starts to rock me. I doze. I could go to sleep anywhere then. I dream that I am sleeping moving in a rowboat with oars that turn into the legs of horses.

A leaf falls on my face. It awakens me. The day has not gone by while I slept. It is still there, with no more lateness in it than before. I jump off the rock.

And then I see the raspberries in the old chopping. There are bushels of them, huge and ripe. No one has discovered them. I have created them. They've never been touched. Wait till I tell Mother! We'll all come back with baskets and pails. I dance to think of leading her and Father to the feast. I pick a handful of the berries and eat them. I taste the wit in them.

The road ends at the hardwood hill. Here the great yellow birches are spaced farther apart than the spruces that cluster branch to branch along the road. I wander through the Sabbath naves that separate them. I see the holiness in the August light that hangs there.

I open my jackknife and make a straight slit down the bark of one of the trees, then strip off a great cylinder of it with my fingers. I stuff the bark inside my blouse, to kindle the first fall fire with in the hall stove. I see the burning pride in it.

And then I see the ash tree. Ash trees are so scarce you never know where they can be found. My father has searched the mountain for days to find one, for ax handles: no other kind of wood will do. He never thought of looking so close to home. Wait till I tell him there is one right here! I have created it. I dance with the thought of leading him to it.

I look around me, to fix the spot in my mind. A flock of crows settle in the dead scrag behind me. I count them. One crow sorrow, two crows joy, three crows a wedding, four crows a boy. My two strokes of luck have stretched my senses to the limit, laid everything wide open to them. I see the entire Mystery in the crows.

They fly away and I touch the scrag. I feel the blankness in it, but I am not sobered or saddened. Swarming as I am with luck and good health, its blankness only makes me feel that much fuller inside myself.

I stand on the top of the hardwood hill, and over the trees on the downward slope and through them I see the brook where it has cut its great circle through the woods and come out here to make the Big Meadow. I see the miles and the leisure in it. And where, halfway to the second hardwood hill, it widens into a pond that has the voice of lakes, I hear in it an echo of the most silent, kindliest thunder. I take a long breath that glories me to the heels, like the first sweet air caught at after running.

I go down the long slope to the August brook. The ferns come almost to my armpits. I see the nobility, the justice in them. I feel the moss beneath my feet, the oracle in it.

There is a narrows where the rocks in the brook are so close together I can hop from one to another to the meadow beyond. I stop midway across and sit on one of them. Here there is a little current beneath the surface. A leaf drifts by, mesmerizing itself.

I dangle my feet in the brook. At first the water is cold, then grows as warm as my blood. I gaze at the brook until I seem to be floating with the leaf. I remember my dream.

And then I see a stir in the pond. Something moving in a long arrow toward the high bank. I am instantly on my toes. Is it a muskrat? A mink? It reaches the bank and starts to climb. It is a mink. But no! It is longer than a mink. Twice as long! Three *times* as long! It is the blackest, glossiest creature I have ever seen. It is an otter!

I hold my breath as it climbs the bank and then slides down again. I *know* it is an otter. My heart bounds. I have created it. No one in the whole place has ever seen an otter. Not even the men. In the days of the Indians there were otters here, but now they were supposed to be gone for good. I see the magic in the word "otter." No other name could fit that sleekness so perfectly.

The otter swims downstream and out of sight— but I have seen it. My heart shouts. Wait till I tell Stan and Jack and Howie . . . that I saw an otter! And Lennie and Dick and . . . And—yes, yes—Laura!

Laura. My pulses stir, as if with news from the sun . . .

We are all scattered now. Stan and Jack and Howie and Lennie and Dick . . . and Laura . . . and all the rest. Some are far off. Some are dead. Some live alone. When two of us happen to meet again one sees in the other's face a mirror of all that has drained out of his own.

We used to laugh at Howie's crazy rhymes. How would he rhyme us now? And could we laugh the same way?

For (he might say) we are caged within age. Our flesh, no longer fresh, is split into features at odds with each other where once its singleness went round and round itself . . . Fats and thinnesses swallow the hollows where the ghosts of how we once looked just flicker. We look at each other and see what the other sees in us: flesh that has seen its own bone.

We try to escape. We talk fast, we smoke, we drink. But time's rhymes have turned against us too. To smoke is to choke a little, to drink is to stink a little. To screw is to rue. Pains stain our brains. Words are now curds. The fair air is now bare. Worries, with their little moles' teeth, nibble the casings off our nerves. The cold scolds. The sun is done. We hear the ears of houses listening for the steps of what's gone by in them.

Some days, loneliness writes the sleepless letters of its name slantwise across everything like a cancellation mark. Sometimes in a hurrying street we catch shop-window glimpses of ourselves mirrored among the throng and for a moment neither reality nor its image has the greater reality one above the other. We have moments (that spring from ambushes as different as a scrap of song and the sunset that looks like the afterglow of the burnt cities of all you ever were, smoldering just below the horizon) when the clock-face of everything seems stopped forever, listening to the shuddering hour it has just struck.

Sometimes, happy in a group, in the middle of a laugh, the self of yourself that has gone its own way with yourself alone (so long that their two faces, turned so jealously toward each other, turn the other faces away) stands suddenly on a vast twilight shore that the others' gaze falls just short of.

We no longer see the things we used to see: our own pulse in the lapping of the lake, our own snugness in the kitchen fire, our own eyes in the window pane. We see things we never used to see: the iron in the band of winter-cloud behind the factory chimney, the prison eyes in the dry blade of weaving sidewalk grass, the death mask of time in the rag of newspaper blowing down the gutter.

Some nights we lie awake, searching for the answers to ourselves in the dark between the bed and the ceiling.

And all days we are asleep, sleepwalking among the things that now are all alike, shorn to their one feature of going from one moment of sameness to the next . . .

But then there were:

Sap spiles and ostrich ferns. Burdock burrs and

Luna moths. Dragonflies and cornflowers. Chimney swifts and screech owls. Puffballs and Northern Lights . . .

There were long white mushroom stalks shaped like sex (sometimes we stuck them down there, clowning) and clouds that looked like the puffs of breath from the figurehead in the corners of old maps and clouds that were black and terrible as a stallion's eye.

There were snowflakes as cozy as locks and sun flakes (under the apple boughs) the image of keys. We had all the locks and all the keys.

Each day the sun came up with a different set of promises, set in a ring around it like opals around a diamond, and each night it went down to gather yet another.

The wind had a thousand different voices, and the rain. (The kitchen fire and the spoon holder and the kettle light stood between us, then, and the homeless dusk when the searching but never finding wind blew the knuckles of the sky blue.)

Wheels went round in the field and sled runners ran straight in their tracks, bearing the loads of food and heat that would go back into the breath and blood and muscle that had gone into the raising of them, while the broad day smiled. Water obeyed its quenchless memory always to boil at a certain heat, the particles of things clung together in the shape their physics said they must, rock was immutably rock, green grew exactly as its seed said—but they did this not as if they were sullen in their implacable yoke (as the steel of ·cities is) but as willingly as if they had made their own laws.

The hawks left the quotation marks of their wings' landing around the mouse blood on the frozen crust. The bag of day-old kittens in the pail drowned with their eyes shut. The leak in the hen pen slimed the droppings on the sodden straw. And old men with a milky film over their pupils tapped their way querulously with their canes to the outhouse they had once swapped the roaring jokes about with the neighbor who was helping them build it, their thin streams now missing the hole.

But the rabbits ran in the calm clear moonlight while the children dreamed of brooks and swings, and the wool and the gingham sang warm and cool against the flesh, and the fir trees prayed with the cows on Christmas Eve.

There were cradle hills and sleigh bells. Rainbows and rhubarb. Catkins and robin hop. Locust eyes and chain lightning. Tombstone moss and lilies of the valley. Summertime and suppertime . . .

And faces in the doorway and faces in the doorway . . .

And there were songs the color of poppies . . . and roofs the sound of sleep . . . and thoughts the taste of swimming . . . and voices the touch of bread . . .

And fireflies and freedom . . .

And fireflies and freedom.